Believe in Me

a novel

*

Jason Warburg

Wonder Wheel Publications
Seaside, California

"Mr. Jones" words by Adam Duritz, music by Adam Duritz, and David Bryson, copyright 1993 EMI Blackwood Music Inc. and Jones Falls Music. All rights controlled and administered by EMI Blackwood Music, Inc. All rights reserved. International copyright secured. Used by permission.

"This Is Your Life" written by Jonathan Foreman, copyright 2003 Meadowgreen Music Company (ASCAP) / Sugar Pete Songs (ASCAP) (adm. at EMICMGPublishing.com).

"Already Gone" written by Jack Tempchin and Robb Strandlund, copyright 1974 Jazzbird Music / WB Music Corp. (ASCAP).

"Jet Airliner" words and music by Paul Pena, copyright 1973 Sailor Music and No Thought Music (ASCAP). Copyright renewed. All rights administered by Sailor Music.

"Stand" written by Bill Berry, Peter Buck, Mike Mills and Michael Stipe, copyright 1988 Night Garden Music (BMI).

"Ramblin' Gamblin' Man" written by Bob Seger, copyright 1968 Gear Publishing Company (ASCAP).

"Lost Horizons" written by Douglas Hopkins, copyright 1992 WB Music Corp. / East Jesus Music (ASCAP).

"When You're Alone" written by Bruce Springsteen, copyright 1987 Bruce Springsteen (ASCAP). Reprinted by permission. International copyright secured. All rights reserved.

"No Better Place" written by Chris Collingwood and Adam Schlesinger, copyright 2003 Monkey Demon Music (BMI) / Vaguely Familiar Music (ASCAP).

"My Mercurial Nature" written by Mark Doyon, copyright 2010 WMM Songs (ASCAP).

"We Are One Tonight" written by Jonathan Foreman and Tim Foreman, copyright 2005 Meadowgreen Music Company (ASCAP) / Switchfoot Co-Pub Designee (ASCAP) / Sugar Pete Songs (ASCAP) (adm. at EMICMGPublishing.com).

All lyrics used by permission. All rights reserved.

Thanks to Stewart Copeland for permission to quote from his 2006 documentary film *Everyone Stares: The Police Inside Out*.

Other quotations used by kind permission of the respective copyright holders.

ISBN-13: 978-0615684796
ISBN-10: 0615684793
LCCN: 2012948510

Jacket design by Wampus Multimedia (www.wampus.com)

www.jasonwarburg.com

For Karen, always

and
in memory of

PRG & LTM

Believe in me
Help me believe in anything
I want to be someone who believes

– Adam Duritz & David Bryson
("Mr. Jones" by Counting Crows)

Democracy is a device that ensures we shall be governed no better than we deserve.

– George Bernard Shaw

OPENER

On the west wall, opposite the circular bar that rises like an altar within the central well of the San Francisco Hard Rock Café, hangs a window into another universe.

The image captures a band onstage mid-song, in full flight, their energy as electric as the megawatt spotlights that have set them all aglow. The angle is low, as if taken from audience perspective at the very front lip of the stage, but off to one side, so that the entire group is seen in near-profile.

The singer, lithe and dark, bends backward with the note at center stage, mouth open to the microphone he holds in his right hand, eyes closed, face constricted in an intense ecstasy that might be mistaken for either spiritual or sexual if not for the worry lines, the deep trails mapping his forehead.

The other four players are spread out across the scene like a loose assemblage of disciples. The drummer rules the back, sandy tendrils of hair flailing along with his muscular arms. The bassist stands close by, small and enigmatic, nearly hidden even in plain sight. The keyboard player holds down the far outpost stage right, only his head visible over the bulk of a grand piano, a scattering of bright curls surrounding a serious face. The guitarist is closest to the camera, bent over his instrument with left foot thrust forward like a runner in the blocks, mouth open in a lopsided grin as long strands of blond hair obscure his eyes.

The five each occupy their own world at this instant, yet their individual orbits are bound together by a fierce intensity, a shared purpose fueled by welling emotion. They've traveled far to reach this moment, and seem determined to live within it for as long as they possibly can. As common as this basic tableau might be in rock and roll photography, there is something distinctly uncommon about this particular image, some concentrated hyper-reality lurking beneath its surface that makes the shot itself not just captivating, but iconic.

This, it says, is IT. The top of the mountain. Stop and look around. You might never be here again.

In the farthest visible reaches of the photo, at the very edge of the wash of light that seems almost to radiate from the band itself, stand two small figures rendered faceless by the distance, a man and a woman, watching from the wings. The one on the right has dark, shiny hair and feminine curvature, and is looking up at the one on the left, who is taller and is looking down at her with a suggestion of longing, and perhaps anticipation as well.

The one on the left is me.

I.

GOING MOBILE

This is your life
Are you who you want to be?

– Jonathan Foreman ("This Is Your Life" by Switchfoot)

Nearly all men can stand adversity, but if you want to
test a man's character, give him power.

– Abraham Lincoln

1

I've always been that guy at the side of the stage. I like it that way. Let someone else hog the mike and the relentless scrutiny that comes with it; I'll stay on safer ground. I'd still rather write these words than speak them, as you can plainly see.

One thing has changed, though. In the old days – which consisted of every day of my working life until six months ago – the figure at the mike would have been an attention addict of a different tribe. Genus *candidate politicalus* rather than genus *singer rockandrollicus*.

How I survived that unlikely leap into another universe is the tale I'm here to tell. And since he's so prone to interrupting anyway, it seems only fitting to give the first word to California Attorney General – and Democratic nominee for the United States Senate – Frank Cassini.

* * *

"Green!"

"Yessir," I said, taking the soft leather briefcase Cassini had thrust at me as he vaulted, blinking, up and out of the back of his chauffered Lincoln Town Car. It was July 5th, four months and change before election day, and I was standing at the curb at Los Angeles International Airport with The Candidate himself. His jet-black loafers gleamed beneath a double-breasted light grey suit of Italian wool, which offered flattering cover for the middle-aged spread that was rapidly conquering his five-nine frame.

"Gimme your phone." His round face was flushed, thick charcoal hair rising stiffly in the breeze, dark eyes darting left and right at the milling herds of common passengers surrounding us. "Mine's outta juice," he muttered as I reflexively obeyed, handing over the new iPhone I had just that week vanquished the campaign bureaucracy to procure.

"Go!" he barked at me, waving with his free hand for me to take the lead as our California Highway Patrol escort (today it was the intrepid Robert A. Falconer, a.k.a. Officer Bob) assumed his post at Cassini's side.

Weaving through the unheeding crowd inside the terminal, we cleared security without major incident courtesy of Officer Bob. As we power-walked the length of the terminal toward Gate 87, Cassini finished his call and began barking questions at me.

"What's new on the Colfax fire?"

"Twenty-four thousand acres burned, thirty percent contained, every air tanker north of Bakersfield deployed. The national guard is enforcing mandatory evacuations east of Interstate 80 and they've set up shelters in Grass Valley and Meadow Vista."

"Meadow Vista? Does that burg even have a traffic light?"

"Their high school gym holds 400 and a hundred volunteers have already showed up to help."

"A hundred people with nothing better to do. Figures. They know how it started?"

"The working theory from Emergency Services is, lightning strikes from a thunderstorm."

"In the middle of summer? In the goddamned Sierra foothills?"

"Climate change. More moisture in the air at weird times of year."

"Yeah, right. More likely some jerkoff didn't bother dousing his campfire. Alright, why's Ostrowitz calling me every day?"

"He wants you to endorse the auto mileage standards initiative. They turned in the signatures two weeks ago. Should get the final word on qualifying for the November ballot any day."

"Dammit, don't any of these clowns understand you've gotta play the middle in the general? I can't let Kendrick sit there calling me a nanny-state job-killer through the whole fall campaign. They should've stuck that crap on the primary ballot where it belongs."

I nodded silently; to do otherwise bordered on recklessness.

"Alright. Middle East?"

"The talks are still going, but they're no closer on the holy places in Jerusalem. Both sides are threatening to pull out if there's more violence."

"Which just makes the crazies on both sides more likely to start blowing things up. I swear, the damn Jews and Arabs are still gonna to be fighting over those piles of rock when my grandchildren's grandchildren are dead and buried. They're nuts, every last one of 'em."

Maybe. Or maybe you just hate them because they believe in something.

"What's the name of the school again?"

"Cesar Chavez Junior High."

"And we picked it to pimp charter schools because…?"

"Biggest year-to-year jump in their SAT-9 test scores in the history of the test. Verbal rose 39 percent and math 31 percent."

"Christ. Anybody think to check if maybe they cheated?"

"Uh, no, sir. The school population is 54 percent Hispanic and 18 percent Asian American, mostly Hmong and Vietnamese. Last summer they instituted a mandatory six-week English immersion program for their ESL students."

"Mandatory summer school. Heh. That'll keep the little buggers off the streets."

* * *

My enlistment as deputy press secretary to Francis John "Frank" Cassini's campaign for the U.S. Senate had come at the urging of Charlie Bond, a hungry-eyed fellow University of California, Davis alum who at the time was the Cassini campaign's Central Valley field representative. "The guy's a sure thing," Charlie had told me in his perpetually urgent way, over watery drinks in a Sacramento bar overrun with navy blue blazers and pleated grey slacks. "U.S. Attorney, Congressman, Attorney General," continued Charlie, ticking off Cassini's resume bullets on his fingers. "Five years in the courtroom making his name as a tough-on-crime Democrat, then a run for Congress, eight years there getting cozy with the money guys he needs to run statewide, then six years as state AG, building name i.d. and solidifying his base. Now he's like a thoroughbred at the gate, waiting for the bell to go off."

I had spent my first six years out of college in a series of low-level legislative staff positions around Sacramento, nothing involving an actual campaign, but enough experience around the fringes of them to recognize that Charlie's cocktail-napkin profile was not without merit. Cassini was a strong public speaker, a canny deal-maker, and a persistent advocate for bedrock middle-class Democratic issues in a state where the Republican Party had spent the last two decades nominating one far-right candidate after another for the Senate – the latest being fire-tongued State Controller Darcy Kendrick – and losing. From a political perspective, Cassini was a consummate pro, one of those guys who seems like he knew exactly what he wanted to do with his life the first time he saw the president on television when he was seven years old.

But leadership – driving positive change, making hard decisions, little things like that – wasn't it. What Frank Cassini wanted to do, I had concluded after more than a year of drafting meaningless pieces of news-release puffery in the man's press office, was to be surrounded at all times by people who needed something from him. Lobbyists, contributors, reporters, staff – it didn't really matter, as long as he was the center of the circle. Issues were necessary nuisances, to be managed dutifully in the manner of monthly invoices that needed to be paid on time. It was the free-floating cloud of need and deference that Cassini craved.

California Attorney General Francis Cassini was a thoroughbred, alright

— a petty, overbearing, thoroughbred egomaniac whose fate my own nascent career in politics was now tethered to in a way that could make me giddy or queasy, depending on the day's polls and the candidate's mood. As for the wager-happy Mr. Bond, he had crapped out one chilly morning in Visalia, fired a week before Christmas after booking Cassini into a poorly-attended labor event where the local union president had exhibited an unfortunate fondness for "Godfather" jokes.

* * *

I parried back as we approached the gate. "Do you have the cards?"

Cassini liked his speeches printed out on three-by-five index cards in sixteen-point type so he could slip the entire speech in his pocket and then, if necessary, refer to them without using his glasses. His memory for the essential points was sharp and he didn't refer to them much, but their presence was a security blanket that helped calm and focus him.

In response to my question, he began fishing through his inside coat pockets without catching anything. Turning with a frustrated glare, he found me waiting with my backup set of cards already out and in my hand. He accepted them with a quiet smirk, about as close as I'd ever come to receiving that rarest of endangered species, the Cassini compliment.

By the time we'd cleared the boarding pass scanner at the gate and started down the ramp to the plane, he had my iPhone out again; by the time we boarded, he was chattering away once more, telling a contributor his previous commitment wasn't going to cut it anymore, not in this race. Officer Bob made sure we found our seats, the first two in first class, and sketched a sardonic goodbye wave as he disappeared back up the gangway. *He's all yours now.* One of Bob's colleagues would meet us at the door in San Francisco.

Cassini had barely sat down, though, when he was halfway out of his seat again, leaning toward the door, nearly shouting into the phone. "Greg? Greg?!" He turned to me accusingly. "What the hell's wrong with this thing? The minute we stepped on board I got a ton of static."

"I don't know, sir, sometimes I have trouble with it on planes —"

"I have to finish that call." He stood and had taken a step toward the door when a nearby flight attendant, a fortyish redhead with long, slender ballerina fingers, intercepted him, touching his arm.

"Sir." Her expression was measured but severe, her intonation that of a patient schoolteacher calming an unruly student. "You can't leave the plane."

He turned and laughed in her face. "Excuse me?"

"Sir, please." Red's guarded expression hadn't changed, but I was amused to note her stance, clenched and ready to pounce. This was clearly not her first time dealing with The Important Passenger Who Declines To Cooperate. She also had terrific legs. "You're on board. We're preparing for departure. You can't leave the plane."

"The door's still open."

"Yes, it is. There are two more passengers just coming through the gate right now."

Cassini's tangled expression spoke of his shock and disgust at such treatment. "This flight was supposed to leave five minutes ago!"

Red stared at him and began to speak slowly, carefully. "Yes, but we held it. A hundred and eighty-seven people on board on time for departure, and we held it." She paused almost a full second before finishing, pointing her line like a stage actress. "For you."

"Well, I'm on now, aren't I?"

"Yes," she said. "And that's where you need to stay."

"Is that right?" sneered the Attorney General of California, and began punching numbers into my phone emphatically, as if daring her to grab it out of his hand. Without taking his eyes off her, he then took three long, exaggerated strides backward, through the doorway, across the threshold and back onto the jetway, where he turned and made a display of hitting the "Call" button.

Jabbing his finger at me for emphasis, he growled a directive: "This door does NOT close until I'm back inside."

Just then two new figures came barreling around the corner and down the last few feet of the jetway behind Frank in a rush of pounding footsteps and out-of-breath gratitude. As Cassini moved back against the wall, they lunged past him and onto the plane like a pair of overgrown teenagers on a joyride. The leader was late thirties, around six-one and instantly magnetic, pale, chiseled cheekbones and laughing blue eyes in a brown leather bomber jacket, well-worn 501s and a navy Seattle Mariners baseball cap. His companion was almost as tall, but broader, thicker, bearded and dark-skinned enough to suggest African royalty. Both wore sunglasses, though Leather Jacket's were perched casually on the bill of his cap.

"Hey!" said Leather Jacket to Red, making it both a greeting and a punchline. *I know him,* I thought, trying to puzzle out his familiarity. *How do I know him?*

"Welcome on board," she replied, all business again.

"Thanks!" he said with practiced ease, clapping large, supple hands together and flashing her another smile as they ambled past and fell into the empty pair of seats across the way from me in the first row. "Thought we'd missed it. Awesome."

"No problem," she said, "You just made it." With this, she turned and, at last, smiled. At me. A feline smile that broadcast her intent as clearly as if she'd used the airplane's public address system.

Oh, shit.

I knew what was expected of me now. I was expected to get up and get in Red's face, explain that she didn't know who she was dealing with and that if she closed that door she might find herself stuck on the Seattle-Anchorage run for the next six months. I had my hands on the armrests, ready to push myself up and into battle, when something shifted inside me, like a heavy piece of luggage coming loose in the back as a car goes around a sharp turn.

Certainly, it had something to do my own increasing inability to reconcile Cassini's public face of pragmatic, can-do Democrat with the private man I had come to view with a mixture of awe and revulsion. Most likely, it had something to do as well with the contrast of Leather Jacket's entrance, the jovial grace with which he had handled his own situation. But I honestly believe what finally reached me was something determined and honorable in the face of our anonymous flight attendant, who wanted only one thing: to do her job, and maybe hang onto a little dignity in the process.

She paused a moment at the door, glancing down at me again. *She's still expecting me to get up and yell at her,* I realized. *Because I work for him, she expects me to be like him. Jesus.* And that was that. I looked up at Red, raised my eyebrows, pursed my lips and sighed. She flashed me the briefest of grins before pulling the handle on the automatic door.

Politics, I thought as the door began its irrefutable hydraulic swing downward, *may not suit me.*

2

Sometimes in the late summer twilight, when the air under the prolific oaks surrounding our back patio grew soft and feathery as a down quilt, my father would begin in his low, rumbling voice to sketch out his vision of the perfect day. Standing over the brick barbecue he'd built by hand, leaning hard against it in his awkward way, he would pass the time while the burgers sizzled by putting his vision into words, drawing it like a picture puzzle.

"Eggs and bacon for breakfast around eight. The eggs scrambled, bacon just crisp, not crunchy, not soft. Kitchen so full of the smell you want to lick the air. Newspaper's on the table waiting. Good news about the Giants in the sports section. A big trade, we finally picked up that ace starting pitcher we need to get past the Dodgers."

Then he'd stir from his thoughts and check on the burgers, thrusting the metal spatula under the patties one by one with a magical-sounding "Shhhing" against the steel grill he carried into the garage and polished every winter like a jeweler.

"Then putter in the back yard for a couple of hours, a little weeding, rake a few leaves, enjoy the breeze in the trees. A smoke or two while I'm at it."

When the patties had achieved the precise coloration and surface tension desired, he would make the exchange, flipping them with exaggerated care, like plump pancakes. After three to five minutes on side two it would be time to add the buns to the grill, gently, using the spatula to ease them on.

"Then back inside for lunch. A turkey club on a french roll, extra mustard and jalapenos, with Laura Scudders barbecue chips on the side. A little time with a book on the couch, maybe Robert Frost or Robert Parker, depending on the mood. Then a long drive down 101 to the Bay, maybe stop along the shore at Richardson Bay and watch the herons peck away at the mudflats for a few minutes, before dinner on the water in Sausalito, melt-in-your-mouth grilled swordfish on top of the tangiest shrimp cocktail you've ever tasted."

When the time came to lift our black-striped charges off the grill I would man the platter, holding on with both hands to keep it steady.

"Last," he would say. "Across the bridge – don't forget to look down at the big cargo ships going under, crashing through the whitecaps in slow motion – and into the city. Down Lombard to Divisadero, then over the hill. Cut over to Fillmore, park in the middle of the block, a little past the dumpster. And then, into Winterland." (The promised land. Here he would stop, fully engaged in his reverie, the last patty still wavering in midair between the grill and the waiting platter, his voice low and throaty with emotion.) "Front row seats. It's a double bill, The Who and Led Zeppelin in their prime, Moon and Bonham both alive and wailing away at their drum kits. Jimmy Page wrings the sweat off his hands and throws a towel down to me. Daltrey windmills the mike so close I can hear it cutting through the air, then snatches it with his other hand and bends himself in half with a scream loud enough to shatter my camera lens."

And then he'd finish, and put the second burger on the second bun, and check the coals to make sure nothing was in danger of catching. And hand me the spatula so that I could carry it back inside, too. And pick up his crutches from where they waited, leaning against the brick counter, and balance on whichever was his good foot that month like the Leaning Tower of Belly before beginning his difficult, stumbling traverse back into the house, and our lonely table for two.

* * *

We were a half hour into the flight and I was two fingers down on my third screwdriver by the time I realized Frank still had my phone. Not only had I ditched the candidate, the campaign wouldn't even be able to track me down now. The day's schedule was a shambles, and I was officially AWOL.

I took another long swig and adjusted my seat back farther, imagining Cassini's volcanic reaction to being left on the gangway at LAX. As the door had moved into place and sealed, there had been one loud thump on the outside and then nothing more. Most likely, security had backed him off and then had to physically herd him up the ramp. No doubt my phone was a lost cause. He'd been known to hurl them into urinals when calls didn't go his way; under the circumstances I imagined him performing some sort of elaborate ritual execution on mine.

I raised my glass in toast to the locked cabin door. "Francis," I said.

"What?" My seat-mate across the aisle had glanced up, curious. I realized in a rush that he'd been sitting silent and nearly motionless all through our preflight and takeoff – ever since the door closed, in fact. No magazines, no earphones, not even idle chit-chat with his voluminous neighbor, who was presently tipped all the way back in his seat, earphones on, thick arms crossed, silent as a Buddha. The only move he'd made in all that time was to take off his cap, revealing a dark, stylish mop of hair. I saw now that he wore a soul patch as well, a triangular tuft of neatly-trimmed beard tucked under his lower lip.

"Ha," I said, momentarily flailing for a response. "Uh, just saying so long to a friend. Nope, not a friend. Jeez. It's a long story. A really long, stupid story —"

My raconteur's eyebrows had raised to half-mast. Thick, assertive things, potentially quite bushy if not tended with care, which they had been. "It's alright," he assured me in a calming tone. "I'm just along for the ride like everyone else."

"What?"

"It's just — sometimes people get nervous, talking to me. I'm just saying, chill. Don't worry about it."

"Nervous."

"Yeah."

I stared at him a minute longer, taking in his firm, symmetrical nose, evenly tanned face and disheveled waves of dark hair that contrasted affectingly with deep-set blue eyes, crow's feet taking hold at the corners like embellishments that only enhance an already-memorable face. Except I couldn't remember it. It was tantalizingly familiar, but in my half-drunk and wholly frazzled state, I couldn't place it.

Whatever. I went back to nursing my drink.

"So, what's in SF? Business?" He was still watching me, bright-eyed and expectant.

"Uh, not really. Not anymore."

"Change of plans?"

"You could say that."

"Was the snarly guy on the gangway with you?" He gestured toward the empty seat beyond me.

"Yeah. Yeah, he was." I couldn't help it. I grinned.

"No big loss, eh?"

I chuckled and shook my head in agreement. "Nope."

He leaned closer and sang his next words to me, softly, conspiratorially, but without a hint of self-consciousness: "'Cause I'm aaaaaalready gone…'"

Instinctively, I finished the line: "'…and I'm feeeeeelin' strong.'"

Encouraged, he tried again. "Big old jet airliner…'"

"'…don't carry me too far away.'" I was chuckling now, feeling warm

11

and relaxed and strangely at home. "Except, no. Far away is good. Necessary, even." I finished off my drink and my thought. "That was my boss."

"Take this job and shove it," responded Blue Eyes in a dead-on country drawl.

I was laughing again, deep into it now. "Oh, what was that Queen song, the one about their ex-manager from the album with 'Bohemian Rhapsody'?"

"Death on two legs," he sang back in perfect Freddie Mercury falsetto.

"Doo-doo-doo-DOO-doo-doo," I followed, singing the guitar chords.

"Yeah, that one's sweet." He eased back into his seat with a thoughtful grin as a companionable quiet descended between us.

* * *

"Chill." "That one's sweet." Not phrases you'd normally expect from a man with flecks of gray coming in at the temples and smile lines etched into his cheeks. I mulled this, and my day so far, for some time as I powered through a fourth drink, moving up to a less disingenuous vodka-rocks just in case the flight attendant was getting ready to cut me off. I typically stopped at two and the alcohol was starting to make me feel hazy in a way that was both unfamiliar and welcome. For a year and a half – hell, for six – I had been focused, ordered and obedient. On track. Now I was off, and this brought me a primitive satisfaction.

Eventually, I realized one of the coach flight attendants, a tiny blonde with small, round hipster glasses, had cornered the fierce Red in the galley in front of us, where the two of them were whispering like schoolgirls.

After a moment Red emerged, no longer severe, in fact now somewhat flushed, and handed Blue Eyes a glass of champagne from a small silver tray. "For you," she said softly, but with a purposeful stare, before retreating back to the galley.

I watched as the frowning Blue Eyes set the glass down on the wide armrest next to him and took a long look at the phone number clearly inscribed on the cocktail napkin underneath.

"That happen to you a lot?"

He glanced up and gave me a curious look, as if calculating how to split a complicated restaurant bill. Then he shook his head wearily. "Too much."

"Uh." I overcame my surprise and the accompanying tinge of jealousy as, without warning, the synapses started firing again. "*Crash*, Dave Matthews Band, song number three." The *–sh* in *Crash* had lasted a little longer than I'd meant it to.

Now it was his turn to grin. "'Too Much.' Uh-huh. They really jam on that one. But the best cut on that album is 'Say Goodbye.' His vocal range is unreal, and the sax tone is godlike."

"Well, sure."

"You know your music."

"Yeah. S'nothin'. My dad. See, he wrote for *Noise* magazine for, I dunno, twenny-five years. Photographer, too. We used to do this all the time, like a game."

"*Noise*. No kidding. What's his name?"

"Bernie Green. One of the boys from the *Noise*, yeah." I shook my head. "He died in January. Six months ago this week."

"Bernie Green." I could feel his eyes on me, but I wasn't prepared to meet them in that moment. "Wow. I'm sorry."

I glanced up and damned if he didn't *look* sorry. My eyes fell to my hands again. I had unconsciously worked the napkin I had gotten with my last drink – the perfectly blank napkin – into a tightly folded one-by-one square. "Yeah. He was alright. A sweetheart, his editor used to call him. Too many cheeseburgers and cherry pies on the road, not to mention the cigarettes. First diabetes, then a heart attack, then a bigger one. He was 55."

"Too soon, man. Way too soon."

There was nothing I could really say to that.

"So, are you a writer, too?"

"Me?" I'd asked myself the question a couple of times in high school and college, but it'd been years since anyone had asked it of me. "Nope." I finished off the dregs of my drink, the ice clattering as I set the empty cup back down.

"Huh. Well, you look like you could use a ride when we get in. Where you headed?"

I considered this for a minute. "Uh. I don't know. I mean, there's this thing I was supposed to go to…" Giggle. "But I don't think I'm invited anymore."

"Well, look. I've got a session downtown this afternoon. If you've got no plans, come along."

A session. The image of a therapist's aggressively comforting waiting room, all pastels and puffy pillows, flickered past. "Huh?"

"We're at Wonder Wheel Studios. Hitch a ride and hang out for a while until you feel better."

"Yeah? Uh, thanks." The conversation had taken one too many weird turns. It was time to clear things up. I stuck out my hand. "Tim Green."

Watching me the whole time, he took it with a careful, sympathetic smile and gave it a quick shake. "Jordan Lee." He nodded back towards his massive companion. "And that's Ray."

Fortunately Ray did not stir, because in the meantime the name Jordan Lee had set my mind churning like an industrial washing machine. It took a few seconds, what with all the driblets of anger and sadness and confusion and alcohol clogging things up. When recognition came, though, it came in a rush.

Lead singer for Stormseye. Four-time Rolling Stone *cover boy, with and without the band. A bunch on the front of* Noise *as well, if I remember right. Frontman for the only act ever to sell out the Oakland Coliseum five nights in a row. A fistful of platinum albums and almost as many Grammy nominations. A bona fide, homegrown California rock star.*

Willing myself to stay composed, I stole another glance at my new acquaintance. He was looking away now, expression clouded, as if he'd done something he knew he had to, but regretted all the same.

3

Terry Valenzuela was the first girl I ever kissed. No, check that – Terry, the dusky-haired neighborhood tomboy and my best friend since fourth grade, was the first girl who ever kissed me. We were eleven. The thermometer out back hit the upper nineties that late June afternoon, and Terry and I were beating the heat down at the creek that ran along the edge of our neighborhood, a semi-rural cluster of homes on the outskirts of Santa Rosa, an hour north of San Francisco. Squatting on the dirt bank of the creek, ten feet ahead of where it ran into a large concrete culvert that cut under our street, we had whiled away half an afternoon chasing and catching tadpoles. I had just finished pouring our last catch into the big pyrex mixing bowl we had liberated from my kitchen earlier when I looked up to see Terry standing in a sunbeam at the entrance of the pipe, waiting. For what, I've never known.

All the same I stood up, wiped my hands on my shorts, and picked my way along the rocky bank, speculating on the way about whether when we were done she'd want to ride bikes down to the Seven-Eleven with me so I could buy some baseball cards. Just as I reached her, expecting to be shown some interesting bug or plant, she reached over, put a hand on either shoulder, and kissed me square on the lips.

Electricity didn't buzz through me. No clouds parted and angels did not sing on high. But the surprise I felt in the moment gave way almost instantly to a kind of exhilarating *Zing!* that tingled in my chest and rang in my ears.

Riding north along the muddy shores of San Francisco Bay in the back of a white limo with Jordan and Ray, for the briefest instant, a rippling echo of that *Zing!* sensation came dancing down my lifeline to the present.

I knew it couldn't possibly be the perfect day of my father's imagination, seeing as though by eleven-thirty I'd lost my job and drunk my breakfast.

But all things considered, it had felt surprisingly decent, strolling off the plane without the slightest fanfare, no CHP waiting, no clustered greeting party of obsequious staffers. It had been a year and a half since I'd joined the campaign, eighteen months of being shackled to a schedule, my entire life regimented by a constant clamor of demands and obligations. As the open sunroof blended the salty sea-breeze with the rich, spunky scent of fresh leather, I began to feel uncaged, alive in a way I hadn't been for a long time.

I'm riding in a limo with Jordan Lee. I shook my head to clear it, but nothing changed, not the shadowed opulence of the limo's interior, nor the wispy fingers of fog being beaten back by the mid-morning sun above, nor the steady murmur of Jordan talking into his cell phone next to me. At one point I glanced at the glass partition that separated us from the driver's compartment and caught my own reflection, the dark-haired, long-faced kid in the charcoal gray suit sitting next to the rock and roll demi-god like this was all completely normal. A moment later I realized the southern reaches of the city had already flown by and we were exiting at the base of the downtown skyline.

Wonder Wheel Studios stood tall amid the wreckage of San Francisco's end-of-the-century tech boom. At its apex, a ravening horde of silicon-based business startups had transformed building after building in the formerly rough-and-tumble commercial district south of Market Street, consuming decaying, inexpensive lofts full of starving artists and spitting back out sleek, modern office spaces haunted by twitchy venture capitalists in thousand-dollar suits. Until the miniature boomtown went bust, that is, when the wind of change suddenly died down from a hurricane to a stiff breeze. Today the neighborhood was an eclectic mixture of the new, the old, and the nearly falling-down.

Ray held the door for us at the base of the graying four-story WPA building that housed Wonder Wheel, trailing me into the lobby. There was no need for him to take the point any more, as we were now officially in Jordan's element. The only threat I detected from the green-haired young receptionist who shot out of her chair to greet us was that she might slump to her knees at any moment, wrap her spidery, tattooed arms around Jordan's legs and never let go. I was glad I'd at least pulled off my tie and opened my collar.

The interior of the studio reminded me of a movie set, a façade masking mysteries both elaborate and mundane. A high-ceilinged reception area with large plants and modern prints hanging on the walls created the illusion of a marginally stylish business office, the only creative touch the cloudy glass bricks that made up the reception desk's front wall. Five steps down the hall past reception, though, you crossed into a new dimension. We passed small rooms crammed with banks of indecipherable electronic equipment, panel after shiny panel of knobs and switches and dials and readouts that could have supplied Salvador Dali with fresh new nightmares to paint. At the end of the hall lay three large rooms, one overrun with a maze of keyboards on trestles and stacked amps and a circled drum set surrounded by open guitar cases. The other two lay virtually empty.

Turning left into one of the apparently deserted spaces, we were met by a line of greeters already emerging from a glassed-in control booth behind the left wall of the large room. One after another they approached Jordan, shaking his hand, slapping his shoulder, thanking him for being there with grateful eyes and, in some cases, an undertone of awe.

We were in the bubble, a place I'd inhabited again and again escorting Frank Cassini through the hinterlands of California politics. We were the center of attention, with deference and accommodation the order of the day as soon as people came within range of our celebrity pheromones. Except this was a different kind of bubble. People approached Frank with a wary mixture of hope and fear, like a football team they'd placed a large bet on but didn't entirely trust to beat the spread. Jordan, by contrast, was the object of out-and-out adulation.

Toward the end of the line he grabbed me by the elbow and pulled me forward to greet a slender, intense man with small rectangular glasses and a shock of straight gray hair falling almost to his shoulders. "Robert, this is my friend Tim. He's along for the ride today. Tim, Robert Pierson. He put this whole thing together." After a moment, Jordan observed my slack-jawed state and elaborated. "We're finishing up a benefit album for the California Conservation Association. It's called *This Land is Our Land*, y'know, the old Woody Guthrie song, except Jackson Browne changed the lyrics so it talks about California landmarks, the Sierras and the coastline and all that."

I nodded and shook Pierson's long, soft, very pink hand. "Nice to meet you. Uh, wow. I'm a fan." *How many acts has this guy produced platinum albums for? R.E.M., the Pixies, Soundgarden... good God, I think he might have engineered for the Who in the seventies.*

One side of Pierson's mouth angled up into a wry half-grin. "Make yourself at home, then," he offered in a clipped British accent that felt both alien and comforting in this strange new world, gesturing toward the far end of the room. Following his gaze I found a large table laid out with a heaping buffet of sandwiches, cookies, fruit, water, beer and wine. "If you need anything, ask him." Pierson nodded toward an equally gangly but decades-younger fellow in ripped jeans and stormtrooper boots who was leaning against the window to what I now recognized as the vocal booth. It was a smallish room tucked into the left wall alongside the control room, empty other than a microphone hanging from the ceiling and a pair of headphones hanging from a rack on the inside wall.

Jordan moved directly into the vocal booth and began warming up, singing a series of scales and nonsense phrases. Trailing him to the door, I stuck my hand out to Pierson's studio assistant, who I saw now had five loop earrings trailing up the side of his left ear, well into the vast recesses of stringy black hair surrounding his sullen face. He stared at me a moment before giving my offered hand a perfunctory shake. "I'm Tim."

"Yeah."

In the booth, Jordan interrupted everyone, holding up a strangely knotted, feathery brown necklace and asking "What's this?"

"Jewel must've left that this morning," said Pierson. "The pendant kept banging against her shirt-buttons so we had her take it off."

"Oh, that's good. For a minute I thought maybe Adam had left one of his dreadlocks in here."

I whispered, half to myself and half to my voluble companion, "Adam Duritz is on this album?"

He sighed, bored with me already. "He was in last week. He and Bonnie Raitt did a duet."

With that, I was officially Alice, slipped down the rabbit-hole.

* * *

Through the 1980s and nineties my father aged, but his musical tastes never quite caught up. He was game to try anything, I'll give him that – I remember catching him unaware in his home office once with his mission control-sized Koss earphones on, jiggering around like an epileptic to Tupac Shakur – but his heart stayed in the seventies. It's one of the reasons he was so excited when Stormseye emerged from the Bay Area scene in the midst of the grunge era. He had hailed them in a review in the back pages of *Noise* as "a group talented and audacious enough to transplant the very heart of rock and roll – the furious noise, the fervent belief – into a new body built for a new age."

The Allman Brothers and Van Morrison were obvious influences in their fluid, heavily melodic approach, and early Springsteen surely informed the raw emotion often poured out in their lyrics. But they were also playful, never taking themselves too seriously. They could blast out a stadium-sized rock song with lyrics purposeful and powerful enough to generate a 50,000-person sing-along, then undercut themselves a moment later with songs like "Green-Eyed Angel," a mid-tempo track that lulls you into thinking it's a love song for two verses, until at the chorus the narrator's girl is revealed as an obsessive nut-job. My dad once compared them to "U2 with less ego and better punchlines."

They were also prolific. In an era when many record labels had come to view two to three years as perfect spacing between albums, and following a period when major artists like Peter Gabriel and Dire Straits had taken five and six years between releases, Stormseye had issued five albums of new material in nine years. Over the course of their first decade they had built a global audience in the tens of millions.

At the pinnacle of their popularity, they had broken up. Or not. The announcement at the end of the truncated *September Serenade* tour had indicated they were "taking a break." But that break had stretched to six months, a year, then two, then five. They had never turned their backs completely on each other; there had been a series of reunion one-off shows at benefits for organizations like the Natural Resources Defense Council and the World Wildlife Fund. They'd done the annual BRIDGE School Benefit in Berkeley twice at the invitation of Neil Young. But until the previous spring, there had been no serious talk in the music press of an actual reformation of the band. Jordan had issued a pair of well-received solo albums during their hiatus, but had remained largely out of the spotlight other than his charity work.

As a result, Stormseye's current reunion album and tour had snowballed into a major cultural happening. The 21st century media machine had welcomed the band back with open arms, ready to tackle someone with a little more substance than the Hollywood celebutante du jour and the latest crop of *American Idol* posers. "Storming Back" was the predictable *Rolling Stone* headline (not that many people cared what *RS* thought anymore, but it still counted as national press). Similar puns played out across the pages of *Spin*, *Noise*, *People* and even *Guitar Player*, whose latest issue featured a grinning Nicky Frost on the cover.

There was more, of course, tidbits of industry rumor and party-circuit gossip from the band's earlier days, but the details were lost in the fog of three hundred artist profiles and three thousand album reviews, my father's Don Quixote-ish legacy, a virtual critical encyclopedia of a creative genre many still can't conceive of as art.

* * *

As my initial awe at my surroundings settled into a contented rhythm watching Jordan work, I began to sober up, clarity leeching back in accompanied by the old familiar strains of worry and regret and guilt. My father had a reputation as a sweetheart, yes, but one whose work ethic was as much a legend in the music-press world as his appetite. He was the sort of guy who, from the day he'd been handed a portable tape recorder, would pack it along to the grocery store in case either inspiration or a chance meeting happened along. The mere act of floating directionless for ninety minutes began to grate on me as soon as the alcohol lost its grip.

Worse yet, as my head began to clear, a wave of buyer's remorse washed in and capsized my mood. Deputy press secretary to Frank Cassini's campaign for United States Senator might not have been the height of political glory to which I sometimes aspired, but it was a damned good job for a twenty-seven-year-old. Less than six years ago I'd been an intern running errands for the Chief Clerk of the Assembly. As satisfying as my choice had felt on the plane, locked in the moment, back in the present it was beginning to feel like the biggest miscalculation of my young life. *What did I just do?*

After Jordan had worked through the song four times, continually fine-tuning his pacing and inflections, he asked for a break. As he left the booth, I pigeon-holed him like the pro I was, or had been until that morning.

"Look, um, this has been great. I really appreciate it. But I need to find a phone now and call my office —" Without slowing he fished a cell phone out of his pocket and handed it off to me, tracking out into the hallway with a little *suit yourself* half-shrug.

"Thanks," I called after him, already backing away into one of the large room's empty corners. Taking a few deep breaths for good measure, I dialed the campaign's LA office, occupying donated space a block north of Wilshire Boulevard.

"Chambers."

"Hi Ame, it's Tim." My erstwhile boss Amy Chambers was Cassini's press secretary, the smartest person in the building for much of her professional life, and as brutally to the point behind the scenes as she could be evasive with a microphone thrust in her face. Her legend continued to grow — she'd had a hand in three consecutive successful statewide campaigns, with Frank lined up as number four. The opportunity to work for her was among the reasons I'd taken the Cassini job.

"Tim." And that was all she said. An ominous sign, coming from someone who was rarely at a loss for words. The faint throb of a midday hangover began to pulse near my temples.

"Yeah. I'm sorry, Ame. I couldn't help it."

"You bailed on the candidate."

In the studio, I began to pace, ignoring my sullen minder's curious looks from across the room. "Um, actually, he pretty much bailed on me. He was on a call when we walked onto the plane and the flight attendant got after him and there was a face-off and —"

"You're supposed to fix this stuff. That's your first responsibility when you travel with him."

"I know. I know. I'm sorry." At that moment, I almost was.

"He's pissed, Tim. REALLY pissed. We had to move the press conference to one-thirty and cancel his lunch. And if Kendrick's people find out he got into it with a flight attendant, they'll be tweeting the crap out of it inside of an hour."

I clenched my eyes shut until multi-colored stars blossomed in the blackness. "Yeah. Look – what should I do?"

"Lay low for a few days."

"You mean he didn't –?"

"No, he did. You're definitely fired. But you know how he is. Give him a few days to cool down. He may come around."

It was true. Frank's record on firing people was decidedly mixed. About half the time it stuck, but the other half he realized after regaining control of his emotions that he needed the person he'd fired at least as much as they needed him. I'd personally witnessed a polling consultant getting run out the door by the candidate one afternoon, only to find him sitting in our conference room again the next morning with a fresh double-latte in his hand like nothing had happened. The man was, like several of the bigger names I'd observed around the Capitol, a little bit of a lunatic.

"Alright. Alright. I'll call again in a few days. You won't be able to get me on my cell, though, 'cause Frank still had it when the door shut."

"I know. Look, Tim, I'm going to see if we can salvage this. But do us both a favor?"

"What?"

"Get it together. You screwed up, and you sound like hell."

* * *

Back in the vocal booth, Jordan was midway through his fifth run at the song, an old '60s tune I couldn't place, something about a mountain and a fire and a soft, smoky sunrise sending shafts of light streaming through the trees. I sank into a director's chair that someone had dragged out and left where I had been standing, just outside the booth. I felt lost again. I had a return ticket to LA and little else to pull me in any particular direction. That in itself was depressing. I was single, parentless and adrift, and had invested my entire professional future in Francis Cassini, only to lose it all to a moment's irretrievable impulse. I couldn't even bring myself to call Terry, the one person I'd always been able to rely on at moments like this to reach down, help me up and dust me off. It was just too humiliating.

A half hour later, Jordan's phone interrupted my sulk, ringing down in my shirt pocket. I stood and glanced around for help, but Jordan was mid-song and Ray was nowhere to be found. On the second ring my sullen keeper began waving frantically at me, gesturing for me to pick it up or turn it off or something, quickly. All I could think to do was power-walk out into the hallway and hit "Talk."

"Ah, hello?"

"Jordan?" The question was full of acid skepticism, the voice deep and strong and on the attack. A wash of noise filled the background, a cacophony of thumps and screeches and hoarse voices shouting indecipherable directions.

"Ah, no, he's in the vocal booth right now."

"So who the fuck is this?"

"It's – I'm Tim. I'm just – at the studio. He gave me his phone."

"Fuck. Well, Mister Tim, give Jordan a message. Got it? You tell him that fucking Seth called, and Glen, and Wayne, and Nicky, too, and if he doesn't haul his ass over here in the next twenty fucking minutes we're going to do the fucking sound check without him. FUCK!"

Returning to the main room yet again, I found Jordan standing just outside the control room chatting with Pierson and one of his sound engineers. I eased up beside him and waited for an opening – another dubious skill honed by hundreds of hours spent at the elbows of Assemblymen and state Senators. As Pierson finished up explaining something I didn't quite catch having to do with emphasizing a certain line in the third chorus, Jordan's attention momentarily flickered in my direction.

I leaned in and whispered "Seth called –"

"Right." He glanced at the clock on the back wall of the control room. "Sorry, Robert. Gotta run – show tonight. See what you've got and if we need to do it again I'll come back next week after Seattle."

I nearly had to jog to keep up with Jordan as he strode out of the room and down the hallway toward the front of the building. Handing his phone back, I asked "So – that was really Seth Lamiroult?"

"The Basher himself. You still with me?"

"I – I mean – where –?" We were out the door and onto the sidewalk by now, Ray having materialized at Jordan's side like a no-necked apparition.

"Sound check, dinner, a little downtime, then the show. C'mon along," he beckoned as the limo emerged from the alley next door, midday sunshine glinting off the windshield like a beacon. "Unless you've got someplace else to be."

4

Needless to say, I did not leave Jordan standing on the sidewalk that day outside the studio. By that point the morning's proceedings had gathered a certain irrefutable momentum; I had been drawn into Jordan Lee's gravitational field like a floundering fragment of cosmic debris yanked off course by a comet. And let's face it – rock stars, limos, bodyguards, famous record producers – it was dazzling, even unemployed and battling a mid-afternoon hangover.

As the limo pulled up to the curb, a crackly, half-strangled voice interrupted us from behind.

"Excuse me! Excuse me! M-mister Lee?"

Jordan and I turned in unison to find Ray already inserting his imposing mass between us and the lanky, tousled high-school kid in a half-sleeved baseball shirt who had materialized from the recesses of the studio's facade. One of the kid's hands was hidden inside the backpack he wore over one shoulder, now slung halfway around in front. Ray was on him instantly, nose to nose, with one hand firmly wrapped around the forearm that corresponded to the hand inside the backpack.

"Ow! What – ?"

"Slowly," said Ray in a voice that was at once quiet, deep and thoroughly commanding.

The kid instinctively obeyed, removing his captive hand from the backpack with exaggerated care, Ray's firm grip loosening only once he saw it held a pair of CD booklets and a thick Sharpie pen, and nothing more. Ray's attention turned next to Jordan. He waited silently, the midafternoon sun reflecting sharply off his dark glasses. I glanced over at Jordan in time to catch him giving an almost imperceptible nod. Ray's hand fell away, though he remained within arm's length for the entire exchange that followed.

Jordan approached the kid, who I saw now was about seventeen and wide-eyed as an acrophobic skydiver. His shirt was decorated with the Stormseye logo and a fancifully painted scene of the band set up and playing on a mountaintop. "Hi, I'm Jordan."

"I – uh – whoa. Chad." Transferring his bounty awkwardly to the other hand, he shook Jordan's offered one.

"Nice to meet you, Chad. Listen, I'm in kind of a hurry today –"

"Sure. Of course. I was just wondering –" He held up the CD booklets in a mute plea for understanding.

"No problem," said Jordan with an easy grin.

"Thanks," Chad said in a voice that suggested he was having significant trouble breathing. "I've been listening to you guys... forever. And your solo stuff, the *Mountain Blue* album, I swear, you have no idea... Thanks. Oh, man."

Jordan looked up from signing the second booklet – "To Chad, All the best, Jordan Lee" – and caught his eye. "You going to the show?"

"Uh, I – I don't know. I missed the presale on the Web site, and then my buddy was supposed to take care of it, but he flaked –"

"You don't have a ticket?"

"N-no." He was actually *quivering.*

Jordan turned to Ray. "Put him on the list. Chad, give my friend Ray your full name. You got a driver's license?"

He swallowed hard and nodded.

"Take it to the Will Call window an hour before the show tonight. There'll be two tickets waiting for you."

"Are you – ? Ohmigod. Are you – ?"

"Have a good time," said Jordan, waving as he backed away and ducked down into the limo's open door, beckoning for me to follow. Ray lingered long enough to collect Chad's full name before boarding last, pulling the door closed behind him and settling into a seat opposite us.

As the limo pulled away, I tried to stay cool. It was a ridiculous proposition. After spending a year at Frank Cassini's side, the whole exchange felt inside out and backwards – celebrity sought out based on admiration rather than need, celebrity reacting with generosity rather than calculation. Finally I couldn't take the silence any more. I exhaled hard and grinned. "Heh. Wow."

A pair of creases briefly dented Jordan's smooth forehead. He shrugged. "Yeah? Well, you know, I did a few stakeouts in my day. Half the time whoever it was would blow right past the kid in the doorway begging autographs. It pissed me off, but once I started getting asked, I understood a lot better how it is. Once you get past a certain point, there's just too many people. Plus, nowadays a lot of these guys aren't even fans – they're just building inventory for eBay."

"But you took care of him."

"Sure. You saw. He was the real thing, and he was polite, and he was alone. Easy call. I wish more of them were that easy."

My dad had a theory about fame. He said that becoming famous amplifies a person's essence, makes them more of whatever they already are. If they're touchy, they become temperamental; if they're introverted, they become inaccessible; if they're arrogant, they became little Napoleons. And if they're innately modest and generous? These adjectives didn't come up too often in my father's line of work.

*   *   *

As we snaked through the hopelessly knotted mid-afternoon traffic, Jordan coaxed more details from me about my dad's career. I told how he'd dropped out of college in the early seventies to become the music editor for Madison, Wisconsin's local alternative weekly before graduating to the ranks of stringer for *Rolling Stone, Creem* and the rest of the emerging national music press. Dropping out was a dangerous path in those days, but thanks to his diabetes, the U.S. Army had already declined interest in retaining his services in Southeast Asia. Within a few years, he'd instead been drafted by a pair of former colleagues to be senior staff writer for their new music magazine, a twelve-page, San Francisco-based tabloid called *Noise.*

"Your dad was good," said Jordan. "One of the things I remember about him is that his name didn't come up much with the guys. When we talked about writers at all, it was usually bitching about the ones who burned us. Y'know, hung out with us for a night and halfway through we all laughed at something Nicky said about a girl, and the story's about what a bunch of total horndogs we are, instead of the album or the show."

"That wasn't his style." He'd told me plenty of stories about the acts he covered, of course. But they rarely made it beyond living-room anecdotes. When he wrote for publication, he wrote about the music. It was part of the reason the work started to wind down about the same time he did. He couldn't adapt to the modern style, where writers inject themselves into the story and trash anyone who crosses them. He actually liked most musicians, and saw his role as helping bridge the gap between them and their audience.

"So, if you're not a writer, what do you do?"

"I —" A rueful laugh escaped me. "I work for Frank Cassini."

"Cassini," he said, searching for a flicker of recognition and not finding it. "Is he with one of the labels?"

I love it. "No, uh, he's the attorney general of California."

"No kidding."

"Yep."

"Big kahuna lawyer."

I laughed. "Yeah, well, in a ceremonial kind of way. He hasn't tried a case in fifteen years."

"Huh. Well, I almost knocked him on his ass back on the gangway in LA. He didn't want to move aside, until he got a good look at Ray."

"That's my guy. Scrappy as hell until someone bigger shows up."

"Wait, he's running for something, right?"

"The U.S. Senate."

Our exchange came to an abrupt halt as the limo pulled down a wide alley and came to a stop at a dead-end turnaround near the edge of the Bay. In the marina on our left, a cornfield of white masts danced to the rhythm of the tide. On our right, a tall brick façade loomed, broken up by a line of arches whose articulated steel doors had been rolled up to accommodate a series of extra-wide tractor-trailers. From deep in the shadows of the loading dock inside came the sounds of metal scraping against concrete, barked instructions and the pulsing beep-beep-beep of a backing forklift.

Climbing out of the limo behind Jordan, I glanced back up the alley toward the street and traced our destination's brick façade all the way to the top, two hundred feet above.

"No way."

For the first time in the five hours I'd spent with him, Ray smiled – a tight-lipped crescent that made his ebony cheeks ride up under his big dark glasses – and spoke to me.

"Play ball."

With that, we trailed Jordan into the bowels of AT&T Park, the 41,000-seat home of the San Francisco Giants.

* * *

"Hey, look who decided to show up for work today! It's Jordan-fucking-Lee!"

Seth Lamiroult was standing on a stool hip-deep in cymbals, adjusting the height and play on the vocal mike that hung on stainless steel elbows down into the center of his semicircular drum kit. The kit itself stood on a two-foot riser dead center on the massive stage a crew had erected in the middle of the ballpark's outfield. Lamiroult's awkward perch, black tee and jeans, and loosely-held ponytail of dirty blond ringlets gave him the aspect of a shaggy gargoyle.

"Hey," said Jordan in Seth's general direction, moving to the microphone stand at the front of the stage. "Everybody ready?"

I hung back at sidestage, lingering by the mixing board, where my inherited knowledge of concert protocol told me a roadie would soon begin tweaking the levels on the sound coming through the stage monitors so that the band could actually hear each other playing. Ray had peeled off before we reached the field, right about the time our entourage had begun to multiply, picking up a lumbering stadium security guard, a pair of rank-smelling stagehands, and a hyperactive pixie of a woman – fast-talking, speed-walking, compact, dark-haired and poured into admirably tight designer jeans. My first impression – mature groupie? – proved sadly out of touch when I picked up just enough of her harried by-play with Jordan to peg her as part of the band's management. She had apparently cut away and headed off around the time we reached the stairs at the back corner of the stage rig, though.

"Been ready half an hour," barked Seth, jumping down off first the stool and then the riser.

"Yeah. Sorry. But my time's worth something, too."

"Then why waste it doing bullshit freebies?"

"So, could we do this later?" said Jordan, nodding in the general direction of the group milling behind me. Seth scowled at me, grunted and went off in search of the rest of the band.

While Jordan surveyed the stage and the three long ramps that penetrated far into the field-level seating, the others arrived one by one. Glen Frazier, the silent, elfin bass player, gave me a curious glance as he brushed by. Wayne Campbell appeared next, flaming red curls riding his pale scalp like a halo as he ambled to his post, a shiny black grand piano backed up to a small bank of electronic keyboards. Last to arrive were Seth and the lanky, visibly strutting Nicky Frost.

"Nicky," said Jordan, hand over his mike, holding it gently like a ripe apple. "How is it?"

Frost held up his absurdly lean and gangly left hand and wriggled the last two fingers on it. "Crappy. Like someone stepped on it and turned their fricking heel." His voice was hoarse and throaty with smoke of one sort or another. Then he grinned, expression all teeth, eyes peeking out from under the wash of blond hair that cascaded forward over the top of his long, thin face. "Let's do it."

As they tuned up, hitting stray chords and running little scales, twisting knobs on their gear like mad scientists, I took in the scene before them. Thousands of padded folding chairs had been set up on sheets of plywood covering the entire infield, the natural grass replaced by carefully sculpted rows of steel and vinyl. Beyond the roped-off baseball dugouts, the grandstands rose like castle walls, their steep aisles leading past uncountable banks of fixed seats, four decks reaching halfway to the sky, protecting us from the steady west wind. Halfway up the second deck I saw a concession worker reclining in an aisle seat, his legs splayed over the seat in front of him. I raised my fist to confirm it – from here I could blot him out with a thumbnail. An image flickered in my mind of the Roman Colosseum, filled with sandal-clad ancients in white robes, gathered to watch gladiators, and Christians, and lions.

A moment later, with everyone plugged in and in place, Seth began pumping the kick-drum, starting with a simple 4/4 backbeat, then doubling it on his snare, then decorating it with a rolling fill that took him the length and breadth of his large kit before Glen's bass and Nicky's guitar jumped in and drove them headlong into the opening bars of "Midnight Moonlight," one of the strongest tracks off their 1995 album *Make Some Change*. Rather than come right in the first time around as they did on the record, though, the final two let the driving opening riff make its statement twice before Wayne's piano joined and Jordan began to sing:

"Long after dark, far down that road
Where you swore that you wouldn't,
But you couldn't say no
There's a sigh in the breeze
There's the moon in the trees
It's just you and me
And we'll never go back"

From the stage, you didn't hear the bass so much as feel it, a low rumbling that started in your legs and spread up to your rib cage. The drums and guitar and Wayne's rippling piano lines washed over me until I began to feel submerged. I had been here before many times, lost in a song, letting it lift me into its rhythms, inviting the singer to express for me those things I couldn't find the words to say. But never this close. Here the music didn't meet you; it swallowed you whole. I was vaguely aware of my scalp tingling, one foot tapping, the waves of sound rocking my body back and forth as they plunged into the chorus.

"I come alive at midnight
When you're shinin' in the moonlight
Please, don't go out of my sight
Stay here because it feels right
And I need you now"

Too late, the song's context came back to me and I closed my eyes tight against the memories that were already seeping in. Dad, shambling down an anonymous, antiseptic hallway, working for every breath, wires emerging from under his robe and trailing back to the heart monitor being pushed along on a cart by a nurse. Julie DeFrancesco clutching my sixteen-year-old hand as a solemn young medical resident explained the severity of my father's heart condition, what his home care needs would be, and the changes he needed to make, as if I hadn't been living with a reckless, stubborn diabetic my entire life. Julie and I, driving home alone for the last time before Dad would return with me, stealing glances at each other, knowing my house would lie empty and unsupervised only one more night, calculating our courage to the tune of a song on the radio.

As the band finished, I opened my eyes again, willing myself back to the present. I half-expected to wake up back on the plane, sitting in my seat, still waiting for Frank to take his. Instead, I was standing at the edge of an enormous stage in the middle of a vast stadium on the edge of the colossal bay, tasting the tangy salt air with every breath while five strangers made a sound together that had brought me to the brink of tears.

5

I was in a strange state of semi-delirium as Julie and I got in the car that night at the hospital, our long, probing, impossibly unself-conscious parking lot kiss still fresh on my lips, the cold chemical hospital smell banished for the night by the musky scent of her hair. I reached over again before I'd even started the car – another kiss, another clutch, another barrier fallen away.

As I drove us through the late-evening mist, watching the light bloom and fade across her profile as we swept past one streetlight after another until they ran out, I wondered how this could be happening. My father, Julie, all of it. Part of me was in retreat and wanted nothing more than to curl up alone in a corner and process it all. But then we were pulling into the driveway, and then we were stopping at the house, and then I was looking into Julie's shiny eyes and we were kissing again in the car, deeper, longer, and then she was moving my hands, and then she didn't need to any more.

I remember the sound her shoes made on our front porch, the gentle squeak of rubber soles on painted wood. Everything seemed loud and distant at the same time. She pressed herself against my back as I fumbled for the house key, reaching around to my chest, holding tight. As we cleared the doorway, she let go, and after I'd reached back and locked the door against the night, I turned to find her gone, the nylon-friction sound of her down vest moving quickly up the stairs, not waiting, leading ever onward.

I hung back in the darkened living room for a split-second, gathering myself. I wanted to follow her – to take the stairs two at a time, in fact – but I couldn't seem to shut off my mind just yet. After weeks of tentative, often frustrating exploration, why now? Did our connection somehow take on new meaning and depth as Julie stood next to me, gripping my arm like a crutch, listening to the doctor explain the seven things I absolutely had to do to keep my father alive? Or did she just feel sorry for me?

And then it didn't matter anymore. Dad was coming home tomorrow. Tonight, we were alone. I was pretty sure I loved Julie, and pretty sure she loved me, inasmuch as I understood the term. Momentum was with us, and the chance we had that night would pass by all too quickly.

As I reached the top of the stairs and peered down the darkened hallway, a ghostly shape passed in front of the window at the other end, moving from the bathroom to my bedroom, silhouetted against the moonlight shining in the tall oak just outside. The flickering image of blue light flashing on the moon-sliver curve of her hip shot through me like lightning. I caught up with her before she reached my bed, kicking piled clothes out of the way, grabbing her bare shoulders and turning her around, pulling her whole, unadorned self into my arms.

The next half hour passed in an instant or an eternity, depending on the mood I'm in when I'm remembering it. Can you say it went by quickly when every new moment, every new sensation felt supercharged with weight and significance? Yet it seems so small now, over so quickly, passed into memory and preserved in amber.

This I do know; from the instant my foot hit the first stair, the question of why then was banished. We never talked about it afterwards, which helps to explain how we came to break up six weeks later in a flurry of misgivings and misunderstandings. In the end, I think the answer wasn't opportunity, or pity, or even plain old teenaged lust. It was even more visceral than that. We were sixteen and death had come for a visit, stared us in the face and recounted in grim detail the fate that awaits us all. The thing Julie and I needed more than anything that night was to feel vital. Clutching one another and gasping for air in the still quiet beyond midnight, if we knew nothing else, we knew we were alive.

*   *   *

After "Midnight Moonlight" the band ran through four more songs, none of the big ones like "Make Some Change" or "I Don't Want to Know," all album cuts instead, lesser-known songs they actually needed to practice playing. The "Storm of the Century Tour" had been getting strong reviews as they mixed in generous helpings of older material with the expected favorites and a couple of cuts from the new album. They'd never been a singles band; even the slightly grungy "I Don't Want to Know," which had been all over college radio in the nineties, never made it into the Top Ten. They had built a career primarily on album sales driven by a relentless touring schedule.

The sound check lasted maybe half an hour, during which time I caught sight of any number of people – roadies, stadium concession staff, security guards – stopping in their tracks to listen for a moment. Even warming up for the real show later on, they played with an undeniable fire. There was a compelling synergy about these five guys as a band, a unique critical mass of sound they were able to achieve together that it was hard to imagine them ever coming close to apart.

When it was over, they spun off in five different directions without a backward glance. Jordan stood alone at center-stage for a moment, looking out over the ocean of empty seats as if searching for something or someone who wasn't there. Then he seemed to come around and ambled over to ask if I was hungry, which I found I was, for the first time in many hours. Weaving through the graveyard of empty equipment cases behind the stage, Jordan led me back along the warning track, around the left-field foul pole, down a green-walled alley and under the bleachers into a large room where a buffet and a series of round tables had been set up. Ray met us at the door. The far wall was festooned with logos, and I recognized it as the backdrop to several post-game news conferences I'd caught on ESPN; dinner had been set up in the Giants' press briefing room.

As we moved through the buffet line, I came to an odd realization; since we'd arrived at the stadium, I hadn't seen a single person speak to Jordan outside of the band itself, and Ray. No, that wasn't true, there was the woman with the tight jeans. But other than her, everyone else on the crew seemed to give him a wide berth. It wasn't that they didn't like him – plenty of them stole admiring glances of one sort or another when he wasn't looking – it just seemed like his presence somehow took up more space than anyone else in the room.

Full plates in hand, Jordan parked us at an empty table with a good angle on one of the flat-screen TVs mounted high up on the wall. Without a word, Ray adjusted the channel and settled in opposite us. Observing what was clearly a regular ritual of some kind, I had to ask.

"CNN?"

"Sure. Just about every day since '91. I was watching when they started bombing Baghdad while the CNN guys were filming from their hotel room. It was the most incredible thing I've ever seen."

I found that statement hard to accept coming from a guy well into his second decade of life as a rock star. But... "Do any of the others...?"

"You mean does Nicky dig Christiane Amanpour? Nicky digs anything he can't have. But, no, the other guys are into cars and gear and Wayne likes to travel but they all think I'm a total geek, watching the news. Notice they aren't exactly rushing over to join us."

The five band members had, in fact, put as much physical distance between each other as they possibly could in the catering room. Glen the bass player was closest to us, two tables away.

We were in the midst of making small talk about the story on the screen, an update on the Middle East talks, when Tight Jeans suddenly materialized at Jordan's elbow. For whatever reason – possibly the electricity that threatened to arc off of her in the course of every brisk movement – when I'd seen her the first time on the way into the stadium I hadn't completely registered how small she was. Standing next to Jordan's chair she barely had to lean over to talk in his ear. She couldn't have been more than five-two, but her wiry frame radiated an intensity that was destined, maybe even designed, to intimidate.

She started out in a low voice that gradually rose until Ray and I could both clearly hear every word she was saying.

"…and Hank called back they can't do the 24th it won't work because of the Chili Peppers' tour Flea and Lady Gaga have to shoot that day so the only day they can take you is the 26th and it has to be in the morning because Lindsay Lohan won't book anything before noon and I told him it wasn't convenient but there's just no other time so if you want to –"

"Fine," said Jordan.

"What?" Straightening now, hands on her hips. Her dark, precisely parted tumble of hair sending off a blinding sheen, her right eye giving a little twitch.

"It's fine. That was going to be a day off, but it's no big deal. We can just move it around."

Blinking rapidly, dark brown irises darting to me and Ray and then back to Jordan. "Alright then I'll change it but don't forget we have to talk about the desert thing in Phoenix next month you said you'd do it but the tour's in St. Louis the day before and Kansas City the day after and I'm not sure there's enough time to get you there and back –"

"Okay. After the show."

"And I know you don't want to deal with it but we seriously have to talk about the insurance situation it's ridiculous the way Jeremy has it set up with each of you guys carrying your own and the band having an umbrella policy too you guys are getting hosed for no reason and I want to fix it for you."

"Sure. No problem. After the show." Jordan looked around the table, casting baldly about for a diversion. His eyes landed on me. "Natalie, I want you to meet my friend Tim."

Pleased with his choice, I stood up to shake her hand, an act which, along with Jordan's interruption of her flow, seemed to throw her completely off track.

"Hi, I'm Tim Green." My hand out, waiting.

"Uh, uh, hi, Tim."

"Tim, this is my manager, Natalie Shaw." We shook, her willowy princess-hand nonetheless gripping mine like a wrestler's.

"So," continued Jordan, "Tim's a writer."

I stared at him a moment, trying to decipher what the protocol might be in such a situation. Correcting authority figures had not been part of my on-the-job training as a political operative.

"Uh, actually –"

"Sorry. I forgot, he's still in denial."

Natalie and I responded in unison. "What?"

"His dad wrote for *Noise*. And he's been hanging out with me all day, hasn't said ten words I haven't dragged out of him with pliers, but he soaks up every single thing that happens like he's saving it all up for later."

I was speechless. And I could feel Natalie's eyes on me again, now, probing, suspicious. I turned, looking down to meet her gaze, yet feeling distinctly like I was the one with an interrogation lamp pointed in my face.

"Ah, I'm a detail guy."

"Really."

"But I work in politics."

"Oh." That seemed to mollify her a bit.

"Or at least – well, it's a long story."

She looked at Jordan again, who gave a little shrug as if to say *he's harmless*. At which she shook her head in exasperation and sped off with a brief wave and an over-the-shoulder "Well nice to meet you see you around."

I turned from watching her go to find Jordan wearing a grin that threatened to erupt into laughter at any second. As his dimples grew, I caught a quick blast of the appeal that had helped Stormseye become an international phenomenon. The band had talent, yes. But they also had a frontman who was charismatic to the point of incandescence.

"You know," he said at last, "Ray used to be really chatty before I hired Natalie."

Ray grinned and shrugged his broad shoulders. I shook my head and sat down, chuckling. "Ten thousand rock bands in America and I end up backstage with Penn and Teller."

"So what exactly do you do for Cassini?"

I let out a long breath. "Deputy press secretary. Media wrangler, advance man, speechwriter, issue tracker."

"So, a lot of p.r. work."

"Sure, yeah."

"Opposite side of the fence from your dad."

It had never occurred to me to think of it in those terms. "Not – I mean – really, I'm just a glorified go-fer."

"More than that, it sounds like."

"On my good days, yeah. On the bad ones…"

"You end up playing hooky at the ballpark."

"Playing hooky, unemployed. It's not too clear right now."

"Really." Jordan watched me without a word until my neck began to itch.

* * *

I almost hadn't gotten the Cassini job in the first place. When the day had arrived for my first interview with Amy Chambers, I was nowhere to be found. Dad's foot problems had been getting progressively worse, until that morning he had collapsed on his bedroom floor. I had gotten the call from my Aunt Ruth just as I was getting out of the shower in Sacramento. By the time I'd made the two-hour drive to Santa Rosa, Dad was in the ER being alternately prodded and ignored by a bored-looking resident. On my way there I left two messages for Amy explaining my situation and apologizing.

In the end, a week later, they took my father's right leg below the knee. The stump looked like the cheek of a particularly chunky newborn's bottom – bright pink with a complex, puckered topography. He came home just a few days before I finally interviewed with Frank Cassini himself. The ever-reliable Ruth, Dad's only and older sister, helped me and Terry get him home and settled in and worked with me to bring order to his new lifestyle, which included three visits a week from a home health care nurse. I had anticipated a kind of avuncular resignation from him, a string of weak puns intended to distract us from the finality of his loss and the progression it represented. Instead, he went silent for hours, sometimes days at a time. Whatever spring of wit and affability he had been tapping into all those years had suddenly run dry. Life had changed, and Dad was too absorbed in processing that change to offer his customary dose of comfort to the rest of us.

The day of the interview I rose from the bed I'd slept in as a child and said goodbye to him early. I was to meet Cassini at the state building in downtown San Francisco, two blocks from City Hall. I had managed to meet with Amy twice by that point, once a formal interview, once an informal lunch, a sort of "get-to-know-you-better" session in which she probed my approach to issues and sense of humor when I was a little less on guard. I had apparently passed both tests, but one remained.

The state building was classic '60s institutional, drab gray with a lot of stainless steel finishes that looked cheap and provincial now. It took me twenty minutes to clear through three increasingly tight layers of security – front-desk guard, CHP escort, executive assistant – to the man himself. He sat behind an elephantine cherry-wood desk with pillared feet carved with bulky geometric patterns that suggested Frank Lloyd Wright in a steroid rage.

"Have a seat."

I did, taking in the sharp division of labor between the walls on either side of his desk, one lined with tall bookcases containing leather-bound volumes of the California Code, the state's entire statutory infrastructure, and the other a disorienting maze of framed photos, some in color, some in black and white, all featuring Frank Cassini shaking hands with, standing next to, or otherwise making time with every manner of celebrity from former presidents to movie stars. Many of the pictures bore autographs. I wondered briefly at how even the famous and powerful crave recognition from those they regard as higher up the food chain.

Cassini was leafing through a file, mine I assumed. I cleared my throat as quietly as I could and took a deep breath, trying to relax. I was as prepared as I could possibly be. If called on, I could rattle off the name of every single state Senator I'd set up a press conference or drafted remarks for in my entire two-year tenure with the Senate Democratic Caucus. In most cases I could cite the principal issue or topic of each media event, as well. I knew Cassini's resume better than my own and was ready to weave in references to every intersection at which our respective career paths had come within shouting distance of one another.

"An Aggie, eh?" Cassini's head was still angled down over the file, but his eyes were peering up over the top of his reading glasses at me now, giving me a cagey look I couldn't read. He'd finished with a J.D. from Boalt Hall at UC Berkeley, big brother to my alma mater of UC Davis.

"Yes, sir."

His gaze flickered back down to the page. "Well, I'll try not to hold that against you."

I shifted in my seat and waited.

"So." He closed the file and set it on his desk, removing his glasses and looking me up and down, as if seeing me for the first time. "I'm on the program at the Sacramento Press Club's annual dinner tonight. What am I talking about?"

"Excuse me?" My neck muscles all tightened at once, as if against a noose.

"Sacramento Press Club. Tonight. What points should my speech hit?"

For a long, excruciating moment, my mind went blank as a freshly-washed chalkboard. Nothing. I had nothing.

"Higher education tax credit." I blurted it out in a rush, but it still felt good. I'd managed to pull out one of his pet projects, a bill to create a state tax credit complementing the federal tax credit for college expenses. It was a red-meat issue for middle-class Californians of all political stripes.

Cassini didn't smile, though. He just kept watching me like a cat watches an injured bird clinging to a low branch.

"School construction set-aside." A key element in this year's budget proposal, and one I knew Cassini supported. The state had been paying for school construction via bond issues for years because there was never any money in the regular budget for it – until the Governor proposed a set-aside.

"Rewriting the Coastal Act." Coastal protection law had been in turmoil since the state Supreme Court had issued a bizarre split decision watering down the California Coastal Commission's authority to regulate development. Cassini's position on it was hazy, but it was too big an issue to side-step before an audience as politically tuned-in as the Press Club.

"Campaign reform." A perennial favorite with the press.

Still, Cassini waited. There was something missing. Something… *ah.*

"Open with a joke about having your press conferences catered by Fat's, and close with a commitment to hold them monthly if elected."

Frank didn't exactly grin then, just sort of let one side of his mouth slide upward ever so slightly, like the marginally lighter half of a set of scales. "Okay," he said.

We waded through a few minutes of small talk after that, mostly him filling in the outlines of my political experience and testing my willingness to travel and be on call twenty-four hours a day for the next twenty-two months. Once I'd answered everything to his apparent satisfaction, he stood and offered me a brief shake of his thick hand, mumbling something to the effect that Amy would be in touch with me soon.

A person more in control of his impulses would have accepted this dismissal and simply departed. I turned back at the door. "Sir?"

He looked up from his desk, reading glasses back on, call sheet in front of him, phone already in his hand. He appeared somehow smaller now, and more vulnerable, though his eyes remained intense.

"The Sacramento Press Club dinner isn't until next month, is it?"

Now he smiled. "February 27th."

"Six weeks."

"Keep your notes," he said, and returned to his call sheet.

* * *

The concert was amazing.

Not that I hadn't been to plenty before; Dad had initiated me when I was fourteen, taking me to a Rolling Stones show at the Oakland Coliseum, and since then I'd been to dozens more, everything from acoustic nightclub debuts to stadium dates with the likes of the Dave Matthews Band and Paul McCartney. The basic components of a well-staged, large-scale rock show were universal. A darkened venue, focusing all attention on the performer. Multicolored lighting that moved and changed in rhythm with the music. A sound system twice as powerful as needed to fill the enormous venue. Giant video screens to amplify the visual piece of the performance to the farthest reaches of seating. And a crowd large enough that individuality is lost and group response takes over. All conspiring to create a sensory overload that, when things go right, can spark a kind of mass fervor in the audience.

All of these elements were present and active that night in San Francisco, but there was more. I'd seen the fire in the band's playing during their sound check, but it was nothing, a match-flame compared to the inferno of Stormseye live on stage in front of a delirious crowd of almost fifty thousand people. Jordan was a transformed man from the even-keeled guy I'd just spent the afternoon with, now wearing a billowing white shirt and skin-tight suede pants, stalking the stage in a controlled fury, gesturing wildly to the crowd, eyes fierce, chest heaving, bending himself in half as he hit the strongest notes. Nicky Frost's movements were similarly larger than life, though his on-stage poses had enough polish that it was easy to imagine him spending hours in front of a mirror getting them just right. Glen and Wayne were the quiet ones, staying in the background most of the time, playing with emotion but a minimum of showmanship. Seth was simply Seth, stripped to a black tank top that emphasized his meaty forearms, abusing his drum set like a tantrum-throwing toddler, hammering the beat home and toweling off sheets of sweat at every break.

Jordan was halfway down the stage's central walkway/platform, a good ninety feet out into the crowd, when it happened. It was hard to see directly from my angle at the side of the stage, but there was a TV monitor by the sound board showing the images being projected on the video screens, mostly close-ups of Jordan.

They were four minutes into the last song of the regular set, the seven-minute mini-epic "Your Time is Now." Jordan was deep into the third verse, head down, leaning into the song, when he noticed a commotion down at the edge of the crowd to his left. He told me later it looked like two people wrestling, until one seemed to lift the other up toward the stage. Momentarily blinded by the spotlights, he took a knee and reached down, only to find himself holding the edge of a double-thick slab of cardboard.

Straightening up, he realized that the "person" being passed up onto the stage was in fact a cardboard cut-out, a life-sized image from a record-store promotion. As the band launched into the lengthy instrumental jam that closed out the song, he stood and stared.

The image, now clearly visible to the left side of the crowd, was of Jordan himself, coiffed and costumed and made-up to cover-shot perfection, teal-and-green silk shirt open, leather pants snug, a sly, come-hither grin planted on his face and a copy of the new album (*Pieces of the Night*) in his hand. The slogan plastered across Jordan's torso was of the ham-handed double-entendre variety ("Stormseye: the new album / Grab your piece").

He stared at the figure for what seemed like minutes – but was likely only thirty seconds or so – as the band moved through Wayne's solo toward Nicky's. From there the jam would build, moving faster and faster until Nicky, Glen and Jordan were supposed to meet between the drum riser and the piano for the final crescendo.

In the meantime, though, something was happening out on the ramp.

Jordan turned away from the spotlight, moving his cardboard twin with him. Another spot from the opposite side of the stadium caught them. The crowd on the right side of the walkway got a clear view of what Jordan was holding and roared its approval.

Jordan looked startled for a moment, then comprehending, then calculating. He maneuvered his cardboard doppelganger directly in front of him. The crowd egged him on, hooting and whistling, fists raised.

He turned back to his left again, moving the cut-out with him, staying behind it, using it like a shield. The crowd on the left side of the walkway roared and began to surge like a wind-whipped tide, up and down and up again.

He turned right again and the mass of humanity on that side of the walkway exploded in a barrage of shouts and screams, nearly drowning out the music for an instant.

Holding tight to the back of the cardboard figure, Jordan continued, turning and turning, faster and faster, the crowd noise on each side swelling to a peak on cue each time he faced their direction. As the escalating roar began to batter the stage from one side, then the other, I saw Glen shoot Seth a quick "What the hell?" look, but they stayed on the beat.

Jordan timed his movements to the music, reaching a crescendo just as the band did. And then, he stopped.

As the band began finishing off the song with a long flourish full of guitar scales and rolling drum fills, Jordan stood side-by-side with his cardboard twin, motionless for several seconds, as if he was imitating it, rather than the other way around. At last he reached over with his far hand, all the way across his body and the cut-out's, grabbed the cardboard Jordan by the hair and, with one hard yank, tore his head off.

The crowd boiled over, a tidal wave of screams and white noise washing over the stage. Feeding off the energy, Jordan went wild, ripping and tearing at the cardboard figure, rending it like a human shredder, shoveling the pieces out into the crowd on both sides. The band finished, but neither the crowd around the walkway nor Jordan even seemed to notice as he continued dismembering his cardboard self and tossing the chunks away until there was nothing left.

Then he stood, alone, ninety feet from his bandmates, hunched over with exhaustion, glaring out at the crowd like a caged animal. They surged at him from all sides, reaching as high as they could (and grasping nothing; the walkway was engineered to six feet high and eight feet wide for good reason). He stood and watched, as if in a trance, sweat dripping off his chin, his once-willowy shirt plastered to his back, until finally, he straightened up and thrust both fists in the air, drinking in a fresh bellow of affirmation from the masses surrounding him, before turning and jogging back up the walkway to the main stage.

In its way it was a classic rock-star tableau, the performer putting everything he had into the show. But watching it from the outside, zeroing in on Jordan's expressions, I was struck with an entirely different impression. Cornered in the midst of a raucous horde of fifty thousand people crying out his name, Jordan Lee had looked for a moment like the loneliest man on Earth.

6

I caught a midnight flight back to LA. After the last encore, Jordan invited me to stay, to hang out backstage into the night and crash in one of the suites the band had reserved at the Mark Hopkins up on Nob Hill. I admit, it was tempting to keep up the charade that I actually belonged there. But besides having brought nothing but a small soft-sided briefcase with me for the day, I was exhausted and pretty well fried emotionally. I wanted, more than anything, to be alone for a while, to crawl off and lick my wounds and try to figure out what came next.

I did make sure to thank Jordan emphatically, and compliment him on his comments to the crowd during the encores. He'd apparently gotten in the habit during this tour of giving a little speech to the audience before the last encore about the difference they could make in the world if they just paid attention, ending with a plea for everyone to register to vote. Not a big surprise, coming from someone who'd been part of MTV's Rock The Vote campaign since its early years, but still another mark on the plus side of the ledger in my eyes.

My plane ride back to LA was considerably less eventful than the ride up that morning. After ransoming my Prius from one of the pay lots near the airport, I navigated home in silence, leaving the radio off and letting my eardrums continue decompressing from the battering they'd absorbed earlier in the evening.

Home – if you could call it that – was an apartment a few blocks off Wilshire and half a block west of the 405, on the borderline between UCLA off-campus student housing and Westside LA opulence. It was a fairly pricey location for a young professional living alone, but as the sole heir of a single parent who'd rarely spent a dime frivolously, I could afford it. I knew renting a nice apartment would make my inheritance run out faster, but part of me wanted it to. When it was gone it would be one less reminder of what I'd lost.

By now you're probably wondering about my mother. Me, too. I have a picture of her and that's pretty much it. Dad had met her dancing in the aisle at a Bob Seger concert at the Oakland Coliseum on New Year's Eve. They had ended the night in a feverish tangle in the back of Dad's VW van, and that had been the last he'd heard from her for eleven months. Then one mild November day he had opened the door to his San Rafael apartment to find her standing in the hallway with a baby in her arms.

"I can't. Do this. I really wanted to. I thought I could. But I can't."

Dad never explained exactly how he responded to this. I imagine he must have protested, asked her why she hadn't told him, questioned whether this could really be happening, all the reactions you'd anticipate. The one thing I doubt he ever did was question his paternity. I don't think there's ever been a baby who looked more like his father than I did, a head swathed in tiny, dark curls surrounding a round face and green eyes that were already squinting. (Dad and I both had glasses before we were ten, though I switched to contacts as a teenager.)

"I'm only nineteen."

Here again I imagine Dad drawing back in surprise; he'd assumed at the time she was closer to his age, twenty-seven. He'd apparently held her off that day, saying there was no way he could start taking care of a baby just like that, with no warning. I'm sure he must have struggled with the decision, knowing how much freedom he would lose by taking me in. But I also think that with just one significantly older sibling himself, he'd been alone for so much of his own life that he might have welcomed the chance at creating an instant family. "I always wanted kids," I overheard him telling friends years later. "I just wasn't expecting to have one show up on my doorstep."

And so, when my mother had returned a week later as they'd agreed, he'd been ready with a crib, blankets, bottles and the beginnings of what would grow into a full menagerie of stuffed animals. Aunt Ruth, who had two sons of her own and had always wanted more, became our lifeline, schooling my father in how to care for a baby and watching me whenever he had to go out of town overnight, which was often. It must have been a bizarre scene when he didn't have help, though – the disheveled music writer interviewing big-haired, leather-pantsed musicians with a baby strapped on his back. But it was us. We got by, somehow, always.

I kept a picture of us on the table in the small entryway my apartment opened into, a profile shot of him holding me up in the air in Aunt Ruth's back yard when I was three, both of us with long, unruly hair and identical smiles. Every time I came home, it was the first thing I saw; I've never lived anywhere that it hasn't traveled with me.

*   *   *

I woke up the next morning shivering and congested. After drinking in the bayside air all the previous afternoon and evening, and breathing stale airline air all the way home, I'd opened a window the minute I got back to the apartment. The change from moist sea breeze to bone-dry recirculated air to LA basin chunky soup didn't seem to have agreed with my sinuses, though.

Lying in bed, snuffling through the gauzy no-man's-land between dreams and consciousness, I had a revelation. As bizarre as the entire chain of events had been, being swept off course into Jordan's world somehow felt right. It was an environment in which I had no history, and in which my baggage therefore became invisible. I could reinvent myself.

Except, I suddenly recognized, there was an echo there, a sensation approaching – maybe even surpassing – déjà vu in its intensity. I wasn't reinventing myself; I was assuming someone else's identity. I was backstage, hanging out with the band, making small talk with the crew while the group warmed up onstage. I was investigating, registering, recording everything I saw and heard and witnessed for later sorting, analysis and retelling. I was thinking like a reporter. I was writing the story in my head already.

Screw you, Jordan Lee.

It took a long shower and two cups of painfully strong coffee to shed this feeling. I wasn't my dad, in fact was in many ways his opposite. He was easy-going and gregarious, one of those socially gifted people who can make themselves welcome in almost any situation – and as a result, whose network of friendships and alliances seemed at times to go on forever. I was solitary by nature; not an island, but certainly a well-guarded peninsula. I thought of myself as being selective, independent, observant. I had a knack for spotting things others didn't, and had learned to make a living by interpreting and sharing this information with my employers. By comparison, Dad seemed like a bit of a dilettante, hanging out with rock bands, helping them sell records to hormonal teenagers with his breezy profiles and interviews. It put food on the table, but was it work that mattered?

I wanted my work to matter. There was so much wrong in the world, so much that caused needless suffering, so much that – bottom line – offended my sense of order. I wanted to try to sort it out, to help make sure the people in power got it right. Early on, around the time I'd decided to major in political science, I'd believed that to accomplish any of these things I would need to find and work for a truly exceptional person, a visionary figure.

But once out of the sheltered college environment and into the real-life habitat of the State Capitol, learning where the levers and pulleys of power

43

were located and how the weights and measures balanced one another, I came to realize that government was primarily in the hands of technicians, not visionaries. Causes came and went, but the entrenched personnel, the committee staff and agency deputy directors who'd survived it all – new initiatives, staff cuts, term limits, changing leadership – they were somehow invincible, as certain and immovable a force as the steel barriers guarding the driveways leading down into the Capitol garage. It was not an exaggeration to say that nothing happened in the building without their cooperation, if not approval. The elected office-holders were in some ways mere figureheads, money-raising and campaigning machines whose major function often seemed to be the maintenance of the existing machinery of power.

Not that I'd become cynical or anything.

I still hung on to the conceit that my purpose was to make a difference, to improve the lives of average citizens. I had just come to see how completely disengaged from and disillusioned by the process most of them were. Anesthetized by a steady diet of *Access Hollywood* and thirty-second political attack ads, they had in some fundamental way stopped caring. The depressing fact was, the average American was more interested in being the first on the block with the new thousand-dollar PDA-slash-taser and seeing who won the umpteenth edition of *American Idol* than in even trying to understand why the proposed new "Forest Management and Conservation Act" would actually result in the ruination for generations to come of thousands of square miles of national forest. Let alone doing anything about it.

If the voters didn't care, what was the point in my holding out for an exceptional leader to attach myself to? Why not work for a Frank Cassini, a politician more shrewd than inspiring? If I was simply another technician tinkering at the margins, didn't it make sense to attach myself to the candidate with the best shot at winning?

Of course it did, I told myself yet again, sipping gingerly at the third cup of coffee I'd just poured in my silent little kitchen. Of course it did.

* * *

Nia Lamar had the biggest dogs I had ever seen at a thousand-dollar-a-person cocktail party. Not having the slightest idea what breed they might be, I immediately began thinking of the trio of tall, shaggy gray beasts collectively as Cerberus, the three-headed guard dog of Hades.

Nia, you'll recall, starred in a string of hit action movies in the years following the turn of the millennium. In terms of looks, she's something of a female Samuel L. Jackson – compact, sculpted and tightly wound, not classically beautiful but exuding charisma from every self-assured pore. In terms of politics, she makes Barbra Streisand look like a soft-spoken moderate.

But the care and feeding of a hundred-million political campaign required that one vacuum up every campaign dollar in sight as efficiently as possible, and Nia Lamar was not a name to sniff at when it came to offers to host campaign events. Indeed, I'd had to park two blocks away from the gates to her spread on the edge of Bel-Air; Frank figured to walk away from an event like this with a cool quarter-million in return for a couple of hours of chowing down on gourmet hors d'oeuvres while mixing with an "A" list of Hollywood names whose checkbooks could fuel his campaign for months to come.

I'd had a momentary setback at the gate, where the security guard demanded that I produce an invitation. But the strategy didn't take long to figure out; I just bided my time until I recognized one of our junior fundraising staff approaching the gate.

"Carolyn."

"Oh, hey, Tim." She paused long enough while digging the invitation out of her tiny, beaded purse that I could actually see the wheels turning in her head. "Aren't you—?"

"Fired?"

She laughed, glancing around nervously. "Yeah."

"That was yesterday. You know how it goes."

She did. As a result, within five minutes I was inside working the buffet line with a twenty-dollar glass of Napa Valley cabernet in hand. Crashing the reception was a risk, but a calculated one. Frank respected people who stood up for themselves and got in his face; he had no use for passivity. My gamble was that he'd be amused, maybe even charmed by my boldness. He knew I was good – had anyone else written a decent speech for him in the last year? And my presence here ought to have the effect of remedying whatever doubts my performance on the plane might have instilled about my willingness to go to the wall for him.

The reception was being held on Nia's expansive back forty, which had been landscaped in the manner of a French country palace, a maze of low, neatly trimmed hedges, three fountains and a series of crushed gravel pathways laid out in precise geometry. The house itself opened onto a wide slate patio where the buffet line and bar were located. Five steps down took you into the garden, where three hundred or so of Hollywood's finest were busy comparing weekly grosses and plastic surgeries.

I watched the crowd from the edge of the patio, catching glimpses of talk show hosts chatting up potential guests, directors quizzing potential stars, stars flirting with potential bedmates. More than likely three or four movies, a couple of TV series and a divorce or two were busy a-borning in the cocktail-hour conversations happening below.

I didn't see Frank anywhere at first, but I had a good feel for how these things tended to play out. This early in the evening he'd be inside somewhere, giving a private audience and pep talk to the cream of the crop, the folks who might go beyond writing thousand-dollar checks themselves and work their own network of friends and associates for contributions. A few minutes from now he'd emerge, mix with the crowd outside for half an hour, then mount the steps to recite the stump speech Amy and I had composed fifteen months ago, making sure to fire a couple of ripped-from-today's-headlines rhetorical missiles at Darcy Kendrick along the way. Then he'd mix for another half hour before slipping away.

I was at the back door, peering in while trying to look like I wasn't, when the dogs first approached me. For a moment I thought I must be hallucinating, they were so massive – three feet tall at the shoulder, four at the head, with long, narrow, horse-shaped faces, their entire elongated bodies covered in tastefully groomed gray curls. They moved in and surrounded me for a long moment, sniffing suspiciously before collectively dismissing me and moving on.

I was back at the buffet, picking at a bunch of grapes and watching the star of CBS's latest *CSI* spinoff laboring to spark the interest of a twenty-years-younger starlet, when I caught a stirring behind me and turned to find Frank standing at the top of the steps, looking down on the assemblage in the garden and giving a little wave as everyone turned to catch a glimpse of the guest of honor.

Trailing him at a cautious distance, I began rehearsing opening lines in my head. Something glib and disarming was what I had in mind, but something that would also remind him of how far we'd come together, the days and weeks and months of toil I'd devoted to the furtherance of his ambition. I had some time still, since my plan was to catch him a few minutes after he'd finished his remarks, as the crowd of glitterati around him was just beginning to thin. In other words, when his ego-fulfillment for the evening was at its natural apex.

I had just reached the bottom of the steps when a firm hand latched onto my left elbow from behind. I turned to find myself looking into Officer Bob's unhappy eyes.

"Hey, Bob, how're –"

"You need to go." His expression was grim, his voice low and taut.

"What?"

"He spotted you the minute we stepped out the door." Here Bob paused and looked around for a moment before continuing. "Tim, I'm sorry. You were one of the good guys. But you're not welcome here anymore. You need to go."

"But I just want to talk to Fr–"

"Walk." He pressed my elbow forward with such surprising strength that I almost stumbled as the rest of my body began following its trajectory.

"What?"

"C'mon, Tim, walk or I'm gonna have to call for backup. You don't want to be carried out of here."

I didn't. I began walking, but slowly, peering through the crowd, trying to spot Frank. Suddenly a lane opened up in the crowd just as Frank turned from talking to last year's Oscar winner for best director to pluck a stuffed mushroom off a passing tray. Our eyes met. I stopped, and Bob stopped with me, watching over my shoulder.

In a low voice, but enunciating clearly so that Frank could read my lips, I said "I just wanted to talk."

The look I received in return was the look you give a cockroach right before you lower your heel onto its head, an expression of utter contempt that lasted perhaps a single second before he dismissed me and turned back to his conversation. As I stared back, the dogs suddenly filtered out of the crowd into the opening just in front of me. One of them turned its great gray snout my direction, stared at me with soulful eyes and began to howl, a long, whinnying cry of infinite distress.

Bob dragged me another five steps before I wrenched my elbow from his grip and strode away without looking back.

7

I sat alone in my apartment for three days. Didn't shave, hardly dressed, ate week-old peaches and month-old Triscuits and whatever else I could find in my pathetic bachelor's pantry. It felt as though my life had come to a dead stop, like a disabled train stranded in the middle of a cornfield somewhere deep in the Plains. I didn't want to talk to anyone, not even Terry, and it seemed the feeling was mutual.

On the first night I drank nothing, just planted myself on the couch and let the television anesthetize me. First the evening news, then *Jeopardy*, then sitcom reruns, then some brainless Bruce Willis action movie. I was actually an hour and a half in and enjoying it a little when I realized one of the supporting players in the movie had been at the reception. His face had registered briefly in the crowd just before I had locked eyes with Frank. In the end I couldn't stand waiting any longer for his inevitable demise, so I switched to cable news and listened to the pundits tear into each other like bitterly divorcing spouses. I fell asleep in my boxers on the couch sometime after midnight.

On the second night I drank an entire bottle of Merlot with dinner (which consisted of several pieces of fried chicken left over in my fridge for I don't know how long) and topped it off around eleven-thirty with a trio of vodka shooters. At midnight I was standing in my bedroom berating the reflection in the mirror behind the door. By one, I was on all fours, chest heaving like a racehorse, fighting back the torrent of self-pitying tears that wanted to come. By two, I was crumpled on the floor of my bathroom, cradling the porcelain.

I got up at noon on the third day and cleaned up, not because I particularly wanted to, but because there didn't seem to be anything else to do. Everything on television only served to remind me that I had crossed over; I was outside the bubble now, just another faceless audience member for Mr. Nielsen's machines to count.

As I washed the dishes I began to calculate how soon money would become an issue for me. I had two weeks' salary in my checking account. The campaign theoretically owed me for some vacation that I'd never used, but I doubted I'd ever see a check for it. I'd been subsidizing my lifestyle with the nest egg that Dad had been holding in an IRA, but I'd burn through that quickly without a salary.

And, of course, I had the house in Santa Rosa. I'd slept there for a week after Dad died, tidying up the essential loose ends, and then walked away. Hadn't been back since. Terry had been staying there for the last couple of months, ever since she'd come home from work early one day to find her husband standing naked in the kitchen with their next-door neighbor's voice echoing down the hall from the bedroom, asking to have her apple cut in wedges, please. The way I figured it, the house might as well be someone's refuge.

At some point, though, I was going to have to make a decision – clean it out and rent it, or sell it. Even after the housing crash, it was probably worth four times what Dad had paid for it in the late '80s. I just hadn't felt ready to make a decision either way about it yet, and I'd felt so bad for Terry that I'd never even brought up any kind of end-date for our arrangement. If I didn't figure out what to do next pretty soon, though, my bank balance would eventually force my hand.

Not today, I finally told myself, sitting at my tiny breakfast table with the fold-down flaps, idly surfing the Internet on my laptop while I pondered my options. *You're not going to make a decision like that today.* Clicking through the online edition of the *LA Times*, I wandered into the Calendar section, where a bulleted list of upcoming events caught my eye.

"Benefit at Staples to raise $1 million," read the link, buried in a boxed sidebar. Clicking in, I found that the fine print for the event, scheduled for that night, ticked off an impressive roster of musical guests, including at least one with whom I had recently dueted in the first row of a 737.

Okay, I thought. *Okay. That's something.*

* * *

The rectangular sign warned me off with stark black letters against a banana-yellow background. Still, I approached the glass-paneled booth inside the vast lobby, ever-hopeful.

"No, we're sold out."

I tried to chuckle nonchalantly, but there was a hitch in it. I was beginning to feel a little like Cain after he was cast out, left to walk alone forever with God's mark upon him. The idea of simply packing a suitcase, going back to Santa Rosa and curling up in the fetal position was looking better and better.

I retreated back out the double doors to 11ᵗʰ Street, where the traffic was continuing its late-afternoon crawl. The show began in three hours; I had envisioned picking up a ticket and then treating myself to a nice dinner somewhere nearby. Instead I was left wandering the downtown streets like a homeless yuppie, weighing a series of unattractive options. I could try to scalp a ticket (too expensive). I could call Jordan's cell phone (too desperate). I could go home and get drunk again (too pathetic). At the corner I glanced right, down Figueroa, across the back end of the center's main parking lot.

Halfway down the block an access road crossed into the parking lot and right up to the back of the building itself. Near the end of the access road there appeared to be a gathering of some sort, a couple of hundred people milling around at the back of the building. I turned in and wandered closer, curious.

There seemed to be no common denominator in the crowd. Some were my age or younger, a small cadre of girls in alarmingly snug halter tops and low-low riders perhaps as young as high school. Others were in their forties, neatly barbered, wearing crow's feet and Rolexes. All were milling around, sunglasses on against the peach-toned late-afternoon sun, elbowing for position along a rope line that was protecting a wide blue carpet leading up to an unmarked door into the arena itself.

As I drew closer several people turned my direction and pointed up the access road behind me. I turned as well, in time to find a white stretch limo bearing down on me. It glided past like a giant waterbug and came to a smooth halt with the back door precisely perpendicular to the rope-line. A moment later Sabrina Kelso, the youngest person ever to win the Best New Artist Grammy, popped out like a champagne cork and waved energetically to the crowd, tastefully highlighted auburn hair shimmering against her white bodysuit. The younger half of the crowd surged against the rope line screaming her name as four security guards I hadn't noticed before held their ground along its perimeter. She stopped midway down the path and quickly signed a pair of the fifty or so items that were being thrust at her by hungry fans calling her name.

It took maybe another sixty seconds for a plan to come together in my mind. By the time the third limo pulled away, I had identified a pattern; the stars, on emerging, consistently ignored the people along the first ten feet of the rope line walk. In their eagerness to be seen first, these folks had positioned themselves where the object of their alarmingly enthusiastic affection was still busy getting oriented as he or she navigated down the carpet through the middle of the crowd. With strategic sideways movements and a judiciously thrown hip-check or two, I was able to work myself to the front of crowd at the opposite end, closest to the building itself.

The fourth, fifth and sixth limos contained more people I didn't care about. When number seven pulled up, however, Jordan and Ray climbed out. All at once the entire crowd was nearly pogoing with excitement, hairpieces and all. Across the way from me I could see a woman with flowing brown hair streaked with gray literally trembling, the t-shirt she was clutching in her hands fluttering as if in a breeze.

Jordan seemed barely conscious of the scene before him as he made his way through the crowd, though. His eyes were hidden behind sunglasses and his manner was distant, as if his mind was somewhere else entirely. Ray led him by two steps, looking back and forth into the crowd, intent, ready. As Jordan drew within twenty feet, I yelled his name. This turned out to be a terrible idea, as my voice was quickly swallowed up by a chorus of "Jordan!"'s from all sides. I waved my arms; everyone else waved theirs. I leaned out over the rope toward them; so did forty or fifty others on both sides of the walkway. Some of them held out signs and albums and programs for him to sign. He stopped on the far side, signed a token few, then moved on, again oblivious, impervious to their cries. There he was, less than thirty feet away, passing me by like the non-person I had become.

They were well past me and approaching the arena door when inspiration struck. I gathered up the biggest lungful of air I could possibly manage and let it all out in one short syllable.

"Ray!"

Their simultaneous turn-around eyebrows-arched double-take was the first sign that my fortunes might be about to change.

* * *

The envy radiating from all sides was palpable as Ray returned, lifted the rope and ushered me onto the carpet. I was briefly concerned that the loud-breathing soccer mom next to me was going to latch onto my elbow Officer Bob-style in an attempt to be dragged in with me, but no. Once under the rope, I moved quickly to the center and jogged up to meet Jordan at the door before anyone could make a move on me.

"Hey. Thanks."

He offered me a quick soul shake while grinning back. "You could've called, you know."

"I wasn't – I didn't want to bother you. It just – I don't know." Barely coherent; all true.

The glasses came off and Jordan gave me a long, appraising look before stepping through the door Ray was holding open for us. We passed into a long tunnel leading deep into Staples' vast backstage area, and as we walked Ray handed me an index-card-sized sticker with the words "All Access" in block letters and today's date. My second backstage pass of the week. Life had definitely taken a turn somewhere.

As we navigated through a maze of white hallways to the dressing room area, Jordan quizzed the entire Nia Lamar reception story out of me.

"That's cold, man," came his summary when I'd finished. By now we were sitting in a ten by fifteen cave of a dressing room with a wall-sized mirror, six or seven chairs, a small buffet and a phone on the counter underneath the mirror. Ray had parked himself against the wall by the door. Walking down the hall, I'd looked over at one point and mouthed a silent thanks to him. He just nodded.

"Yeah," I agreed. "But it's him. He demands complete loyalty. You're either with him or against him. I failed the test."

Jordan was adjusting his hair in the mirror, the lights surrounding it setting his square-jawed face aglow. I waited, thinking he hadn't heard me. Still looking in the mirror, he finally responded. "That's a fascist line."

"Hmm?"

"That's the kind of talk the dictators of the world have always used to keep their people in line.'"

"Well," I considered, "a campaign is kind of a dictatorship."

"A military dictatorship. Think about the words people use talking about running for office – it's a campaign that uses footsoldiers and weapons and attacks on the opponent."

I got it. "– and the documentary about the Clinton campaign was called –"

"*The War Room*. Yep. Your guy thinks he's General Petraeus."

I let out a rueful chuckle. "Except he's not my guy any more. I may have to vote for the Green candidate or something."

"The Greens. Perfect. 'This is George Stephanopoulos and our guest this morning is spokesperson Tim Green of the Green Party…'"

I was laughing, not at his surprisingly passable Stephanopoulos imitation, but at the memory this exchange triggered. "At one point my dad almost had me convinced that R.E.M. named their *Green* album after us. He even got Michael Stipe to call me up on my birthday –"

With barely a glance at each other we both began to sing to the mirror, me badly, him in perfect pitch: "Stand in the place where you live / Now face north…"

I fell away, laughing harder as Jordan continued, throwing wild inflections into every other line.

"That was the coolest song in the world when I was eleven," I said when he'd finished the chorus.

Jordan nodded, but didn't say anything. Instead he just watched me for a long beat until, at length, he spoke. "So, what're you really doing here?"

I glanced up at his reflection in the mirror. It was a bizarre, disorienting effect, sitting next to him and facing almost straight ahead, yet also looking directly into his penetrating eyes. My gaze darted to Ray's reflection. He appeared oblivious, focused on something fascinating on the opposite wall. I glanced at my own entirely unremarkable reflection, dark brown hair shoveled to one side with the help of a palmful of gel, nose a little large for my taste, mouth a little small, grim expression. A college girlfriend had once told me I looked like Ross from *Friends*; I broke up with her the next day. Tired of my face, I next studied my hands, which had once been shaken by some of the most powerful men and women in California and were now stained by my shortcomings. In the end, the truth bubbled out on its own.

"I've got nowhere else to go."

I felt Jordan's left hand come to rest gently on my right shoulder just as a fresh presence burst into the room.

"Jordan there you are oh hi Tim nice to see you again sorry to interrupt but they're saying the state senator who was supposed to talk about the Santa Monica Mountains thingy isn't going to make it his wife had to go to the hospital or something and so they really really need someone to take his place on the program and somebody from Train I think it was Pat Monahan said they thought you could do it and I said I'd ask."

"Hmm," replied Jordan. I glanced over at Ray again, who appeared to have swallowed something that was tickling his esophagus.

Natalie, in a dress this time, a black-with-red-triangles knee-length sleeve that clung to her wonderfully, waited with one foot tapping – no, vibrating – against the smooth carpet. Her dark hair shone brightly in the horizontal light reflecting off the mirror.

"The only problem," Jordan eventually replied, "is I don't know anything about the Santa Monica Mountains thingy."

"Well neither do I of course!" She crossed her arms and shifted her weight – what there was of it, anyway – to her other foot. Then she released her arms to wave around as she finished her thought in a burst of pent-up frustration. "I hate this! I know music I know tour logistics I know negotiating royalties I know managing investments but doing these events drives me crazy because I don't know a thing about all this political stuff!"

Jordan nodded with a mixture of sympathy and boredom – which I took to mean this was not their first time having this particular conversation – and glanced over at me in the mirror. The minute our eyes locked it was as though I was a skipping jukebox someone had just given a swift kick.

"Senate Bill 278 by Senator Carl Perreia (Democrat of Simi Valley) would provide – six? – no, five million dollars in funding for trail and habitat restoration on the San Fernando Valley side of the Santa Monica Mountains reserve. There's a rare bird species – I think it's some kind of coastal hawk – that nests in the foothills on that side. To date the development on that edge of the reserve has been residential with a couple of small pockets of light industrial, but now there's a developer who wants to build a factory – making those big roof racks for SUVs, if I remember right – on open land within the buffer zone. He's claiming in a lawsuit that the adjacent part of the reserve isn't used at all, so the environmental impact would be negligible. Adding trails for day use in strategic locations in that part of the reserve would blow the developer's argument out of the water without further litigation and without significantly disturbing the hawk habitat. It's actually a pretty clever strategy. Provides public access while preserving environmental values and potentially saving the state years of fighting with the developer in court."

Jordan turned slowly away from Natalie. This time he wanted to look me in the eye directly.

"Dude" was all he managed before he and Ray both burst out laughing.

* * *

With my hand-written notes ready and Jordan's assurance that he would be fine with the earlier call to the stage, Natalie departed, leaving with a glance at me that was just long and considered enough to make me smile inside. Ray followed her out with the understanding he'd return in half an hour. For no rational reason I suddenly found myself nervous, left alone in the dressing room with Jordan. My solution was to get up and graze the small buffet supplied by the venue, picking at the veggie tray before moving on to the Chinese eggrolls and barbecued chicken wings.

"So, you live in LA?" he finally asked, changing shoes from the shiny black half-platforms he'd arrived in to more practical low-heeled, rubber-soled Eddie Bauers.

"Kind of. I have an apartment down here. But I lived in Northern California my whole life before a year ago. Still own my dad's place up in Santa Rosa."

"That where you grew up?" He stripped off his navy turtleneck tee and began putting on a marginally more formal lime-green button-up shirt.

"Yeah."

"Was your dad into politics?"

"Him? No." My plate was full now, and I was snatching bites between pieces of our conversation. "I mean, all the writers and people he worked with had an opinion, for sure, and sometimes I'd walk into the room and catch him talking back to the news on TV. But it's not something we talked about much."

"You talked music, though."

"Sure, all the time."

"Go to a lot of shows?"

"Probably a hundred or so between when I turned fourteen and when he died in January."

"So you know the scene."

"Sure. Mostly as a fan, but I've been backstage a few times over the years."

He nodded, adjusting his shirt and tossing the old one on top of a canvas gym bag I hadn't even noticed before, sitting in the corner.

"Your work keep you on the road a lot?"

"Yeah, a fair amount, moving around the state doing press events." I tried to lick the barbecue sauce off my fingers gracefully. It wasn't working.

"You get tired of that?" He was adjusting his pants – black jeans, boot-cut – in the mirror now, pulling the creases tight in the right places.

"No." I let that thought settle for a moment. The travel had actually been a blessing, the complex logistics becoming one more thing to keep my mind off Dad. Less time to mope when you're always on the move. "No, it's been a good time for me to be on the road."

"Oh lord I got to ramble," sang Jordan, catching my eye in the mirror.

"Oh lord I got to gamble," I answered back, using my eggroll for a mike and laughing. "But it isn't the same without background singers." I wandered back over to the buffet and grazed a little more.

"No," he agreed, putting the final touches on his hair in the mirror. "You gotta have support for that one." He turned to face me then, dressed and ready, the energy and anticipation of performing in front of 18,000 people emerging on his face. My expression must have slipped back into awe as I suddenly became conscious again of standing alone in a small room with a bona fide star, a man whose very presence was sufficient to drive entire stadiums full of people into a frenzy. He grinned for a moment, letting himself enjoy it.

Then he turned serious. We faced each other like that in silence for so long that I could feel the individual beads of perspiration beginning to form under my shirt. Finally, Jordan began to speak.

"I'm sober and healthy and have more money than I could ever spend in my lifetime," he said. "And the only thing I give a shit about anymore is these charity gigs. But I can't have Natalie stressing out on me like that all the time, and she shouldn't have to. She's great at handling all the regular business and touring details and I never should've asked her to do this, too. What I need is someone to coordinate my charity work, do the research, make the connections, manage the details, make sure I get it right."

I nodded. I might have swallowed loudly if I had a thimble's worth of spit left in my mouth. In my career thus far I had been interviewed for jobs by two assembly members, three state senators and the attorney general of the State of California. Jordan Lee was the only person who had ever managed to do it without me even noticing.

"And it has to be someone I trust."

I forced myself to breathe.

"Come work for me, Tim," he said, stranding his words in the vague no-man's-land between entreaty and command.

I had been lost all day. No, that wasn't right. I had been lost all year. Nothing I'd done since Dad died had felt right. It had all felt artificial somehow, like I was an actor playing a part. I thought I had played it pretty well, despite the review Frank had ultimately given me. But something was missing the entire time. It had fit, working for Cassini, but in some fundamental way, it hadn't felt right. It hadn't felt *true*.

And now Jordan Lee – Jordan Lee! – was offering me the chance to clean my slate, to start over. In that moment I could hear Charlie Bond's voice in my head again, offering his analysis of my situation, ever succinct: *Duh!*

II.

BAND ON THE RUN

Maybe I could use you to reassure myself
I wouldn't wish this indecision on anybody else
Drink enough of anything to make this world look new again
And when the sin smiles how could it be wrong

– Douglas Hopkins ("Lost Horizons," by Gin Blossoms)

The thing about democracy, beloveds, is that it is not neat, orderly, or quiet. It requires a certain relish for confusion.

– Molly Ivins

8

I don't believe in fate. I don't believe that the random things that happen in the course of anyone's life aren't random, that we spend our lives stumbling through some predetermined master plan. I'm nobody's chess piece. And I don't see how you can believe that stuff and still buy into evolution, quantum physics, the law of averages, gravity. There are too many contradictions.

Dad did, though. He carried a quiet air of belief through his life, a certain assumption that where he was and what he was doing and what was happening to him was all intended, all part of a plan beyond his knowing. He was Jewish but we didn't go to temple; when I met Jordan Lee I had in fact never been in a house of worship in my entire life with the exception of a few friends and colleagues' weddings. Hell, I didn't even know what religion (if any) my mother was; I'd never asked Dad. All I knew was that a certain intense quiet would come over him at times, whether sitting in his study, watching a squirrel clamber around in the oak trees out back, or just after the lights went down at a concert. At those moments you could see in his eyes that he was otherwise engaged, communing with something larger than the two of us, something mysterious and presumably benevolent.

This all comes to mind because I felt my dad's presence a number of times over the first few weeks I worked for Jordan Lee. The sensation was something like that tingly fugue state you fall into just before something happens that you've anticipated completely, that actually triggers a sort of instantaneous déjà vu, a sensation that you saw it happening before it actually did. I didn't hear a voice exactly, or see a face, just felt a presence, like a warm breeze carrying a familiar scent – Marlboros and jelly donuts and sweat, perhaps.

Those weeks were also infused with an unfamiliar yet undeniable sense of satisfaction. I had been pretty well convinced up to that point that six years of doing political scut-work had extinguished my capacity for juvenile awe. I understood the system, its checks and balances and potholed morality, that motives were always partially hidden, that virtually anything could and would be bargained. These were the givens, the laws of behavioral physics to which all things in my professional political universe held. Over the years a silent assumption had grown in me that they must therefore hold everywhere, that self-interest was in fact the driving force of humanity as a whole.

This amplified the sense of unreality that periodically swept over me. My eyes and ears were telling me day by day that I was working with and for a man whose motives appeared to fall somewhere between unknowable and – there's no other word for it – pure. I knew one thing; he wasn't in it to sell more records. If that wasn't obvious from the care and commitment with which he approached his charity work, it became a no-brainer once I had the opportunity to better appreciate the band's financial situation.

Among other things, I observed that Seth "Basher" Lamiroult was in the habit of wearing an earring in his left ear in which was set a diamond the size of a pea. On his right pinky he wore a thick gold ring studded with rubies. In place of baby pictures, Nicky Frost liked to show off snapshots of his fleet – the Ferraris (when I met him, he had four), a silver Rolls, a black Bentley and a canary-yellow Lamborghini Countach. In contrast, Wayne never went anywhere without photos of his kids – his son atop the Eiffel Tower; his daughter in front of the Taj Mahal; the whole family on top of the Great Wall of China; his entire 14-person entourage – fully a third of them as pale and carrot-topped as he was – on safari with a coterie of bemused Kenyan guides. According to Jordan, quiet, modest Glen had a collection of autographed bass guitars (Jack Bruce? Check. John Paul Jones? Check. Paul McCartney? Check. Bill Wyman? Check times two.) that was coveted by the Rock and Roll Hall of Fame.

If the other players had that much money to burn, Jordan – who had written a third of the band's material by himself and had written the lyrics for every single original song they'd ever recorded, thereby ensuring a steady stream of songwriting royalties for the rest of his life – had to have exponentially more. Sitting in my Kansas City hotel room late one soggy night, I tried to do the math. Using conservative guesstimates for royalty rates, album sales and concert grosses, I was up to 2005 and $190 million when I stopped calculating; there didn't seem to be much point. Even after you subtracted management fees and taxes the guy had to be far into nine figures for his career, and they'd never even sold a song for a car commercial – yet.

I had a hard time believing he'd parted with much of that, though, because he appeared to spend nothing on himself. The band's transportation, food, drink and lodging while on tour were all covered by their record label. Jordan apparently had a house in the Oakland Hills, but in the two months I'd known him he had yet to visit it, and he never talked about any other property anywhere. I wasn't even sure if he owned a car. He could be generous to friends, but was more thoughtful than extravagant; on my one-month anniversary with him, he'd reached into his duffel bag in a Dallas dressing room and tossed me a brand new iPod Touch already loaded up with The Band, Pearl Jam, Coltrane, Mary Chapin Carpenter, Hendrix, the Gin Blossoms and Mozart.

When he ate out, his tastes were simple; he was as likely to get takeout from the closest Chinese restaurant – shrimp potstickers were a particular favorite – as anything fancier. He was always carefully dressed in something both stylish and casual, but he wore almost no jewelry other than a simple silver band on his right ring finger. I'd never seen him drink more than two beers in a sitting, and if he had a secret drug habit he was covering it like a champion. He wore no makeup and did his own hair.

His entourage was laughably small, too. Nicky traveled with six staff members and a dozen hangers-on. Wayne held reams of tickets for family and friends at every show through the Midwest. Jordan had Ray and Natalie and now me, and that was it. No one trailed him around the country, not so much as a wayward brother or a sponging cousin or a high school friend from back home whom he'd taken pity on.

For all his affability and down-to-earth nature, though, Jordan Lee remained at his core inaccessible. I'd done a cursory search through the music press archives and read a few of his old interviews, trying to glean what I could about Jordan the person, as opposed to Jordan the public figure. But there just wasn't much out there in the public record. Interviewers could count on an engaging discussion of the music, the band, the album and/or the tour, with a punchline or two and hints of a party-hearty atmosphere, but nothing more revealing. As much as he fed off the attention when performing, Jordan seemed reluctant to engage at all with the media when he was off the stage.

I got a hint there when I ran across some old tabloid articles panting over sightings of Jordan with a couple of different actresses on the Hollywood party circuit. But those were over a decade old, and the rest was standard stuff, predictable band profiles and album reviews. He had one of the most recognizable faces on the planet, yet over the course of fifteen years in the public eye, no one seemed to have gained any real insight into what was going on behind it.

It was a contradiction of the kind that always drove me in search of the deeper truth behind it. But this time, I was coming up dry. Jordan Lee was too good to be true, and yet having seen what I had seen, I couldn't bring myself to doubt him. I don't believe in fate. But life has a way of making you believe in something.

* * *

Of all the reasons I'd said yes to Jordan, the one I'd had frustratingly little return on in the early going was my interest in getting closer to the supersonic Natalie. The distance that Jordan created with savoir faire, she achieved with pure velocity. I could barely keep up with her, let alone pin her down long enough to have a real conversation. My first real break there came at a late-August fundraiser for American Rivers' Great Lakes Project in Chicago, the day before a pair of sold-out Stormseye shows at the United Center.

Everything was in place and we were ten minutes ahead of Jordan's stage cue – introduced by Harrison Ford, then a little patter about the importance of the lakeshore ecosystem, then two songs with the "house band" of semi-retired rock and roll pros – when I just about literally ran into Natalie as I approached the modest green room sidestage right. It was at the Chicago Theatre, a historic venue with narrow backstage passageways, so when I tried to dodge her missile-like trajectory and guessed wrong, we pulled up just short of a head-on collision. She was in a pantsuit tonight, a deep navy shade with a lighter blue open-necked blouse offering a hint of cleavage, an outfit that might have impressed me as very professional if I hadn't immediately fixated on the rich, sweet scent of her perfume.

"Where you headed?" I asked, taking a deep and pleasant breath. Lilacs beat the hell out of the vague eau de locker room that even the nicest backstages seemed to carry.

"Looking for Jordan he's not in there and I need to let him know about the change tomorrow morning we need to roll for Indianapolis at nine instead of ten and –"

"I'll let him know."

Her eyes, a honeyed brown the tone of deeply tanned leather, finally found mine. "Thanks but I should really find him I have a message for him too and a couple of other things I need to –"

"He headed the other way. Said he wanted to talk to the musical director for a minute. Something about the tempo of 'Water's Edge' from sound check. I'll tell him after, it's okay."

She stopped and watched me for a moment, assessing me so frankly and unforgivingly that I had to stifle the urge to laugh. Instead, I quipped.

"The cell phone doesn't do much good, does it?"

She looked away and shook her head. "It might if he'd answer it once in a while like a normal person."

"I don't see that happening any time soon."

She was still focusing down the hall past me, assessing options, calculating her next move. I took another intoxicating breath and decided the moment was right to try to change the game between us.

"So, do you ever slow down?"

She gave me a brief, sharp look before glancing away again. "I'm working."

"No, you're not."

Her eyes widened. "I'm working!"

"No, this is *my* event. *I'm* working. You're *fussing*. Relax. Have a drink. Chill out."

She flashed her eyes at me, an accusation on her lips, and then relented. I enjoyed watching her face change as she for once looked directly into mine.

Before she could invent a new protest, I hooked my arm through hers and began gently pulling her towards the green room. It was mostly empty now, with Jordan the headliner having long since deserted it. The ancient, white-suited bartender appeared glad for the company.

"What're you drinking tonight?"

"I don't."

"Ever?"

"Not when I'm working."

I gave her a look that was half commanding, half tongue-in-cheek, trying to press my way into her good graces. "I realize people rarely listen to me – it's how I got into consulting – but didn't we just cover that subject?"

She gave me a look withering enough that I almost took it seriously, at which point she turned to the bartender. "White wine." Grimacing inwardly at the thought of drinking eight-dollar-a-bottle chardonnay when a liter of Stoli lurked just behind the bar, I ordered the same.

"So," I asked, dropping a bill in the tip jar, "what do you do when you're not working?"

"What?"

"When you're not working. Do you ride a bike? Go to the ballet? Clubbing? Crosswords?"

Natalie continued to stare at me like she either didn't understand the question or was deeply insulted by it. After a long silence, she looked down at her untouched wine, took a slow, deliberate sip, and sighed.

"I have a cat."

"Really?"

"No, I just made that up. Yes, I have a cat."

"What's his name? Or is it a her?"

"You ask too many questions," she said, and bolted for the hallway.

* * *

She has a cat. It was the first scrap of personal information I'd coaxed from her in six weeks on the road. But what kind of cat? Was it a shorthaired grey male or a long-haired white female? Inside or outside? What kind of people are "cat people"? Would she like her men aloof and independent? Moody and sensual? Low-maintenance, but affectionate? On the furniture or on the floor?

And who took care of the cat when she went on the road for weeks at a time? Mother? Sister? Neighbor? Boyfriend?

"Look at him," she said, standing between me and the silent Ray in the wings a few minutes later, watching Jordan do his thing. I did. It was hard not to when 3,600 other people were already busy doing it. He stood at the edge of the stage in a wide stance, hips thrust out, one hand holding the mike to his mouth, the other raised high as his face contorted around the note he was holding as he and the band hit the crescendo of "Water's Edge," a song he'd written about a road trip to Lake Tahoe, but that had exactly the right vibe for this particular event. Camera flashes went off in brilliant, flickering waves every time he moved.

"Yeah," I said.

"He has no idea."

"What?"

"He has no idea of the effect he has on people." I glanced over, but she was still watching Jordan with wide, fixed eyes. Ray meanwhile checked his watch, checked the stage door, and returned to watching Jordan.

I sipped at my wine, which was rapidly warming and souring. "C'mon. After fifteen years?"

"You'd think. But, not really. He knows people follow him around and cheer and want his autograph and all that, but he doesn't see how different it is from how they treat other celebrities. They don't just love him, they practically worship him. The women all want to sleep with him and the men all want to be him."

This was true, of course. I knew it as surely as I knew in that moment that I was out of my league, whether the question was divining Jordan Lee's motives or bluffing my way past Natalie's defenses. Her singular focus and determination was one of the things that had attracted me to her, but it seemed clear now that it was trained elsewhere.

As Jordan finished up, the band going into a brief, ascending flourish, the crowd noise hit a new crescendo along with it, the waves of sound building as Jordan paced the front of the stage, bowing and applauding back at them. Turning away from the crowd, he approached each member of the event's house band and thanked them with a shake or a high-five, pointing to each as he went, encouraging the crowd to spread their love around. Finally he gave one last wave and ambled offstage into the wings. One of the roadies tossed him a towel as he approached us, tousled hair perfectly askew, muscled neck glistening with sweat, aquamarine eyes twinkling, a soul-patched Michaelangelo sculpture come to life.

"Good crowd," he said, and wandered off toward his dressing room with Natalie and Ray trailing in his jet-stream wake.

9

I was out of my league, but that didn't mean I couldn't enjoy the ride for a while. Day after day I found myself rising up through the clouds, emerging into the brilliant sun above and apart from the rest of the world. What was the rest of the world to me at that point, anyway? A handful of relatives and old friends, an empty apartment and a house full of memories that I couldn't cope with. No, I wasn't missing much riding along at 36,000 feet with my iPod on, a drink in my hand and Jordan Lee across the aisle.

That illusion held up for the better part of two months, until one day I was standing in the security line at an airport somewhere in the Midwest, watching a young couple say goodbye. The man was maybe a year or two younger than me, just an everyday average guy in a button-down short-sleeve shirt and jeans, carrying a garment bag and a computer case, leaving for out-of-town corporate training or something. The woman was about the same age, a little shorter but not much, broad-shouldered and solid, one of those naturally physical types who probably played softball or field hockey in college and still ran five miles a couple of times a week. One who would carry herself with an easy confidence under almost any circumstances but these.

He set his bags down at the side of the terminal hallway, just past the newsstand's last spinner rack, and turned to her. They not so much embraced as fell together, arms wrapping around one another, pulling them into a union as complete and intimate as any you could find on pay-per-view. He buried his face in her hair and whispered in her ear. Her back trembled, her breathing came fast and sharp. They somehow drew even closer, finding new purchase, disappearing into one another like two bodies of water.

And then she stepped back and their eyes met for a brief, charged moment before she turned and walked away, not brushing the tears from her cheeks, just moving again, propelling herself in the other direction in an act of pure will. He stood and watched her go with emotion rippling across his face like a neon sign – Passion, Regret, Longing. By all appearances his pain was exquisite and would last a long time.

And all I could think was: *you lucky bastard.*

*　*　*

As the airports and hotel rooms accelerated to a blur, and my mood continued to fray, the question became less of an interruption than a steady drumbeat. *You're earning a steady paycheck. Great. But what, other than that, are you doing here?* When I ran away with the circus, had I simply traded one cage for another – a bigger, shinier one?

On September 25th the circus stopped in Detroit, where I sat alone after midnight at the bar of yet another upscale hotel lounge drinking yet another Stoli on the rocks. I threw in a lime twist this time, just to shake things up. Mostly, though, I watched in the mirror behind the bar, simultaneously repelled and fascinated, as Nicky Frost and Seth Lamiroult preyed on a herd of willing females ranging from half to three-quarters their age.

Nicky played the hummingbird, flitting from one nubile blossom to the next, spreading his attentions around, laughing raucously with one, whispering in the ear of another, toasting yet a third across the low table, continually flipping his straight, almost pigment-free hair back over his shoulders, only to have it fall into his eyes again. Just holding his hands up to his face and playing peekaboo with them might have been subtler.

Seth, by contrast, played the lion among his pride, a man apart, intense, feral, brooding. He ignored Nicky completely – seemed, in fact, almost embarrassed by his constant ministrations to his flock. After watching them for twenty minutes or so, though, I noticed that every so often he would steal a glance at the particularly tall and curvy halter-topped brunette two seats to his left, waiting until he caught her eye, then glancing quickly away in a near-pantomime of the bad boy caught looking. From the way she kept glancing over and then away herself, wearing a more and more obvious smile, it was clear he'd already plucked her from the herd and was just toying with her now.

I sipped my drink and continued to wallow. Jordan and Ray had headed straight for the elevators and their rooms the minute we'd returned from the show, and I'd given up on locating the ever-elusive Natalie twenty minutes before. A couple of other night owls sat scattered down the length of the bar, but I had purposely chosen the less populated end.

As the only child of an itinerant parent who was something of a loner himself, I was used to spending chunks of time alone, and often welcomed it. It replenished me, giving me time to sort through all the emotional, physical and mental inputs of the day. There was a peace and sense of order that came with solitude. The only downside, as Bruce Springsteen observed, is that when you're alone, you're alone.

And I did want to connect. I just wanted it to be meaningful. I was repelled by the superficiality I heard in the chatter between longtime couples in college, the kind of inane verbal goo-goo eyes they were constantly making at one another lest, God forbid, there ever be a moment of silence – awkward or otherwise – between them. I wanted to understand and be understood on some deeper level, one that involved less mindless jabbering and more genuine connection.

The one place I ever found that kind of connection was with Terry. The kiss she had stolen down by the creek had been an anomaly, a momentary fluctuation in the force field that bound us together. Through middle school we were the lone bridge between the otherwise sharp boy-girl divisions in our class. By the time we graduated from high school, we were finishing each other's sentences and half our friends were convinced we were just faking not being a couple. But they were wrong. We'd connected first as pals, and then grown into foils, that one ever-reliable friend you went back to, needling and commiserating, after your romantic initiatives with others had crashed and burned – which both of ours did with regularity. Terry was forever crushing on the wrong guy, the one with the attitude or the one who didn't like her back or the one who already had a girlfriend. Whereas I was the type to be enraptured by a girl walking by and spend two months yearning after her without ever actually speaking a word aloud in her presence (too risky, too self-revealing). Julie had been the exception, and I'd still managed to screw that up.

College could have pulled Terry and me apart – she went to San Francisco State, went through a hippie phase and tried going by Teresa for a couple of semesters, while I went to Davis, left my name alone and drank a ridiculous volume of Sierra Nevada Pale Ale – but we e-mailed all the time and got together back home in Santa Rosa at every holiday. There had been a period of weeks towards the end of college when I had mulled over the idea of seeing what unexplored territory there might be for the two of us beyond the comfortable, familiar boundaries of our friendship. But I could never get past the risk factor. Do you gamble the sure-thing, lifelong friendship you have for a chance at the great unknown? I couldn't stand the idea that I might lose her, that the relationship that we had both come to rely on so much through all the other ups and downs of our lives might be damaged beyond repair if things went sideways. The stakes were too high.

Three months after graduation, Terry had met Michael, known in those early days as "Sweet Cheeks," as opposed to the more recent "Apple-

Slicing, Neighbor-Screwing Son of a Bitch." Two years later they were married. How close were we still? Terry had insisted on me being one of Michael's groomsmen even though he and I had never progressed beyond a kind of wary détente. I stood there before God and most everyone I had ever known, looking across the dais at Terry as she pledged herself to the man she loved, and was ashamed that I felt nothing – neither happiness for her, nor the urge to "speak now." I held my peace. I'm good at that.

For my part, in college and beyond I'd run through a series of dead-end relationships lasting weeks to months, friendly interludes that never seemed to lead anywhere. At times I felt like an observer in my own skin, watching myself seek out companionship, only to withdraw once I'd secured it. It wasn't that I didn't care; it was just that whenever things settled into any sort of routine, I lost interest. No, the truth: I got bored. Can you have relationship ADD?

Sitting there at the bar watching Nicky and Seth weave their pheremonal spell, I thought again of Terry, sitting in my father's house two thousand miles away, licking her wounds. The impulse hit me to call a cab and just leave. I could be home in six, seven hours, far from the funhouse-mirror parallel world I had slipped into, that seemed to have no real place for me in it. All I had to do was pull out my phone and call.

I waited until the feeling passed, and ordered another drink.

* * *

I woke the next morning in a tangle of sheets atop a mattress I'd nearly stripped in my restless sleep. Showering and dressing happened in a head-throbbing blur; I stumbled down to a late breakfast in the lobby atrium, thinking food might improve my situation, but the minute I shuffled out of the elevator and caught the first whiff of undercooked eggs I lost all appetite. I was considering turning straight around and heading back upstairs when I spotted a familiar figure navigating the maze of tables, headed for the buffet line.

Some sixth sense caused Ray to glance my way. Our eyes met and he nodded, simultaneously beckoning for me to come along and pointing ahead. I traced his path forward and there was Natalie, waiting in line already, right hand tapping against her thigh while she spoke quickly and softly into the phone in her left.

In that case... I waved back indicating I'd find a table.

The big man was already in his standard-issue gear – earth-toned turtleneck tee (olive this morning), dark casual slacks, black tennis shoes. Despite being nearly as broad as he was tall, there didn't seem to be the slightest wasted space on his frame. Chiseled he wasn't, but he was strong and solid and moved with unexpected fluidity, always balanced, ever-alert. I chose a table opposite the elevators, away from the artificial fountain/waterfall that filled the atrium with a gentle burbling, and against the side wall; I'd long since taken note of Ray's habit of sitting where he could see the whole room.

Natalie was still on the phone – full plate in her other hand – when they approached, leaving the table talk to Ray and me for the moment.

"So how'd you end up with this gig, anyway?"

Ray was focused on working the margarine into the crannies of his English muffin, which he then piled with scrambled eggs. "Worked corporate security for a few years after I got back from the Gulf in '92. Hated it. Dropped out and moved to Jamaica. Spent my savings, came back a few years later looking for work and heard J needed someone. Simple job. Pay's good. Get along with the boss." He shrugged, like that was all there was to it.

"When'd you start with him?"

"'Bout five years ago. The band was huge. Had another tour coming up and things were getting crazy. You know." Another shovel of muffin and eggs.

"So, when did he start doing all these charity events?"

"He'd always done a few. He just kinda dove in after –" Ray caught himself mid-sentence and shot me a brief, assessing look. Next to us, Natalie continued to murmur into her phone, absently waving a forkful of cantaloupe as she spoke. "Why you asking?"

"Oh. Ah, just curious. Seems like a lot of celebrities get involved in causes out of ego or boredom or wanting people to take them seriously. Jordan's different."

"Right." Pointing at me with his fork. "Right. Dude's real, as real as they get. Worked for a lot of bullshitters before J. Known him a long time now." Looking me right in the face now, his big brown eyes wide and intense. "There is no bullshit in that man."

I nodded. I believed it.

Natalie hung up at last. "Hi Tim. Sorry. Working on some details for LA next month."

"Oh, sure. I need to make some calls today about a thing there, too. There's a Save the Bay group that's been bugging me for two weeks about getting Jordan to appear at a rally."

I started to feel guilty about how quickly I'd transferred my full attention from Ray to Natalie. He, on the other hand, seemed completely indifferent. So I continued.

"So what did you think about the –"

Her phone rang. In quick succession she checked the caller ID, sighed, held up her index finger to ask me to hold on a minute, gave me a little sideways grin, and took the call.

I glanced over at Ray again, whose half-resigned, half-amused look spoke of many calls interrupting many breakfasts. After a moment of companionable silence, another little scene caught my attention thirty feet away. First Seth marched up, striding through the crowd like a general surveying his troops, and took a place in line at the buffet. Then Wayne ambled in from the gift shop area, checked out the scene for a moment, took three halting steps toward the buffet, spotted Seth in line, turned around, and disappeared back into the hallway leading to the first floor rooms.

I turned back to Ray, who'd been watching me watch Wayne and Seth. "Can I ask you something?"

He shrugged and took another bite.

"Do they really hate each other?"

"The band?"

"Yeah."

"Nah. They're just – they're like a family that's been tight for so long they've started to drive each other crazy. Fifteen years of hotels and busses and airports and studios. All of 'em stubborn, all of 'em with different reasons for being here."

"So, how'd they get together in the first place?"

"Mmm, it started in Berkeley. Jordan was at Cal, but he hated it, spent all his time singing in coffeehouses and staying out all night. Nicky and him, they met at a party or something. Then they found Seth in a music store. Came in for some strings and Seth was hammering on the kit they had set up in the back of the store. J asks the guy behind the counter 'Who's that?' and the dude looks over at Seth and just goes 'No, man, he's too heavy for you.' I think J took it like a challenge."

"How about Wayne and Glen?"

"No keyboards at first, and they had a couple different bass players. Nick and J found Wayne playing in a jazz trio on the strip after they decided to go less grunge, more classic rock. Some dude named Dom was playing bass when they got signed, but he was so strung out he barely made it through the first session. Then the label brought Glen in and everybody liked him. Quiet, mellow, no ego. You know."

I did, as well as I knew most of the band's bio already from there – five increasingly successful albums, steady touring moving quickly from opening theaters to headlining arenas. But there was one big, obvious question that had never seemed to have been answered.

"So, why'd they take that long break after *September Serenade*?"

Ray went silent. I realized after a beat that Natalie was watching me now, too, even as the person on the other end of her phone continued chattering away.

And there it was. The longer I hung out inside Jordan's bubble, the more obvious it become that there were actually two layers surrounding the man, and I'd only made it through the first. As much as I wanted to be a part of Jordan's road family, in some fundamental way I was still an outsider.

"Never mind." I wasn't ready to surrender the conversation entirely, though. "So, you said they all have different reasons for being here. Why's Jordan still here?"

Ray looked away toward the milling conventioneers in the buffet line, watching them silently for a moment. Finally, softly, he said "I think they guilted him into it."

"The tour?"

"The whole reunion thing. He was fine solo. Not as big as when they were together, but not such a zoo either. Two busses and a truck with the whole band and crew, instead of ten tractor-trailers criss-crossing the country while the big dogs fly in city by city. But without him, those guys've got no face, no voice. They need him. And they know it. And he knows they know it. Gets intense."

Soon we were finishing up. Natalie was still on the phone, though she'd somehow still managed to clean her plate. I thought of one more question.

"How long do you think he'll keep it up?"

Sharp glance. "The band?"

"Yeah."

"Want to say 'til they get enough, but these guys? No such thing. Basher, seems like that dude wants to die lyin' in a pile of money with a nose full of coke and a whore on top. Frost, too, 'cept it'd be a case of champagne and twins. The other two, I dunno. I think it's down to, this is the only thing they're good at." Looking down at his empty plate now, a single deep furrow bisecting his broad ebony brow. "My guess is one day J will just decide he's done."

"And that'll be it? He'll just walk away?"

Looking up again, relaxed, matter-of-fact. "Oh, yeah, man. J decides something, that's it. End of story. That is one dude who knows what he wants."

* * *

The familiar rhythms of my day – hotel, bus, airport, plane ride, airport, bus, hotel, bus, arena, eighteen thousand delirious fans screaming Jordan's name at the top of their lungs, blah, blah, blah – carried me through to another midnight, another city, another hotel room, where I sat nipping at a vodka-rocks hijacked from the lobby bar and surfing the Internet. Checking e-mail I found the usual scattering of junk, a couple of Google news alerts, and a note from Terry.

Smiling and yawning at the same time, I clicked into Terry's message, which was both brief and vaguely alarming: "Need to talk when you can. Don't worry, house is fine."

Ten p.m. on the West Coast – late, but not too late for Terry and me. *Alright, you got me this time.*

"Hey!" Her voice was warm and sleepy. I imagined her curled up on the couch in front of our antique picture-tube TV with the digital converter box balanced on top, full waves of shiny, jet-black hair pulled back and braided, wearing PJ bottoms with bunnies on them and a Rolling Stones t-shirt.

"Hey yourself."

"How are you? *Where* are you?"

"Cleveland. Doin' alright."

"Cleveland." A little chuckle of disbelief at my city-hopping lifestyle. "How was the Hall of Fame?"

We'd talked before I hit the road about the places I needed to visit in each city on Jordan's itinerary. Cleveland's top pick was the Rock and Roll Hall of Fame. But our flight in had been late, the show finished up after eleven, and we were due back at the airport before noon that next day.

"Didn't happen. Too busy. Schedule's tight all week."

"Oh, bummer. The job's still good?"

"Sure. Sure, Jordan's great. And lots of events for me to work on. And in between, I'm like an extra roadie."

"Riding with the band."

I chuckled at her gee-whiz tone. "Sure."

"Setting up the gear."

"No, I don't go near the instruments. They have guys who actually know what they're doing for that."

"Fending off the groupies."

"The ones that need fending off, anyway."

"Oh yikes."

"Kidding. No, really, they come on to Jordan all the time, but he never takes it seriously. Just makes small talk and walks away."

"Really?"

"Yep."

"That's kind of weird, don't you think? I mean, I'm sorry, but the guy is *smoking* hot."

"I hadn't really noticed."

"Shut up, you know it. So, he's not married and he's not getting busy with the groupies. Gay?"

This stopped me for a minute. *Hmm. But* – "I don't think so. There were some articles about him dating actresses and models back when the band first got big, and I've caught him checking out the women backstage sometimes, even flirting some. I just never see him, y'know, following through."

"Girlfriend at home, maybe?"

"Maybe. He never seems to go home, though. And he barely uses his phone. I don't know."

"Huh. Vow of chastity?" We shared a laugh at the unlikely sound of that idea. "What about you? You fending them off?"

In truth, there had been opportunities – there often seemed to be women backstage more than willing to settle for bedding someone close to Jordan if the man himself wasn't within their reach. A tube-topped, collagen-injected blonde in Des Moines had been especially aggressive, but I just couldn't see myself spending two hours answering questions about Jordan in between bouts of sloppy drunken sex. It was just so obvious that anything that happened there wasn't going to be about me.

"Pretty much."

"Well, be careful."

"I know."

"You don't know where these girls have been."

"Gee, thanks. And yeah, I do. With Nicky Frost, most of 'em. The guy's an animal."

"Lovely."

"Sorry." *Real sensitive, Green.*

"No, it's alright. Whatever. Anyway, the reason I wanted to talk."

"Yeah." I took in a big breath. "What's up?"

"I need to start making plans for the rest of the year."

"Already?"

"It's been four months, Tim. You know how much I appreciate it, being able to stay here, but it's time to start getting my life together."

"Yeah, I know, but – well, what're you saying?"

"It's time for me to move on."

The entire contents of my chest cavity sank. I stood up and paced over to the window. The city spread out before me, glimmering and indifferent.

"Like, out of the house? Or out of town?"

"Not out of town, not this minute. I still want to finish my teaching credential. Two more classes at Sonoma State and I'm done."

"Campus is twenty minutes away."

"I know."

"Just stay, then."

"Tim." Heavy sigh.

"What?"

"It's just – I don't know, I'm sitting here in your old house and it's cozy and familiar and full of good memories, and I love that. But it's not mine. I lost – everything." I caught the hitch in her voice and looked down at my shoes, feeling, for a minute, very small.

"I left with three suitcases of clothes and books and pictures and I don't ever want to see anything else that was in that place again. It hurts too much. I left it all behind and I just need to start over now, and I can't do it here. This is your home, not mine."

"I –" *Crap.* "I understand. No, I get it, Ter. I'm sorry."

"I am, too. I love the big oak trees. I watch the squirrels in them all afternoon sometimes. And I love being down the street from where I grew up, even if Mama doesn't live there anymore. And –" a choking laugh "– I love seeing all your old high school stuff in your room."

"Been reading my comic books again?"

"Only *Superboy.* He was pretty cute back in the '80s, before they tried to make him all Hollywood."

"Remember when you wanted to be Lana Lang?"

"Yeah! Lana, that great Latina role model. Always getting in trouble so she could get rescued."

"That's how it works with heroes."

"Mmm, I forgot, you're into that whole damsel in distress thing."

"Is that right?"

Her laugh occupied the neutral zone between agreement and resignation. "I had you figured early on."

"Maybe you could explain it all to me sometime, then."

"Sure. It'll only cost you 95 bucks an hour."

"How about instead of rent?"

"Deal!"

We laughed again, together. "Ter –" I took a deep, gathering breath. "Don't."

"Don't what?" Knowing, but making me say it anyway.

"Don't leave. Stay until fall semester's over. It makes so much more sense. And I should be off most of December, and we can get through the holidays together, and then you can start over in the new year."

"I don't know. Tim, I don't know. I need – something. Something I can't have here, sitting alone in your house."

"Just – look, is there any reason you need to make a decision about this tonight?"

A sigh spilled out across the miles of empty airwaves between us. "No. No, I guess there really isn't."

"Then don't. Just stay a little longer. I'll be there in two weeks and we can talk about it again then."

"Two weeks. Alright. Alright. At least I can keep listening to your dad's record collection."

10

Before the hospitals and nurses and tubes and monitors took over our lives, before the cane and the stump, before I left my father and before he left me, Dad and I used to go camping every summer. We established a few favorites in my middle school years – the dunes at Bodega Bay; Gualala Point Park above Sea Ranch; and way up the coast among the redwoods at Patrick's Point.

We'd pack up most of the gear on Thursday night and leave as soon as I was done with school that Friday. The gear was always the same: the "three-person tent" that barely slept two; a pair of down sleeping bags Aunt Ruth had passed on to us; an ancient Coleman stove with a football-sized propane can for fuel; a few battered pots and pans; the pillows from our beds and a couple of bags of food. We kept it basic, but that was fine. The point was to get away for a couple of days, just the two of us.

On the drive we would talk, and when we talked, our conversations almost always came around to music. By my early teens song titles, song lyrics, little musical fragments and liner notes trivia had already become the foundation of a secret language Dad and I shared. Riding up the coast in our sputtering Toyota with two missing hubcaps, anytime we got bored one of us would start twirling the radio dial, looking for a classic rock station. It was a contest every time, in which victory went to the person who guessed the song first, either from the first few chords or the DJ's shorthand description. On longer trips we'd turn the radio off and go deeper: "Who was the Beatles' original bass player?" "Who were the Eagles the backup band for before they got signed?" "Where was Jimi Hendrix when he lit his guitar on fire?" It had made for some weird moments in high school, when my peers were all into Smashing Pumpkins and Rage Against The Machine while I was immersed in the finer points of Janis Joplin and the Flying Burrito Brothers.

There was kind of sacred rhythm to these dialogues, a sense of significance far out of proportion to the actual content. We argued the finer points passionately, quoting source material, betting each other five and ten and twenty bucks we were right, never collecting. Music was the one bridge between us that never closed.

Music, and the night sky.

Sitting close by a crackling fire late into a spring or summer evening, we'd wait for the last vestiges of sunlight to leave the sky and then set out with flashlights for the nearest unoccupied meadow or coastline, pushing away from our fellow campers into the dark, finding a place of stillness where no artificial light would interfere. Once we got established – sitting or standing or lying flat on our backs, depending on the terrain – the flashlights would go off and we'd wait a ten count for our pupils to adjust and the show to begin.

There were two elements to this ritual. The first was rather basic, the puzzle portion of getting oriented and picking out the constellations one by one. "There's Polaris!" "There's Orion's belt!" "Cassiopea's bright tonight." "D'you see Hercules, down over there?" We'd go on like this for five or ten or fifteen minutes, depending on how talkative we'd been just before and how tired Dad was. Then gradually, quiet would set in as we stopped imposing our arbitrary, Earth-bound sense of order on the universe laid out above us, and allowed ourselves to simply gawk at it, to let our awe in.

For all my misgivings about religion, I'll say this; the night sky seen from the wild feels indisputably sacred. The enormity of it, the utter unknowability of even our little corner of the universe, is so instructive. We humans walk around in daylight thinking we know so much, that we have somehow mastered our world. The night sky tears away the false façade of control we have constructed and exposes the absurdity of our arrogance. We are gnats, every one of us, in the face of the infinite.

Lying in the grass, sitting on a rock, standing at the end of a trail with necks craned skyward, Dad and I would soak in the tableau, pinpoints of light scattered across the heavens like fairy-dust, stars and planets and galaxies turning gently, eternally above us. It was a silent and almost certainly holy moment, our communion, our consecration. We were tiny, Dad and I, but we were two, and we were together.

* * *

I caught a flicker of one of those moments, just a quick flash of time and place and shimmering melancholy, while riding on the band's chartered bus the next day between the airport and the Cincinatti Hyatt Regency.

Staring out the window while listening to the voice mails that had stacked up during our flight, I spotted a star-speckled billboard advertising the Cincinatti Planetarium just as a rep from the Wilderness Society was explaining in my ear that they still needed to confirm Jordan for an upcoming event. The irony of that internally contradictory name – "The Wilderness Society" – had always amused me. Was that what Dad and I had been, lying on our backs, attempting to impose our human desire for order on the chaotic heavens?

The image faded again, though, as we negotiated the usual check-in mob scene at the hotel, pandemonium being the normal result when 19 high-maintenance guests all belly up to the registration desk at once. After a long wait for a key, I stashed my bags in my room and rode up two floors to knock on Jordan's door.

His cell phone at his ear for once, he waved me into the room and kept talking. I busied myself studying the view out over the Ohio River, trying hard not to look like I was eavesdropping.

"Cincinatti."

Jordan seemed to only use his phone for outgoing calls, so chances were he'd made this one.

"A week. I think the first date is on the 4th."

Telling whoever it was when we'd be in New York.

"Yeah."

La-di-da-I'm-not-listening-except-I-am...

"I always do."

I pulled the curtain farther back, craned my neck and pressed my forehead against the window glass as if straining to get a look at the building next door. I doubted I was fooling him, but at least I was making an effort.

"Because I have to."

Hmm?

"That's not what I'm doing." Pause. "I just have to." Pause. "Yes, every time. I owe her that."

A sudden urge to clear my throat came; I stifled it.

"I know. I know. Look, I've gotta run now. Just wanted to check in. Thanks, babe. Hugs to the kidlets."

Babe? Kidlets?!

"I will." Pause. "You, too. Lots of love. Bye."

Jordan hit "end," tossed his phone on the bed – a four-poster with nine pillows and an elaborate woven spread – and turned to me, still bright-eyed, but maybe a bit more subdued than usual. "What's up?"

It took me a second to unclutch. But then: "The Wilderness Society called about the dinner in New York."

"Oh, yeah. Which night is that again?"

"The 3rd, right after we get in from Philly."

"Right. That one's tight. But no performance, right?"

"Right, they just want to confirm an appearance – no remarks or performance. You know, just looking to nail it down so they can wave a list of confirmed guests in front of the ones they're still working on."

"Sure," he said, moving to his big travel bag and digging out a fresh set of clothes for the night's show. "Go ahead and confirm."

"Alright. Back on the bus in twenty minutes."

"No problem." Jordan suddenly stopped what he was doing, a black t-shirt in one hand and a pair of dark socks in the other, and shot me a quizzical look. I realized in a rush that it probably had to do with the fact that I still hadn't moved an inch from my spot by the window, rooted there as I was by my curiosity.

"So, um, you do use your phone. Natalie's not gonna believe me." Straining to make a joke out of it. He didn't laugh.

"I pick up sometimes. I just don't let it be a leash."

"Sure." I let the silence hang between us for another interminable second, then gave up and broke for the door. "Alright, see you in a few –"

"It was my sister."

I turned at the door and looked back down the narrow entryway into the large part of the room, where Jordan stood in silhouette now, backlit by the window behind him.

"Your sister?"

"Sharon. She lives in the East Bay – San Ramon. Two years younger than me. Couple of kids, one in third grade, one still in preschool."

"Oh. I – I didn't know you had a sister."

He smiled and shrugged. "You never asked."

It wasn't until much later that it occurred to me how, by surrendering one significant piece of information, he'd succeeded in diverting me from any pursuit of the other. *What's in New York?*

* * *

Two floors down, the elevator doors opened and I stepped out, intending to cut left towards my room. Glancing right for a split-second, I spotted Natalie halfway down the hall, standing by her suitcase at the door to her room, working the door handle fruitlessly and looking frustrated.

"Hey," I called and headed her way.

"Oh hi Tim this isn't working maybe the key card's bad or something I think I'm going to have to go back down and get another one." She was back to jeans and a casual pullover blouse, comfortable travel clothes. I speculated briefly on what she might wear to the show that night and came up with several pleasing possibilities.

"Want me to give it a try?"

"Sure." She handed me the card and started digging in her shoulder bag while I took a look. Standard key card, standard hotel room door card slot, in and out it went and the light stayed red. *Brilliant, Green. Another genius move. Imply she's incompetent and then look like an idiot when you can't do any better.*

I turned to hand the card back to her just as she fished a second, identical one out of her purse, saying "Oops." More or less elbowing me out of the way, she thrust the second key into the slot and got a green light on the first try.

Before I could offer to help she'd grabbed the handle extension on her suitcase and started wheeling it into the room. I leaned forward next to her and held the door open until she and her suitcase had passed through, and then stepped into the doorway myself. Parking her suitcase by the dresser, she turned and seemed surprised I was still there.

"Thanks. All set now."

"You always get two keys?"

"Um, yeah. Good to have a, you know, back-up, I lose them all the time and they all lock, I mean look the same so you know…" *Stumbling over words? What? And – is she blushing?*

"Yeah. Okay, well, see you in a few."

Her relief at my willing retreat was palpable. After I let the door shut, I stood there in the hallway for a moment staring at it, letting this entire odd exchange replay in my mind. And then, passing the elevator again going back the other direction, as I caught a glimpse of my rankled reflection in the mirror hanging in the little foyer area, it hit me.

The problem hadn't been that she had two keys to her room and one of them didn't work. It was that she had keys to two rooms.

* * *

Back in my own room, I left a snippier-than-necessary return message for our contact at The Wilderness Society, threw my phone charger in my laptop case and decided I'd rather use the ten minutes remaining before the next band rendezvous returning another voice mail than brooding about my latest romantic pie-in-the-face routine. Next on my call-back list was the one and only Gene Ostrowitz.

I'd crossed paths plenty of times in the past with Gene, who'd been an advocate for one progressive cause after another over a twenty-five-year career working the hallways and committee rooms of the California State Capitol. He was one of those unique characters who might have foundered elsewhere, but became a minor star in the firmament of Sacramento iconoclasts. He had lobbied or advised virtually every Democratic Governor and Senator since Ronald Reagan had left Sacramento for

Washington, D.C. There had been frequent talk of him joining one office-holder or another's team on a permanent basis, but temperamentally, Gene was better suited to play the role of consultant-savant than staff member working within a hierarchy. Late in a career spent dabbling in multiple different areas of policy, he had decided to devote himself full-time to a single cause, and accepted the position of executive director of the California Climate Change Coalition, an aggregation of environmental groups focused on promoting efforts to combat global warming.

"Tim!"

Gene was also the only man I'd ever known whose voice sounded like it was permanently under the influence of helium. For safety's sake I held the phone an inch from my ear as I stood at the window of my own room, taking in the view of the roof of the parking garage next to the hotel.

"Hey, Gene. It's been a while. How's it going? What can I do for you?" Questions that, in the political context, amounted to one and the same.

"Great! Always great! And how're you? Good? Excellent! Listen, I ran into your pal Charlie Bond at Frank Fat's the other day and he told me about your new thing." *Charlie. Predictable.* "Pretty neat, Timmo! Out on tour with the biggest band in the land! Dancing with the stars!" He laughed at his own joke.

"Just helping out with some charity stuff. It's pretty interesting, actually."

"Where are you today?"

"Cincinatti."

"Cincinatti! What a disgusting ignorant little backwater! The only thing worth even talking about in that entire city is this little place on Madison Road that serves the best pesto linguine outside of Venice."

"Sounds great, Gene. Wish I could make it out there. The schedule just doesn't leave us much down time."

"Too bad, too bad. Well, you tell that Jordan Lee hello from me. He is just too cute for words!"

I should mention also that a lot of peoples' first impression of Gene was of a cartoonish dilettante. After watching him work a crowd several times, though, I came to recognize this face—"the gayest man you'll ever meet"—as a character he played in order to disarm his audience. The more outlandish he was, the less threatening he was, until he made his move, always in a quiet huddle, off to one side. In public he was Puck the jester; in private, Machiavelli reborn.

The other key to Gene's little kingdom was a virtually photographic memory. The man could recite clauses buried deep in the Political Reform Act like long-treasured poetry, and recall the name, spouse's name, mistress's name, pet issues and personal vices of every person he'd ever met. The running joke among Capitol staffers was that if Ostrowitz was ever called to testify in front of a grand jury, there would be a riot at the airport from all the legislators trying to flee the jurisdiction at once.

"I'm sure he'll appreciate the thought, Gene."

"Oh fine, maybe I'm a little old for him, but every fella needs a dream, you know. Anyhow, Charlie told me what you were up to, and the first thing I thought of was how great it would be if we could get your new boss out front on the Clean Futures campaign."

Of course. Clean Futures was Gene's brainchild and the CCCC's first big media splash, a ballot initiative that would require every consumer vehicle sold in California to get at least thirty miles to the gallon within the next seven years. Any model that didn't make the cut by the deadline would get hit with a twenty percent markup, with the fee revenue split evenly between funding mass transit and providing competitive grants to support alternative energy research. It was a no-brainer for Jordan – he'd endorsed it months before I'd even met him.

Before I could respond Gene went on, as he tended to. "You know, your old boss still won't even meet with us. Claims he doesn't have time. What a bozo! He thinks he can sit it out, keep both the enviros and his corporate pals in his corner with a bunch of two-faced happy talk. Did you see the *LA Times* editorial last week? No? I guess you really did check out. Anyway, the headline was 'AWOL' – saying what an outrage it is that a major-party Senate candidate has no position on the biggest environmental initiative in California in the last fifteen years. It's pathetic, absolutely pathetic. So what do you think? Could we get Jordan to do some appearances, maybe cut an ad?"

"Well, I'll have to check with him. I know he's on board and I'm sure he'll want to help. I just don't know how much more we're going to able to pack into his schedule at this point."

"Of course not. He's a busy guy! But this is big, and he's such a natural for it. I mean, California boy, national profile, years of activism – c'mon. And we need him. We're pushing hard, but it's looking like a photo finish, and that's the scenario where a Jordan Lee could make the difference, get out the eighteen-to-thirty-five vote and all that."

"Sure."

"Anyway, what's the calendar looking like? I know you guys're on the road, but where're you scheduled between now and election day?"

I realized I could hear Gene clicking away on his mouse in the background. *Probably checking the tour dates on Pollstar while we talk. No point in playing games.*

"We're on the East Coast for another ten days, then a short break, then we finish next month with twelve shows out west."

"Out west – ?"

I cut him off before he could try to pin me down with appearance commitments I wasn't in a position to give. "Traveling all month. It's pretty tight – we start in San Diego on the 12th, two shows there and then three in LA, up to Sacramento, jump over to Vegas, and then five in Oakland at the end, finishing on the 29th. They always close with a big homestand."

The phone was suddenly quiet. I glanced at the time and realized I'd need to finish up soon to catch the bus to the show. "Gene?"

"I'm here, I'm here. Just let me rewind the tape a second. You're telling me Jordan Lee is already committed to being in San Diego, LA, Sacramento and the Bay Area the last three weeks of October?"

"Well—yeah."

"That's perfect! If he'd do some appearances for the initiative, I mean."

"I understand. Look, I'll try to check with him tonight. With luck I should be able to get back to you within a couple of days."

Another pause.

"Listen, Gene, I should go. I need to catch the bus to the show in a minute here."

"Sure, Tim, sure. You've just – you've got to understand, I've heard – everybody's heard – how things went with you and Frank at the end. The man is without grace."

This was so unexpectedly kind that I didn't know what to say. And then…

"No one would blame you if you wanted to put a little fear of God in him."

"What?"

"Oh come on, Tim Green. Frank throws you under the bus and you resurface working for a ridiculously good-looking, ridiculously wealthy celebrity activist, a guy with a Q rating Oprah would smother kittens for, and he just happens to be on the opposite side of the biggest political dogfight going. You can't tell me that's a coincidence."

"Except, Gene, it pretty much is."

"Well then, one of the following two statements is true: either you're an even better liar than I thought, or someone upstairs is trying to tell you something."

11

Down in the lobby — yet another tastefully carpeted, faux-pillared tomb — I found I was once again the first to arrive, a habit born of fifteen months doing advance work for a boss who would have taken "snarly" as a compliment. Standing there alone for a minute, I couldn't really figure which knotty issue I wanted to start working at in my head first: Jordan, Natalie or Gene.

I didn't have long to commiserate, though; no more than a minute after I pulled to a stop near the registration desk, Seth came striding out of the elevator, waves of sandy curls bobbing against his black leather jacket as he moved, eyes raking the lobby, impatient before he even came to a stop a few feet away from me. He gave me a brief assessing look, then turned away, scanning past the potted ferns and picture windows for the rest of our troupe. I adjusted the shoulder strap on my laptop's carrying case, took a deep breath, and waited. Eventually, without warning, he spoke.

"What's shakin'."

Seth Lamiroult, Master of Small Talk.

"Nothing much."

Seth shoved his hands in the pockets of his two-hundred-dollar, hand-stressed, stone-washed black jeans and began shifting his weight from one leg to the other in the dance of a man about to either wet himself or jump out of his own skin. Three or four shifts later, he weakened again.

"You hear how fast tonight sold out?" He still wasn't looking at me — I wasn't of sufficient caste to be shown that level of respect — but at the moment he clearly couldn't tolerate silence.

"No." Most of the shows on the reunion tour had sold out within twenty-four hours of going on sale.

"Sixty-seven minutes, man. As fast as they could process the fucking credit cards." He shook his head in mild disgust. "We should've done two here."

I gave him a sharp look, then thought better of it and just shrugged. It was already a six-month, eighty-three-city tour. They'd started in Europe, jumped to the West Coast in early July and played four nights a week almost every week, with only three breaks of more than two days between early May and the end of October. It was a grueling schedule for a bunch of kids, and they were all pressing forty now.

"Jordan going straight to sound check?"

"As far as I know."

Seth grunted and side-stepped over to the once-again-orderly registration desk, where he found a dish with wrapped, minted toothpicks. He fished one out, peeled off the plastic wrapper with a single deft pull and commenced to chewing the end, making the toothpick dance along the line of his mouth like a Rockette in full swing.

After a moment he turned to face me head-on for the first time in all the weeks we'd been traveling together.

"You don't like me much, do you?"

I froze, startled, as Seth loomed directly in front of me: six feet, two hundred and twenty pounds of professional rock drummer, ruddy-cheeked, thick-armed, richer than sin and more than likely coked to the gills. And had just spent eight weeks treating me like a fly he simply hadn't bothered to swat out of existence yet.

The only sane response seemed to be nervous laughter. "Well – I mean – does it matter?"

He stared at me, eyes boring in, pupils dilated. One eyebrow began to arch upward. Then he stopped and shook his head. "You don't get it, man. You just don't fucking get it."

"What?" I asked, now genuinely curious.

"We're a band." He turned away and began to pace, gesturing with both arms as he spoke, as if conducting music that only he could hear. "We've been a band since I was nineteen. When Jordan called timeout, it was – man, I'm no junkie, but I've known a few, and I'm telling you, it was like going cold turkey. One minute you're doing the thing you love more than anything else four, five nights a week, the next you're sitting on your fucking couch staring at your fucking TV and wondering why you bothered getting out of bed that morning."

Just as Seth stopped pacing and turned to face me again, I spotted Jordan, Natalie and Ray approaching from one angle, and Wayne and Glen from another. He had maybe ten seconds to finish before they were upon us.

"Jordan thinks he needs all this other bullshit." Waving his hand at me, like it's all my fault. "I just want to play, man. That's it. That's all."

* * *

That's all. Why couldn't it be that simple for me, I wondered? To want one thing, and want it so much that everything else fell away to insignificance. What would it be like to be that focused? To have your work feed not just your bank account, but your soul? There had been a time when I'd thought I was getting close to that, that my shilling for others had a deeper meaning, a genuine purpose behind it. It had just gotten hard to keep that feeling alive after spending a year and a half in the trenches with a guy who'd molded an entire world around him toward a single objective – the glorification of self.

For the past eight weeks I had watched Jordan do the opposite, wading through situation after situation in which he was the object of that glorification, without ever treating it as anything more than a nuisance. If I couldn't find meaning in my work standing beside a man like Jordan Lee, it was probably hopeless, and if it was hopeless, I had no idea what I was going to do with the rest of my life. Thus it came to pass that, while riding to the arena on a chartered 40-passenger bio-diesel bus, I found a purpose again. Gene was right; Clean Futures was the most important environmental initiative to surface in California in a generation, and thanks to Jordan, I might be in a position to affect the outcome. All I had to do was pick myself up, dust myself off, and get moving again.

At the arena, we were immediately surrounded by the swirl of pre-sound check set-up activity. Speaker and amp connections were being tested, wiring bundles rigged, lighting cans on the main rig tended to, changing out bulbs and gels. In a few more minutes they'd hoist the lighting rig up above the stage and finish setting up the stage monitors. Roadies swarmed everywhere, yelling back and forth with and without the benefit of walkie-talkies. The stage mixer and his assistant stood sidestage wearing full-ear headphones, adjusting levels, twisting knobs, lost in their own cacophonous interior world.

At the back corner of the stage I came across the road manager, a balding, fiftyish guy named Bill who looked like it should really be William and he should really be nose-down in a cubicle in some big corporation's accounting department – until he turned around and you spotted the sword-blade tattoo running up the back of his long, thick neck.

The first thing I needed was an Internet connection for my laptop. Bill steered me to Arjun, the nebbishy East Indian lighting director, who steered me to Denny, a wiry, haunted-looking twenty-something who naturally had jet-black hair, a black t-shirt, ripped-out black jeans and a silver nose ring roughly the size of a cow bell. Denny gave up the venue's wi-fi password like I was the face of capitalist oppression in the world.

Weaving around the stage to the arena floor, I grabbed an empty seat in the front of the floor section and fired up the laptop. While I busied myself clicking and keying, the crew began raising the lighting rig, stationed at the four corners of the stage using winches and pulleys while Arjun called out instructions. At the same time, a huge racket went up from the side of the stage thirty feet from me, steel hammering on steel as two burly guys worked to force a recalcitrant stairway fixture to connect properly with the raised stage floor. It would have been quieter sitting next to a jet engine.

A moment later all was forgiven as Jordan and the band materialized out of the wings. The hammering ceased and soundcheck was on. It was the one part of my daily routine with Jordan that I couldn't imagine ever getting tired of, taking my pick of seats in an empty arena listening to Stormseye blaze through four or five songs for no one but me and the crew. They'd been working for three shows now on a new arrangement for the outro section of "Make Some Change" – heavier on Wayne's piano, with Nicky picking out a nimble, pungent solo underneath rather than slamming power chords – and tonight it was sounding ready.

Twenty minutes later they finished up and dispersed, leaving the crew to continue their preparations and me to pick up my computer again. Clicking into the CCCC Web site, I started jotting notes, bulleted phrases I would repeat to Jordan to remind him of the key provisions of the Clean Futures initiative. As usual, California was out front in an area where others might soon follow. Not that increasing fuel efficiency was a new concept, but pushing it at the state level – in the state with the most cars in the nation, yet – was a new approach that was bound to cause a ripple effect. If California went for it, it would ratchet up the pressure significantly for a greener national energy policy.

I'd been in my seat for over an hour and was well into my third page of notes when my phone began vibrating on my hip. I took a peek and didn't recognize the number, but the area code was 310 – LA, which was intriguing enough to send me scampering for one of the side tunnels that led out onto the cavernous arena floor. In that quieter space, still able to keep watch over the laptop I'd left sitting in the eighth row, I took the call.

"Tim Green."

"Tim, glad you picked up. Jessica Turner with the *LA Times*."

"Hi, Jessica. I don't think we've met. I used to work with Matt Hennessey and Ed Chavez pretty often." "Work with" being a euphemism for "shamelessly pimp my boss' press releases to."

"Sure, on the political desk. You were with Cassini, right?"

"Guilty as charged."

She chuckled and I liked the sound of it, genuine but with a knowing edge. "We probably wouldn't have crossed paths, then. I usually write for the magazine."

The LA Times Magazine? Are you kidding me? A feature story in the *Times'* glossy Sunday insert was a California public figure's wet dream, the kind of exclusive, in-depth free media placement you could pursue for two years and still come up empty. And here she was, calling me. Of course, chances were she was checking up on a filler item for the gossip column or something.

"So, I understand you're handling media for Jordan Lee these days."

"Depends on the focus – the band has its own publicity team. What are you working on?"

"We want to do a cover profile of Jordan. It seems like he's the new prototype for the politically active celebrity, trying to use his fame to make a difference. We want to talk about the activism, his commitment to the Clean Futures campaign, things like that."

"His –" *Gene. Gene! You didn't waste any time, you little s.o.b.!* "Oh. Well, I'll have to check with him, but that sounds interesting. What'd you have in mind? We're on the road another ten days on the East Coast, but he'll be in LA for a few days in mid-October. If you're on deadline, I could try to set up some phone time."

"Thanks, but I'm looking for an in-person. If you can hold some time for me in the next couple of days, I'll fly out."

* * *

A moment later I hit "end" on my phone, did a quick fist-pump, and scrambled out to retrieve my laptop. I found Bill again sidestage, got directions to Jordan's dressing room and took off into the beige concrete tunnels that snaked through the bowels of the arena, weaving through Nicky's milling entourage and down a short side passageway. Finding the door to Dressing Room C cracked open, I gave it a soft push and stepped in.

"Jordan?"

A tinny half-echo was the only reply from the still room before me. This particular space was relatively small and bare, with a modest makeup mirror and counter on my right and a single, narrower full-length mirror on the far wall. A rolling wardrobe rack had been pushed against the wall on my left; on its lower rack Jordan's canvas athletic bag lay open and askew. His tweed Converse all-stars sat nearby, socks thrown casually on top.

I was still standing there contemplating the image of Jordan wandering barefoot through the backstage halls when I heard movement of some sort, quiet and near. Stepping farther into the room and peeking around the back of the door, I found him. He was standing, eyes closed, arms stretched high over his head, palms flat together and pointing at the ceiling, balancing with little apparent effort on his bare left foot. His right knee was bent sharply outward, with the sole of his right foot planted high against his left thigh. His breathing was deep and steady, his concentration total, holding position with little apparent effort.

A moment later he released his right leg, lowered his arms slowly, and moved into a neutral stance. After three more deep, measured inhales, and without opening his eyes, he said in a soft, toneless voice, "Two more."

I closed the door behind me and sat in the single chair by the makeup mirror. Jordan now assumed the mirror image of the awkward position I had found him in, balancing on his right leg this time, left knee out, left foot pressed high against his other thigh, and held it for the space of ten long, steady breaths. Then he released, rested, and repeated the cycle. When he'd finished, he held the neutral standing position for a long time, concentrating, it seemed, on nothing more than his own breathing. It was at least a minute later when he finally opened his eyes, focused on me, and came back to life.

"What was that one?"

"Vriksha-asana," he replied, clearing his throat a bit. "The tree. Great for balance."

Jordan tried to do his yoga in hotel rooms whenever possible, but on occasion I'd walked into dressing rooms and found him in a variety of odd positions, most memorably one afternoon early on, in Houston, when I'd walked in to find him doing savasana, a.k.a. "corpse pose." Charging in with an update about his appearance at a New Orleans charity event the following night, I'd found him lying flat on the floor, arms at 45 degrees from his body, every muscle in his body appearing loose and relaxed. Only his deep, steady breathing had kept me from checking for a heartbeat. Natalie had laughed knowingly when I'd asked her if Jordan often took naps on his dressing room floor.

Grabbing a towel off the wardrobe rack, he settled against the wall opposite me. "What's up?"

"A couple of things. You remember the Clean Futures initiative?"

"The fuel efficiency thing? Sure."

I explained about Gene, ran through a few of the key bullets, and told Jordan what he was asking for. Jordan listened intently, with genuine interest.

"Any details about the appearances – how many, where, when?"

"No, but he's seen the schedule. He knows you'll be in California the last couple of weeks in October and he's pushing for as much time as you can give him."

"Sure. What else've we got booked then?"

"Around the California dates, just a fundraiser for the Yosemite

National Institutes in San Francisco between the second and third nights in Oakland. Right now you're pretty clear otherwise between San Diego and the end of the tour."

"Okay. Alright. Tell him I'll do whatever I can and if he wants to try to do radio or TV spots and can send crews out here to get my parts, I'll make it work. What?"

He was giving me a funny look, most likely triggered by the grin I could no longer suppress.

"It's just a little different here."

"Has your old boss endorsed it?"

"Nope. And I'm sure he's gotten a lot of pressure to stay out of it from his friends over at the Chamber of Commerce."

Finished with the towel, he flung it over the top of the wardrobe rack, leaned down and began rummaging through his bag for his show clothes. "He has friends over there?"

"Sure, there's a few moderate pro-business Democrats left in California, just like there're still a handful of moderate social-liberal Republicans in the Northeast. Frank's really cozied up to that crowd the past three or four years. There's a lot of cash there to spread around."

"And that's what counts. Who has the cash."

"Sure. As long as campaigns are privately funded, money's going to be huge. To be a viable candidate you either have to raise it every single day or have deep pockets of your own."

Jordan shook his head and peeled off the light cotton tee he'd been wearing. He wasn't exactly muscle-bound, but the yoga had left him toned enough that there was no sign of middle-aged spread creeping in.

"Okay. Anything else?"

"The *LA Times* wants to do a profile."

Shirt still in hand, bent over his bag, he stopped cold for a minute.

"The *LA Times*?"

"Yeah, a writer with their Sunday magazine called. Jessica Turner. I've seen a couple of her pieces. She tends to go pretty deep. And she's good, knows how to frame a story."

He straightened and turned to face me again, antennae now fully extended.

"What kind of profile?"

"They want to focus on the whole celebrity activist angle."

"With me? That's – why not somebody like Bono?"

"They probably think he's overexposed. Plus, you're from California, so there's the whole hometown-boy angle to play."

"Mmm. When?"

"As soon as you'll agree to. She said she'd fly out and do it in person."

He seemed to hesitate for a moment, and I couldn't fathom why.

"It's a chance for you to reach a whole new audience. And it could have a real impact on the initiative."

"Have you ever worked with her before?"

"No, but –"

At that precise moment, the door blew open without a knock and Wayne steamed in breathless, with Natalie on his heels.

"Jordan, you've gotta get out here, man – Seth's gone psycho and somebody's gonna get their ass kicked."

* * *

We followed Wayne and Natalie back down the long hallway at a steady jog toward the stage area. As we cut through into the main hall I could make out the sound of several different voices all shouting at once. All work had ceased; even Denny, now perched high in the lighting rig thirty feet above the stage, had stopped what he was doing and was staring down at the gathering below him.

Wayne and the rest of our trailing posse took the back stairs up onto the stage two at a time, every thudding step on the metal frame echoing through the empty arena. At the top we moved past the drum riser where Seth's kit was now fully assembled, and melted into a circle of milling spectators surrounding three figures.

In the center of the group, Seth and Arjun were circling slowly, Seth the aggressor, Arjun in defensive posture. Standing between them, watching Seth intently, was Glen. Considering he was a good five inches shorter and sixty pounds lighter than Seth, this could be considered an act of extraordinary bravery.

Jordan pushed immediately through to the inner edge of the circle. "Hey," he said in a calm, neutral tone, gliding forward to line up alongside Glen. "What's going on?"

Arjun and Seth both tried to speak at once, but Seth shouted him down, still circling, tensed and ready.

"They won't fix my fucking spots! My head's been pounding for a week because they can't get the goddamned angle right! So I told Bombay Bob here –" pointing at Arjun "– I was going up top to fix it myself, but then he had little Johnny Rotten –" pointing at Denny "– pull the fucking ladder up behind him!" Sure enough, I could see the rope ladder bundled in a heap a few feet from where Denny was crouched on top of the lighting rig, watching the scene play out thirty feet below.

Wayne couldn't contain himself. "So, what, you're gonna pound on our lighting director two hours before show time? What the hell, Seth?!"

"Shut your fucking pie-hole, Liberace. You spend the whole show looking down at what you're playing. Try hitting cymbals when you've got a thousand-watt spot in your face!"

"Seth." Jordan took a single step toward him, right hand out in a calm-down stance.

"*Se-eth*," he spat back, slapping Jordan's hand away. "What? You got a new mantra for me? A little organically-grown green tea to calm me down? Get outta here, Jordan, you're a fucking joke and everybody knows it."

"And you're a bloody lunatic!" shouted Glen, bringing the entire tableau to a crashing halt.

In the two months I'd been on tour with Stormseye I'd never had a single conversation with Glen Frazier; I had in fact never once observed him speaking above a murmur. I hadn't even realized he was British until that moment. But he was, and he had now drawn his entire five-foot-seven wisp of a self up into Seth's face, nose inches from Seth's chin, fists clenched at his sides, visibly trembling.

What happened next, I can't really explain. Seth seemed about to explode with rage for a moment. Then his whole body went slack. In the silence he stared at Jordan for a moment, then turned again to Glen. For a brief instant he looked the smaller of the two, wounded somehow by Glen's outburst.

At last he turned and stalked off, directly at me. I sidestepped away from Wayne to make a path between us. As Seth passed us he shot Wayne a quick, savage look and muttered "Pussy."

Wayne turned and lunged after him, but then Jordan was there, holding him back in a bear hug until Wayne finally threw off Jordan's grip and stomped off in the other direction, through the crowd, down the sidestage stairs and out into the empty arena, where he could still be found fifteen minutes later, sitting high in Section 114, staring at nothing.

12

Although in most of my memories it's just Dad and me, he did have a few girlfriends over the years.

There was Lily, the woman Dad's friends at work fixed him up with when I was in kindergarten, a stick-legged, fair-haired ex-hippie who made a badly mismatched set with my stocky, dark-haired pop. In her post-hippiedom she had taken to wearing perfume, though, so she smelled good, and we got along fine even if she didn't seem to be able to find anything to talk with me about other than baseball. She lasted from opening day through the all-star break.

Carolann was another parent at my school, a divorced mother of three girls whom we got together with a number of times over the course of several months in second grade, until the day the seven-year-old daughter and I decided it would be a great idea to trade clothes and then run downstairs and surprise our parents. I don't remember seeing Carolann at our house again after that.

There were a couple of others after Carolann whose names I don't recall – they weren't really around long enough to register as more than passing acquaintances. I remember one always carried a large off-white canvas bag from which she would produce candy bars and Lifesavers in truly remarkable quantities. And another, a bubbly, heavy-set brunette, insisted on hugging me every time she arrived or left, even if she'd only stayed five minutes. I remember an involved conversation with Dad one night about whether a person could be "too huggy" and what that would be like.

Finally, there was Rochelle, who lasted longer than most – I remember her being around for Valentine's Day *and* Thanksgiving one year. A round-faced African American woman with a mysterious smile, Rochelle loved to play board games like Monopoly and Life and checkers. We spent half the summer between fifth and sixth grade at the dining room table, locked in playful competition. Eventually, though, one gray winter day she came up to find me in my room and told me with serious, shining eyes that she wouldn't be coming around again for a while. She promised she'd visit me, and she did return once the following spring, but that was it.

After Rochelle faded out of our lives when I was eleven, there was no one of note. An odd blind date here, a dinner with a friend there. As Dad's health became progressively worse and my teenaged bullheadedness became progressively more entrenched, the very idea of welcoming another person into our duo seemed unlikely if not impossible. We were entwined in a primal way, caught in a net of affection and need, dependence and desire, each of us wanting more than the other could ever provide.

* * *

Two days after Seth's eruption, the tour's full complement of principals and retainers had descended on the Grand Hyatt Washington, an atriumed Emerald City four blocks west of the arena where the band was scheduled to play, and four blocks northeast of the White House. The bus was stashed for now somewhere nearby, awaiting the signal to pull up and take us on the short ride over to the Verizon Center, formerly known as the MCI Center, soon to be known as some other faceless corporate sponsor whose name would doubtless quickly be lost to the ages.

In the meantime, we remained trapped inside, some of us moreso than others. Press conferences were not routine in the middle of this or any tour, but the Stormseye reunion was a national story, and we were less than four days from diving headlong into the omnivorous media maw that is New York City, so the band's collective management team – both Nicky and Jordan had their own personal managers in addition to the band's manager, Jim Dowland – had prevailed on them to spend half an hour in front of the mikes.

Inside the meeting room we'd reserved, Jim had the band seated in a line behind a draped table set up on a low stage. Most of our coterie of staff was strung out along the near wall, watching as Wayne labored away answering a question, something inane about the last time they'd come to D.C. six years ago. Arriving late for once, I had slipped into an open spot along the wall just behind Natalie. In front of us stood Wayne's assistant and Dowland; in front of them was Ray, nearest to the stage.

The audience spread out before the band consisted of fifteen or so reporters scattered among six rows of folding chairs, a notably ragtag group of daily-paper feature writers, independent weekly arts editors, an Associated Press stringer, a small cluster of bloggers and a couple of freelancers who'd probably compete to sell a blurb to *Rolling Stone* or *Spin* or maybe even *Noise*. It wasn't exactly the political reporter crowd I'd grown accustomed to in my former life; no blue blazers and a lot of tennis shoes, not to mention tats, piercings, a high-school-age-looking girl with cropped purple hair, and an older guy who bore a remarkable resemblance to Tommy Chong, which is to say, you expected to pick up a contact high just standing near him.

"Question for Jordan."

Jordan leaned into the mike set up on the table in front of him. "Yeah?"

"Have you been writing new material on the road?"

Jordan took a second before answering, those impossibly deep blue eyes focusing on the reporter, a twenty-something kid in the second row with thatched brown hair, a wrinkled Korn t-shirt and blue jeans with both knees ripped out. "We're always writing. Sometimes we just do it without actually writing anything down." Affable grin. *Next.*

Jordan's questioner – not to mention several others in the crowd – did not seem appeased. The woman next to him, black-haired, pale and wearing thick-rimmed granny glasses, shot her hand up. "Carly Ishikawa with the *Village Voice*. This is for Nicky. *Pieces of the Night* is really a continuation of the same sound you guys have had since *Make Some Change* in 1995. Will the new album stay with that sound or do you see it evolving?"

Nicky was motionless, the usual screen of blond hair shielding his eyes, elbows on the table, hands together, fingers entwined in front of him like a battering ram. His palpable irritation with the event, the questioner and the question itself filled the room for a long moment, until at last he spoke in sharp, clipped bursts. "'That sound,' as you call it, has sold like twenty million units. But sure, we could change it around. What do you want, maracas? Mellotrons? Maybe Seth could switch to rhythm guitar and we could all rap over a beat box." He shook his head as if disgusted to breathe the same oxygen as his questioner.

I looked over at Natalie, who stood, tight-lipped, arms folded, weight on her left leg while her right twitched as if electrified. The band's management team had agreed to make them available for twenty minutes, no more and no less. As the clock ticked past minute fourteen, Natalie began checking her watch every thirty seconds or so.

Back on the floor, Granny Glasses would not back down. Her follow-up question was sharper. "This one is for any of you. Let's be honest – one album of new material in the last five years, and your sound hasn't changed at all. Is there actually going to be another new album? Or are you guys basically a nostalgia act now?"

Wayne and Jordan leaned forward simultaneously to respond, but Seth was too quick.

"Congratulations! That's the stupidest fucking question I've heard this entire fucking tour!" The staring contest between Seth and Granny Glasses achieved laser intensity inside of three seconds. "We've played, like, sixty shows so far, and every single one sold out. That's a million people. *Pieces* went platinum the third week out and it'll be double platinum soon. Does that sound like fucking 'nostalgia'?"

To her credit, Granny Glasses did not flinch. "What about the new album?"

Seth's glare could have melted steel. "Gimme your address and I'll send you a copy when it's done."

She looked like she'd rather give him a restraining order, but kept silent. Behind her, Tommy Chong saw an opening and took it.

"Ken Leonard with the *DC Weekly*. What about the rumor there was a fight backstage in Cincinatti?"

Seth grinned, a dark sparkle in his eyes. "What about it?"

"Was there a fight?"

"Yeah, a couple of the girls got into it, fighting over Nicky. Or was it me?" A scattering of nervous chuckles rippled through the room as Seth feigned searching his memory.

Jordan had his hand on Seth's shoulder now. Seth shot him a hard look for a minute, but then gave in with a little shrug. Jordan leaned into the mike again. "There are always little disagreements on the road. Sometimes they get loud because we're tired and we all take a lot of pride in what we do and sometimes there isn't much time to make decisions. But we've been through all this before, and we're all still friends, and the tour goes on. It's just part of life on the road." Glen and Nicky were nodding. Seth looked bored again. And Wayne kept perfectly still.

The purple-haired girl sitting next to Granny Glasses had her hand up now. As she began to speak, I suddenly focused on the woman sitting just beyond her, a stylishly-coiffed blonde about my age, wearing a sharp navy pantsuit over a classic pink silk top. Her Italian pumps alone would have made her stand out in this crowd.

While I was busy checking out her seatmate, Purple Hair sputtered through a long, convoluted paragraph of a question, the gist of which seemed to be "How dare a bunch of major-label corporate tools like you guys run around pretending to care about the environment?"

Glen and Wayne kept silent. Nicky picked at his fingernails. And Seth stared at Jordan, who didn't even bother looking around before launching into his answer. "We've always believed in the power of music to connect people. It's what brought us together as a group and what brings us together with our audience every night. That said, we're five individuals and I can't speak for anyone but myself. For me personally, I feel like I have an obligation to try to inspire people to be aware and get involved. Too many people spend too much time complaining about our government doing things they don't agree with, without taking any kind of action to try to change it. I try to commit time and energy where I can to support groups who are working to preserve the environment. Other people in the music world and in this band have other causes they support. The point is, if I can use the fact that people know my name to get them involved in issues, engaged in the process, I'm going to do it."

The room was quiet. The reporter seemed to take a moment to absorb the nuances of Jordan's response. Then, just as Jim stepped in front of the table to bring the press conference to a close, she called out her facetious follow-up: "What're you, like, running for Congress or something?"

Jordan laughed, hard and loud, and it quickly became contagious. First the rest of the band joined him, and then Jim was laughing, and half the writers as well. After a few more seconds, Jim broke in, thanked the audience and told them that was all the time the group had today.

*　*　*

In the midst of the post-press-conference hallway milling-about, I spotted Italian Pumps standing off in a corner on her cell phone. As the knot of band-plus-entourage moved steadily for the elevators, I peeled away and found a column to lean against while biding my time.

I studied her as she chatted away intently. On the tall side, medium build, strong forehead, delicate nose, angular chin, precise makeup. Definitely highlights in her close-cropped hair, but they looked good. Small rings on her left pinky and right middle finger. Simple pearl studs in each ear. A thin gold bracelet on her right wrist that was probably plate, but you never knew. Classy, understated, confident.

I scanned the rest of the crowd for a moment, searching through a mix of strangers and familiar faces, and then turned back to find my quarry standing two feet away, phone in hand, blocking my way with big gray-green eyes and a smart-alecky half-smile.

"Can I help you?"

Willing myself not to blush, I held out my hand. "Hi, I'm Tim Green. With Jordan Lee."

She gave my hand a firm, professional shake without taking her eyes off mine, her grin growing even more playful. "I know." Lifting a small flap on her shoulder bag, she clipped her phone into one of the outside compartments with practiced precision. "Jessica Turner. Thanks for saving me my next call."

"I wondered if that might be you. We weren't expecting you until this afternoon."

"Decided to catch the red-eye, start with the press conference."

"And?"

"And that's quite a collection of characters you've got there. Sleepy, Dopey, Surly, Nasty… makes me wonder if Doc is really the one I should be interviewing."

Thirty seconds in and I was already playing defense. "Had anything to eat yet?"

"My last meal was a stale muffin on the plane three hours ago."

"Want to grab some lunch? We've got time before the band heads over to the arena."

"Sure. I should check if I can get in my room yet, too. Left my bag with the bellman."

The twelve-story central atrium held a scattering of café-style tables around a lagoon with a piano set on a platform in the middle. We settled in by the railing amidst more road-warrior banter, before Jessica deftly steered us back around to the topic at hand.

"So, I hear Jordan's agreed to emcee a Clean Futures rally in San Francisco on November 1st."

I stared at her for a minute. He'd agreed to that after the show the previous night. In the interim I had informed Gene and Natalie and no one else, and Jessica had been on a plane half the night.

I smiled and shook my head. "You're good."

She took this as entirely a matter of course. *Nice try, though*, her dancing eyes seemed to say.

"Or at least, Gene's finally learned how to text."

Now she smiled. "You know a reporter never reveals her sources."

"Not even when they're as obvious as the purple hair on the girl you were sitting next to."

"Not even then."

We ordered – a BLT for me, a southwest chicken salad for her, a couple of iced teas. I looked over at the piano again, perched on a pedestal in the middle of the shallow tiled lagoon, a ridiculous Hollywood affectation ready for its close-up. Still, I could see that later in the evening it would have a kind of cheesy, inevitable romance to it, a Nat King Cole melody echoing off the cavernous interior walls all the way up the skylights.

"Been to D.C. before?"

"A couple of times. Followed the mayor out here last year when he came begging for federal money for the subway extension. That, and a family vacation in high school."

"You from LA?"

"No, Bay Area. I went to UCLA, though. Got on with the *Torrance Daily Breeze* for a while before I moved to the *Times* four years ago."

"And you like working at the *Times*?"

"Sure, it's one of the last great big-city papers left."

The impish grin she had worn when she'd first snuck up on me in the hallway an hour before was back. I liked it. "What?"

"For a minute there I forgot what you used to do."

I raised an eyebrow. *Meaning…?*

"You're asking all the questions." She shook her head as if to say *What am I going to do with you?* "Once a flack, always a flack."

13

Day two in DC was an off night before a second show the night of day three. An "off night" meant that all Jordan and the band had on schedule was a testy early-morning appearance on a live drive-time radio show, followed by a lunchtime in-store acoustic performance at a warehouse-sized downtown music emporium that nearly triggered a riot when a loud argument broke out between two groups of fans halfway back in the autograph line.

By the time Jordan had finished up with the thirty-turned-to-seventy-minute "drop-by" at an early-evening fundraising reception for the National Geographic Society, a normal person would have been ready to crawl into a cave somewhere and hibernate for a week. Instead, at 7:08 pm Jordan turned to me in the back seat of the hybrid SUV Natalie had arranged for and asked, "What's next?"

Though he remained as impenetrably still as ever, I did catch Ray checking my reaction in the rearview mirror. I glanced at my watch, rubbed my temples and responded. "Dinner with the *Times* reporter at 7:30. Then the interview. I told her we'd block out two hours, but really, it's as long or short as you want to make it."

"Great."

Natalie met us among the milling early-evening lobby crowd of bone-weary tourists and ravenous businessmen with two messages and three decisions for Jordan to deal with. He blew them all off with the same simple diversion I'd used just the day before: "Come to dinner with us." She gave in on getting answers, but didn't budge on joining us.

With Natalie staying behind, Ray dropped Jordan and me at the curb down the street at the entrance to Tony Cheng's Seafood Restaurant, a DC institution just across from the arena. Jessica was waiting outside, her outfit strictly LA casual chic, a suede blazer over a snug silk blouse, sharply-creased tan slacks and another expensive-looking set of dark leather pumps. She and Jordan had seemed to hit it off fine the night before, though it had been a brief introduction amidst the usual after-show backstage chaos. Today she'd skipped the radio appearance but – for better or for worse – attended the in-store mob scene.

At our table inside, steps away from the circular Mongolian barbecue that dominated the restaurant's downstairs area, I quickly established with Jessica that our dinner conversation was off the record and she'd save her tape recorder for some mutually agreeable time after the meal was done. Ray appeared minutes later with a little nod to Jessica as he took the fourth seat at our table. Being surrounded by three men didn't seem to bother her in the least; if anything it appeared to elicit a sort of feline contentment. I caught myself watching her delicate, moist lips as she talked and struggled to regain focus.

Over dinner we chatted amiably about the in-store debacle and the previous night's Stormseye show for a bit before turning to the day's chief news headline – the first gas stations in the continental U.S. to push retail gas prices over five dollars a gallon. An Exxon station in West LA had earned the dubious honor, followed quickly by a BP location across the street. The Administration was talking about tapping into the Strategic Petroleum Reserve for the second time that year. Meanwhile, the number-two headline in the *Times* was about the fact that sixteen of the offshore rigs off the Santa Barbara coast were being managed by the successor firm to the one that had been held responsible for the infamous Gulf of Mexico deepwater well blowout. You could say what you wanted about Gene Ostrowitz's tactics, but his sense of timing was impeccable.

As our meals arrived and we began picking away at them with chopsticks, Jessica pushed the conversation in a new direction.

"Have you heard about the latest polling?"

Jordan glanced across the table at me. I hadn't.

"The environment now ranks ahead of everything but education in the latest *Times* poll. It's even ahead of gas prices."

This got Jordan's attention. "You think people are finally figuring out you can't just drill your way out of dependence on a finite resource?"

Jessica flashed a brilliant smile that again told me something about her effectiveness as a reporter. *Why not use everything you've got?* "I wouldn't give them that much credit yet. Gas prices still come in at number three and there are still plenty of folks out there who'll give up their SUV when you pry it from their cold, dead hands. What's interesting is that it seems like environmental issues might be starting to affect the Senate race. You know all the enviros've been beating up on Tim's guy Cassini –" I grimaced at the reference "– because he won't endorse the Clean Futures initiative. He lost five points in our latest poll. Meanwhile Kendrick stayed flat at thirty-six percent and the Green candidate picked up three. She's at six percent now. Fifteen percent undecided."

I had to break in there. "He lost five?"

"Yep. Lead's down to six points."

"And the margin of error on the poll –"

"– is plus or minus three."

"Damn."

"Exactly."

* * *

A half hour later, safely shuttled back to the Hyatt atrium, Jordan and Jessica settled into a quiet booth in the lounge area and sent the rest of us off for the evening. As we walked through the lobby I made a half-hearted try at convincing Ray to grab a drink with me, but he demurred and headed upstairs. I glanced around the lobby for a minute on the off chance that Natalie might be lurking nearby, but no.

Fine. Great. Perfect.

I stalked across the brightly lit lobby past the island piano to the sports bar at the other end, found an empty table, listened to my messages, found nothing of consequence, glanced at *Baseball Tonight* on the big screen, secured a bowl of mixed nuts, ordered a drink and settled in for a high-grade sulk.

I knew it was obscene to be feeling sorry for myself – I was drinking imported Russian vodka in one of the nicest hotels in Washington while people were sleeping on steam grates a few blocks away – but that didn't keep it all from welling up anyway. It was Saturday night, I was alone and rootless, and though I'd carefully hidden the fact from everyone around me, I was in the process of spending my twenty-eighth birthday feeling even more isolated and helpless than I'd felt on my twenty-seventh, which had been celebrated at the side of my father's sickbed. A hungry voice inside still whispered to me that I didn't just want more, I *deserved* more.

An hour later I had moved up to the bar proper and was sitting on a stool whistling Sam Cooke's "Another Saturday Night" to myself when Jessica climbed onto the stool next to me. I stirred and drew on the reserves I had left.

"You guys finished?"

"I got what I needed. Might have a couple of follow-up questions over the next few days."

I watched the sharp outlines of her jaw work in profile as she called over the bartender, who spun a cocktail napkin in front of her with a flick of his wrist and took her order – tall bourbon, neat, not even a twist. Hardcore.

"Yeah. Sure. They've got one more here tomorrow night, then to Philly Monday morning, a day there and then to New York on Tuesday. You've got my number. Whatever we can do."

"Thanks."

I rubbed my forehead, ran my fingers through my hair, and instinctively tried to keep the thread moving. "So how'd it go?"

She took a moment to consider this, glancing down the bar and then turning back to me as the bartender delivered her drink with an elaborate flourish. "He's an interesting guy. A lot of times these celebrity pieces end up fluffy not so much because that's what you're shooting for, as because fluff is the only thing that ever comes out of their mouths. He actually seems pretty smart, and engaged, and, I don't know. Sincere." Like this was an alien concept.

"Surprise, surprise."

"I'm not saying I totally buy this persona, this selfless activist millionaire rock star. There's something else going on there. Poke at him enough and he gets dark around the edges."

"Well," I parried, "you do get paid to be skeptical."

She closed her eyes and masked a little smile by taking another pull from her drink.

"And you get paid to spin. But c'mon. What do you really think of him?"

"Are we still working here?"

"No. Just curious."

"Off the record?"

She reached over and gave my shoulder a push. "I said off!"

The little jolt her touch delivered tingled up my shoulder and neck.

"Can't be too careful when you're talking to the *LA Times*."

I thought she'd laugh at this, but instead she gave me a hard, assessing look and took another swig of her drink. "That's the part I hate."

I nodded. "That people are careful."

"The minute I tell people what I do, most of them want nothing to do with me."

"You've got a lot of power in your hands."

"I used to believe that. But newspapers are dying, even the *Times*. The only guys on our staff whose jobs are secure these days are the bloggers."

"Start a blog."

At which Jessica Turner executed a complete one-hundred-and-eighty-degree eye-roll, flagged down the bartender and ordered us another round. Turning back, she focused in on me and transformed for a moment back into the steely inquisitor I'd met the morning before. "So, answer the question. What do you think of him?"

I grinned at her persistence and nursed the dregs of my drink for another minute, letting the familiar warmth and looseness seep into every corner. "I think he's a freak."

She raised an eyebrow mid-sip.

"Not him personally – the guy's totally for real. Totally. It's just the context. He's just so out of place in a time like this, a country like this. I mean, who actually believes in anyone anymore? Half the time the hype around celebrities seems like it's just designed to – well, could I quote a song for you?"

I could.

"The title song on the second Counting Crows album is called 'Recovering The Satellites.' And it might be about something else, but I've always thought it was about how all the hype around their first album sort of shot them into orbit, and then people turned on them and were just standing there looking up, waiting to watch them fall back to earth."

"Sure, I know that one." The second round had arrived and Jessica was attacking hers like a thirsty sailor fresh from the open sea. I struggled to keep pace, then gave up and just talked.

"People these days don't want to believe a guy like Jordan Lee is for real. That he actually treats people with respect and keeps his word and gives a crap about something besides getting rich and going on *Cribs*. For a while I had a hard time buying it myself. Some of the stuff I saw working at the Capitol – it'd make anyone cynical. But the thing is, everyone in this country has gotten so used to our heroes letting us down that we don't even recognize the real ones anymore when they're standing right next to us. Someone does something good and selfless and meaningful and everybody's first reaction is to look for the catch. People think no one like that actually exists anymore, not here, not now. But Jordan Lee – I swear to God, this guy is different. I swear." Not the elegant finish I was shooting for; my speech circuits were starting to bog down.

She watched me with eyes that had lost none of their vibrancy, but certainly some of their focus. From this close, their gray-green tint felt not just unusual but exotic, almost otherworldly in a way that fundamentally contradicted their owner's groundedness. The silence between us extended and grew awkward until finally, she blurted out the words dancing on her shiny lips.

"A true believer."

I thought for a minute she was mocking me, but then she smiled, closed her eyes, shook her head and shifted on her stool in a way that seemed entirely casual, yet left her thigh pressed up against mine under the bar.

The only sensible response to that seemed to be to order another round. As we waited, I caught her stealing a glance at the late-night edition of *SportsCenter* running on the big screen at the far end of the bar.

"Goddammit."

"What?"

"The Dodgers won again."

"The – what?"

"The Dodgers." The next round arrived, interrupting her thought as she stopped to drink deep once again. "You've gotta understand, Green, I grew up in San Mateo. Giants all the way. The A's, I don't care. The Dodgers, poison. I love everything about living in LA except having to listen to all those goddamn Dodger fans."

No way. A test was required.

"Who was your favorite player growing up?"

"Are you kidding? Will Clark. That sweet swing, that game face, the '89 playoffs against the Cubs…"

I stared at her while she drank until she noticed and smiled back. There was something in it, some flickering mixture of playfulness and need, that invited me to lift my drink and clink my glass against hers. "I think I'm in love."

She laughed and shook her head and pounded the rest of her drink in three long draughts and set the empty down hard, drawing a glance from the bartender as she turned to face me head-on, eyes now sleepy and sparkling all at once. "No you're not. But you're alright, Green, and it's a long time 'til breakfast."

* * *

I woke up to the sound of the shower running in the bathroom. A thin strip of light from under the door fanned out in the early morning darkness of my hotel room to trace the greyed-out outline – no more – of the closet doors. I rolled over and checked the clock radio: 5:37.

The shower stopped. I heard the curtain pulled back and allowed my thoughts to dwell on the image of Jessica drying herself off. *Need help with that?* After a minute or two of slumbering fantasy, I reached over and grabbed a pillow from the heap on the floor and propped my head and shoulders up against the headboard, trying to will myself back to consciousness. Before I got more than halfway there, the bathroom door opened and she stepped out to stand in the wash of light and steam now escaping. She was already wearing her slacks and bra. I remembered the lace. Lace is always nice.

"You awake?" she said softly.

"Yeah."

"Sorry about that." She moved to the dresser and began feeling around for her blouse. I could see she was a foot off in her calculations and groping blindly after emerging from the brightly lit bathroom, but I didn't offer help.

"S'okay. You in a hurry?"

Finding her blouse, she flipped it around, slipped one arm in and then the other. "Deadline." She began buttoning up in a series of quick, efficient twists of her hands. Her strong hands that had gripped my back tightly just a few hours ago.

I stretched and sat up farther. "Time for breakfast, at least? We can get room service."

"No, gotta run."

Her tone was perfectly neutral. No annoyance, no regret, nothing. Just another day at the office. Which was, if anything, worse. "I thought you had a few days on this."

She finished, glanced around, found her shoes and stepped into them. "Four days, and they gave me six thousand words. I'm gonna need every minute."

"When's your –"

"My flight back's at nine."

I let all of this sink in for a minute before shaking it off and trying again. "What about – I'll be back in LA a couple of times next month. Can I call you?"

"Tim." She found her blazer, folded it over one arm, lifted her shoulder bag over the other and just stood there, a ghostly figure in the half light. I wished I could see her face more clearly. I wondered if she could see mine, or if it would have mattered. Probably not. I've wished for a lot of things in my life, and wishing has rarely been enough.

"I had a good time last night. But it was just one of those things that happens on the road sometimes, that's all. If we got our signals crossed somewhere, I'm sorry. Really. But I've gotta go." Stepping lightly through the minefield of pillows scattered across the floor, she leaned over and gave me a quick, companionable kiss. "Take care. I'll see you around."

14

I allotted myself forty-eight hours of scowly, inarticulate brooding after Jessica's exit and was surprised to find that it seemed to be enough. The truth was, she felt like a stranger even after several hours of banter spread across two days; so hardened to the bruising nature of the world she moved within that she was nearly closed off. In a weak moment I had wished for more, but it wasn't going to happen, and there was in fact a coolly rational part of me that accepted this was for the best. One-nighters weren't a habit of mine, but maybe there was a lesson to be learned there; not everything in my life had to be imbued with rich layers of hidden meaning. Sometimes things – including sex – simply were what they were. As for the sex itself, it was fine. If that doesn't sound like a ringing endorsement, it isn't. The truth is, sex with Jessica sort of reminded me of a trip to Starbuck's – efficient and of good quality, but you got the feeling no matter how many times you repeated the experience it was unlikely to vary much.

The time also passed quickly because we were on the move throughout – the last show in DC that night, then up on the early side (nine a.m.), into Philadelphia for barely a day and then on to New York. The band was set to occupy the Ritz-Carlton for the next week, around a three-night stand at the mother of all rock arenas, Madison Square Garden. There had been talk of alternative bookings – Jordan had actually wanted to stay at the Algonquin, and Seth's vote was for the Trump International – but in the end the consensus fell behind Nicky's sentiment: "We dragged our asses through all these other shithole towns for three months so we could earn a week at the Ritz."

The ride in from JFK was revelatory. Nothing actually happened, mind you. But as a New York virgin there was a certain amount of shock and awe involved for me in riding over the Brooklyn Bridge into Manhattan in the blazing sunshine of early fall, spying the Statue of Liberty off in the harbor as the Wall Street skyline rose before us. A sort of hush came over the bus as we crossed over into the city, past the U.N. building, down onto 37th Street and then up Third Avenue towards the park. Canyons – they really were canyons of steel and glass, just like the news anchors always said. The sheer scale of the buzzing honeycombs of life surrounding us on all sides made the mind reel. Fountains of Wayne have a song about a lover splitting town that goes "And now you're leaving New York / For no better place" – as if no better place could possibly exist. It wasn't hard to buy the conceit on an afternoon like this.

I had no time to contemplate the surge of energy that shot through the bus during the ride in, though; in Jordan's and my case, our arrival was a blur of tossing bags in rooms, changing clothes and rushing off to make happy talk with the cream of the Wilderness Society's contributor crop before collapsing into blessed, dreamless sleep back at the hotel.

The second morning started early with another drive-time radio appearance. Two bus rides and one painfully stilted interview later, the Stormseye entourage stumbled blinking into the sunlight in front of the Ritz again, where things promptly took a turn for the weird.

I'd asked Jordan a couple of times during the previous forty-eight hours about the middle of that day's schedule and gotten nothing back but diversions and doubletalk. When I had asked Natalie the same thing that morning, she'd insisted it was just free time and he might "go walk around the Met or something." At that moment I needed to feel a part of something, and the more I was marginalized, the more urgent my need became. It surely didn't help that Jessica had called me a true believer and here I was again, thirty-six hours later, outside looking in.

My agitation ratcheted up yet another notch when I spotted Jordan and Ray lingering at the curb while the rest of our traveling troupe filed off the bus and back into the hotel. Not knowing what I was doing, not even really thinking anymore but just going on instinct, I trailed the herd inside but then peeled off at the registration desk, feigning interest in the gift shop. When the rest of the group had cleared the lobby I doubled back to the front window and found Jordan and Ray had disappeared from sight.

Brushing past an incoming flock of dark-suited Japanese executives, I hurried out to the curb and looked both ways. I was on the verge of giving up when I saw what looked like it might be Jordan's Mariners cap bobbing amongst the Central Park South sidewalk crush half a block down. Taking off at a slow jog, I wove and dodged through the crowd like a bike messenger navigating bumper-to-bumper traffic. As I gained ground on the baseball cap I caught a glimpse of wavy brown hair bobbing out from under the back, and slowed.

By the time I got close enough to get a clear view of Ray keeping pace at Jordan's side, they were turning south onto 7th Avenue, still almost half a block ahead of me. Rounding the corner a moment later, I momentarily thought I'd lost them before catching a flash of Ray ducking into the rear of a white limo waiting at the curb twenty yards up the street. Jordan was nowhere in sight; I had to figure he was already inside.

Crap.

I could easily have given up at that point and just figured the outside was where I belonged. Hell, I wouldn't have minded a couple of hours' free time to knock around the city myself. But then I spotted a cab behind them just dropping off a fare, and instinct kicked in again. The second the limo pulled out, I sprang from the middle of the crowd, wrenched the rear door of the cab open and threw myself in.

"Follow that car!"

The face that turned to greet me from the front seat was round, full, darkly bearded and rich with a sort of quizzical wisdom, eyes brown as almonds peering out from under a carefully wrapped turban. "Kidding me. No?"

"No! No kidding. That limo, the white one. Follow it. Quick! Please." In the interest of inspiring a shared sense of urgency, I pulled out my wallet and flashed the wad of bills I'd picked up at an ATM in the airport terminal the previous afternoon.

"Okey-dokey" came the calm, sonorous reply from the front seat as my new comrade faced front, flipped on the meter and pulled away from the curb.

Moving in fits and starts through the moderate mid-morning traffic, we tracked south for twenty minutes, past Carnegie Hall, past Madison Square Garden, onward towards the sword-point of Manhattan Island. At 14th Street, just above Greenwich Village, we cut over to the West Side Highway, riding the shoreline with the wide expanse of the Hudson River spread out to our right, busy with barge traffic, Newark's dingy hardscape lurking beyond.

Soon we encountered a dizzying sequence of signs offering the choice between Wall Street and the Brooklyn-Battery Tunnel; the limo was on course for the latter. My driver turned to me as we slowed with the traffic. "Still follow?" I glanced at the meter, doubted whether this was really going to be worth half a week's pay, swallowed hard and decided I'd gone too far already to back out now. "Still follow."

Diving into the tunnel's maw, we barreled nearly a mile through the dim fluorescent cave-passage, hundreds of feet down under the crushing weight of the river. Halfway through, the traffic thickened briefly and as we slowed I felt a tightening in my chest, the first clenching hint of claustrophobia. *What am I doing here?* It was a question I'd been asking myself a lot lately.

Emerging on the other side, rebirthed into the bright midday sun amongst the low-slung, densely-packed suburbia of Brooklyn, we sped toward its center only briefly before exiting the freeway, moving down dense rows of weathered brownstones out of a Spike Lee establishing shot, and arriving at our apparent destination.

What the –?

"Stay back," I said, suddenly conscious that the traffic had lightened considerably, leaving us too close to the limo for my comfort.

"Back? But still follow?"

"Yes. Slowly. Slowly."

He shook his head as if I was crazy, a perfectly reasonable suspicion, but did as instructed, easing up and leaving ten or twelve car-lengths between us and the limo as it crossed one final urban intersection before entering an expansive, leafy oasis. As we followed in its tracks I instinctively rolled down the window, taking in air that was both lighter and more filled with portent as we glided down the quiet, tree-lined lane that led into the heart of Woodcrest Cemetery.

* * *

We buried my father on a Tuesday. The day dawned late and unenthusiastically; it was early January and the sunlight was not just scant, but filtered. The fog that pressed inward along the north coast through the depths of winter had been creeping inland for two weeks by then, making steady advances on Santa Rosa and the valleys beyond. I awoke that morning in my childhood bed, disoriented and alone. Shuffling down to the family room, I peered out the sliding glass doors into the dull grey thickness that had enveloped my world.

I showered in silence, wondering if tears would come, but they didn't. Two days past my father's death, I felt as if I were traveling inside of some sort of cocoon; everything was gauzy and slow. I dressed and made it to the breakfast table by eight, lingering over a bowl of Cheerios. I stared at the colony of tan circles floating atop the milk, observing their patterns, watching them swirl and rearrange themselves with each spoonful I took, as if magnetized. There was a gentle, hypnotic rhythm to my eating, lifting the spoon and dipping it again, over and over. After a while I became acutely conscious of each breath I was taking, of the steady in and out, of the sensations of nose and mouth and throat and chest and lungs at work. My body, it seemed, was perfectly capable of continuing through its necessary routines with no input from my mind. And it was a relief; consciousness felt impossibly burdensome. *Is this what shock feels like?*

At eight-thirty Aunt Ruth and Terry arrived, simultaneously but in separate cars. Her slender frame covered in soft, layered folds of black,

Ruth fussed around the house for an hour, transferring platters of food from her car to the refrigerator, cleaning counters and windows that were already clean, covering the mirrors, and setting up the shiva candle in the middle of the table at which I had just finished my breakfast.

The weeks leading up to that day had been tense. With three months remaining before California's early primary, I was expected to be on the road with Frank five or six days a week. Through December I managed to get home every time we had an evening or morning event in the Bay Area, but Frank lived in Los Angeles and worked in Sacramento, so the opportunities were irregular at best. Meanwhile, as Dad's condition became more and more obviously dire, Aunt Ruth became more and more assertive in managing not just his physical but his spiritual care. It was as if she saw his final illness as her calling to bring her brother home to the faith they had once shared. She read psalms at his bedside, kept the Sabbath with him, stopped answering the phone on Saturdays. The closer he drew to death, the closer she drew them both to her God.

As far as I knew, Dad hadn't been to synagogue since he was in college. I kept expecting him to object, but the veil of silence that had descended over him after they took his leg was by now nearly complete. He was noticeably calmer, though, when Ruth read or sang to him in her thin, pretty voice. I doubted he was getting what she intended from her ministrations, but he was clearly getting something, enough so that after a few minor skirmishes with Ruth I backed off and let them be.

Terry came over and sat with me as Ruth flitted around the house. She had always dressed in bold, unashamed colors, red and yellows and deep forest greens. Seeing her in dark monochrome – black skirt, black knit top, black button-up sweater, left open – was like seeing a color photo suddenly transferred to high-contrast grayscale. I had no idea how much I needed her until she was there. Where others might have filled in the silences with empty platitudes ("It's okay." "You'll get over it." "He's in a better place now."), she seemed to recognize instinctively that her quiet presence at my side was the only real salve she could offer in that rawest of moments. After several minutes of perfect stillness, she reached over and took my left hand into both of hers, holding it in her lap.

Ruth had arranged for the rabbi from the temple she attended twenty miles south in San Rafael to come up for the services – a small ceremony at graveside. Ruth's husband Abe and my cousins Max and Aaron were there, as well as Max's wife and young daughter, Terry's mother, a handful of Dad's closest colleagues from the magazine, and a couple of loyal neighbors.

As I got out of the car at the cemetery, Ruth handed me a kippah to wear for the service. My reflexive instinct was to hand it right back, but I didn't want to make a scene. Abe and Max and Aaron had all covered their heads before the Lord. It seemed like a small price to pay for peace in this moment.

There were no flowers at graveside – a further signal of Ruth's quiet dominion over this day – only a gathering of solemn faces all dressed in shades of black and white. How many movies had I watched with funeral scenes, characters full of subtext, their machinations continuing uninterrupted. How absurd. How obscene. How could any living being fail to be consumed by the weight of this moment?

Once we had all gathered in a half-circle around the gaping brown hole scarring the surrounding expanse of lawn, the rabbi began to speak. I soon became lost in the rhythm of his words, unsure after a while whether he was speaking English or Hebrew or some invented hybrid. It was the cadence that captured me, the steady, sing-songy rhythm by which he propelled us through the congealed depths of our grief. I watched over the simple wood casket immobile, entranced, as a memory bloomed in my mind.

In third grade we were given an assignment to create our own storybook. I knew the story I wanted to tell – a space adventure that owed more than a little to George Lucas – and working on the illustrations was fun, but coming up with the words was agonizing. Trying to organize my thoughts, to choose the right nouns and verbs and puzzle out the punctuation felt like an impossibly large and precise task. I stalled and procrastinated and finally developed a massive case of what I would later learn to call writer's block. I ended up approaching my father in his study one Saturday morning, two days before the assignment was due, having spent a largely sleepless night fretting over the fact that my "book" was still nothing but a sequence of wordless drawings.

Dad looked over what I had and found something positive to say about almost every illustration. Then I explained the assignment, the story that was in my head but not yet on the page. "I don't know what to do!" I blurted, on the verge of tears. "It's too hard, and if I mess it up –"

"You won't mess it up. It's *your* story. There's no wrong way to tell it."

"But it's too big. I don't know how!"

"One page at a time, buddy. One sentence at a time. One word at a time. Start small, and stay small, and keep going. That's it. Just focus on the page you're working on right then, and keep going. Don't stop. Don't think too hard. And don't worry about getting it perfect the first time. Just let it flow."

I came out of my reverie with the realization that the rabbi had at last fallen silent. I kept still, staring down at the wooden vessel that now held my father, until Terry took my hand again and gave it a quick squeeze. I looked over at her, and at Ruth's pinched expression, and remembered. A shovel lay at the side of the grave. "Use the back," Ruth had instructed me the day before in her gentle yet forceful way. "The front is for digging; the back is for mourning."

As I stepped forward, a fresh wave of unreality swept over me.

This isn't happening. This is not me picking up a shovel. This is not me lifting dirt from the heaping pile next to my father's grave. This is not me holding it over my father's coffin as it lies in the ground, waiting. This isn't me. That isn't him. It can't, he can't —

A rock hidden inside the clump of dirt I was scattering struck the coffin and the sudden, sharp report hit my ears like a gunshot.

Max's daughter let out a little yelping cry and began to sob. A shudder ran through my entire body. I stepped back and let the shovel fall from my hands. Leaving it, I shuffled unsteadily back to Terry's side. She took a deep, ragged breath and once more wrapped both her hands around mine. The rabbi began again, reciting what I knew must be the Kaddish, the prayer for the dead. Ruth's voice joined his, and Abe's, and Max's, and Aaron's, becoming a kind of chorus, singing my father to sleep.

And I couldn't join them. I didn't know the words.

* * *

"Stop here." The limo had swung off to the side of the road a quarter mile ahead, pulling over halfway around a gentle curve. I watched through a stand of oaks that partially shielded our position as Ray and then Jordan emerged. As they began to move off on foot, deeper into the cemetery, I was gripped by conflicting impulses. One told me I was already way out of bounds and needed to butt out before I risked making the situation worse. The other told me I'd come much too far already to stop now. And there was, still, a thread of frustration, even anger running through all of these thoughts. I had hidden nothing from Jordan, had been thoroughly exposed, and yet he continued to pick and choose what he shared of his life with me. I didn't just want to know what was inside that last circle; I deserved to know.

I reached over and opened the door. My driver's head swiveled the minute he heard the latch.

"Please wait," I asked.

"Wait here?" Skeptical; concerned.

"Yes, please."

"One minute, one dollar."

I stopped halfway out the door. "A dollar a minute?"

"Yes." No emotion, simply stating a fact.

"Fine." I pulled out my wallet and handed a pair of twenties over the back of the seat between us. "Here's a deposit."

I closed the door behind me as quietly as I could and watched through the trees as Ray trailed Jordan down a path on the far side of a pair of large mausoleums two hundred yards away. Using them as cover I advanced, walking carefully among the gravestones and markers, catching little flashes of Ray's jacket up ahead and then ducking back until I was pressed up against the cold marble facing of the first tomb. Peering around the near corner, I could see Ray had stopped just over a rise a hundred yards ahead and was scanning the horizon in all directions. So far as I could see, though, we were alone.

Circling back around to the other side of the mausoleum, I found a path that paralleled the one Ray and Jordan had used, with a line of scrub oaks and birches running along it until both disappeared around the far shoulder of the small rise ahead. Moving carefully but steadily, I made my way up the path, willing myself not to look in their direction until I'd put the rise between us and could plot a further course forward using the cover of the tree line. Moving tree to tree now, I advanced only another twenty feet before Jordan came into view. I froze behind an old birch, its thick, once-white trunk now gray, cracked and pitted, and watched.

He was standing in the middle of a long row of graves, cap now in his hands, white Oxford shirt blazing bright in the midday sun, eyes fixed on a solitary headstone. He stood like that for at least five minutes, quiet and motionless, and then he began to speak.

I was too far away to make out anything he was saying, especially turned three-quarters away from me as he was, and there was no cover any closer, so I was left watching from a distance as he went on explaining, cajoling, at times seeming to admonish the crisp fall air in front of him.

This continued for several minutes, a performance both heartfelt and macabre, until he seemed to freeze up suddenly mid-thought, his left hand a fist at his side, his right open and extended before him, staring down at the headstone with a fierce intensity.

And then, without warning, he fell to his knees and began to sob, deep, hitching wails released from the depths of his being. My breath, by contrast, had slowed to a whisper.

Unbidden, another memory rushed in. One night out at Patrick's Point, lying snug in our tent with my father I heard a wolf's howl, a long, piercing, feral cry repeated over and over. After a minute of listening flat on my back, I sat up. Dad stirred and rolled over. I couldn't make out his face in the darkness, but chose to assume he was awake.

"What is it? Why does he keep doing that?"

My father's slumbering reply came back from below. "He's alone. Probably looking for his mate. And she's far away, and that's the only way he knows to find her."

Jordan crumpled forward now onto his hands and knees and stayed there, chest heaving, arms shaking, hair hanging forward across his face in long weeping strings. After a moment more Ray appeared next to him and began talking to him so quietly that I wouldn't have realized it if I hadn't seen his lips moving. Soon Jordan's whole body seemed to sag. Then Ray took a knee at his side, reached around and half-lifted, half-guided him to his feet, and began leading them back the way they had come.

III.

INSTANT KARMA

Is that supposed to be your poker face
Or was someone run over by a train?

– Chris Collingwood & Adam Schlesinger
("No Better Place," by Fountains Of Wayne)

The most common way people give up their power is
by thinking they don't have any.

– Alice Walker

15

I rode back to Manhattan in silence. The light seemed different now, the afternoon sun casting deep shadows across the cavernous corridors, framing every tableau in tones colder and more stark than before. The scene I had witnessed in the cemetery forced me to confront the reality that, as much as I liked and even admired Jordan Lee, he was still fundamentally an enigma to me. I knew of him only that which he allowed, and that had been doled out in measured portions at times of his choosing.

The name on the headstone was Maya Jean Baptiste. (Of course I went over and checked it after they left; you think I'd make a lease payment on a cab and play secret agent in a graveyard without at least getting a name?) She had died five years before, at the age of 25. The only other information on her gravestone was a single word, stating the obvious: "Beloved."

Back at the hotel, wallet considerably lighter, I found myself with barely half an hour left before the bus would be leaving to take us to the Garden and the night's show. The good news was, what a generation before might have taken me a week to research instead took five minutes. I googled "Maya Jean Baptiste," got 78 hits, added "New York," got 23, added the year she died and got nine.

The first two clips were from the *Village Voice* and a small alternative paper, both blurbs mentioning her as a singer-songwriter playing small clubs in Manhattan. The *Voice* found room also to mention that she was a graduate student at Columbia, leaving the snotty dismissal of her bourgeois value system implied.

The third was from the Columbia student newspaper, an op-ed piece blasting the current federal administration for its attempts to open the Arctic National Wildlife Refuge to oil drilling, authored by Maya Jean

Baptiste.

The fourth, a captioned photo from deep in the *New York Post* archives, was the bingo moment. A group of dark-suited mourners stood at graveside in the same small grove of trees near the same gentle rise that I had been lurking around an hour before. One of the faces in the photo had been circled to highlight it. The shot was fuzzy – probably taken from considerably farther away than I had been that afternoon – and the person pictured wore dark wraparound sunglasses, but the hair, cheekbones and chin were unmistakable.

LEE ATTENDS FUNERAL – Stormseye lead vocalist Jordan Lee took time out yesterday from finishing up work on the band's forthcoming album at Virtuality Studios in Manhattan to attend the funeral of local musician Maya Jean Baptiste. Lee jumped onstage at Club Guadeloupe just ten days ago to introduce Baptiste's set, calling hers "the most amazing voice in the city today." Baptiste's accidental death last week shocked her peers on the city's busy club circuit.

Her obituary in the *Times* was no more or less illuminating. Scholarship student at Columbia's graduate school of journalism, talented singer, leaves behind parents, two brothers and a sister, uncles, aunts and cousins, most of them in Brooklyn. No mention of Jordan. And nothing more about the circumstances of her death.

I looked up from the screen, stretched and considered my surroundings for a moment. Nine pillows decorated the raised bed, which was outfitted with a carved oak headboard and 400-thread count fine linen sheets. The elaborate drapes were held back with four-inch thick twined golden cords. The desk I was sitting at was real stained cherry wood with Queen Anne legs. Fresh flowers on the table in the sitting area, a marble tub in the bathroom, fine art on the walls.

The Ritz. I should be enjoying this. But instead all I wanted to do was figure out what the hell was going on.

* * *

Why was that?

Natural curiosity was part of it, but there was also that thread of resentment. After knowing me for a matter of hours, Jordan had already figured me out to the point where I had felt at times like a butterfly getting pinned to a cardboard display. Meanwhile, after living inside his vapor trail for two months I knew almost nothing about the man that the rest of the world didn't already.

Rightly or wrongly, in that moment it felt like he owed me something. As we rode to the show that afternoon I found myself stealing glances over and over, watching him from across the aisle and a row ahead as he alternately looked out the window and made murmuring conversation with Natalie. He gave no sign that anything was out of the ordinary, gaining energy steadily as the afternoon wore into evening and the band went through its pre-show paces individually and together. By eight o'clock he seemed positively jacked up at the prospect of putting on a show in one of the world's premier indoor concert venues.

And it showed in the result.

Andreas Katsorous of the *Times* called that first Garden show "the concert of the year." The set list varied from recent shows as they threw in a few older album cuts, both to keep the hardcore fans happy and to make sure there was some variety among the three concerts they'd be playing there over five nights in town. But it was more than just mixing up the set. They played that night with a kind of controlled ferocity, pressing the tempos while still keeping the arrangements tight, pouring all the power and majesty they could muster into each and every song.

Nicky had gone on and on during dinner about how great New York crowds were, about how bands and fans would feed off each other's energy until it gets explosive, and the audience that night did not disappoint. At one point Jordan actually had to ask them to cool it ("We need your help with this next one. It's a quiet song, so if you supply the quiet, we'll supply the song."). They did, and for four and a half minutes of the band's big ballad "Riverside," Madison Square Garden was as silent as a classical music concert hall, right up until the final, rising, quivering note from Nicky's closing solo began to fade out, at which point 18,000 people rose as one and erupted in screaming, whistling, hooting applause. Leaning against a beam by the stage mixer's table in the wings, I could actually feel the steel vibrating. Jordan looked over at Nicky, who gave a little nod and grin, then at Wayne, who was smiling wider than he had in at least a week, and then back at Glen, who actually jumped up on Seth's drum riser and demanded a high five.

They closed out the night with a powerhouse trio of encores: "Midnight Moonlight," a blistering cover of Led Zeppelin's "Rock And Roll," and the freshened-up arrangement of "Make Some Change." Jordan was everywhere during the encores: flat on his stomach at the front lip of the stage singing right in the faces of fans who looked like they might faint from excitement, stalking the farthest corners pumping his fists and twirling his mike by the cord during Nicky and Wayne's solos, leaping up to balance on the edge of the drum riser and air-drum along as Seth hammered through the powerhouse break between the first and second verses of "Make Some Change." The crowd ebbed and surged in feverish rhythm with the band the entire time, but the pulse of the evening belonged to Jordan, whose every move was greeted with roaring affirmation until the final seconds, when he fell to his knees at center stage, head down, arms in front, palms raised to the crowd, a supplicant at his altar. A single white spot shone hard on each of the five as the music crescendoed and finished. Then the house lights came up full and the entire arena was bathed in bright light as the other four made their way to center stage, Wayne and Nicky arriving on either side of Jordan. As they reached down and lifted him to his feet, the crowd's still-building roar sent the needles across the length of the stage mixing board dancing into the red. Red for danger, red for blood, red for the thrill of that singular moment.

* * *

I joined Jordan as he slipped away through the wings toward the backstage tunnels. He was moving a little slower than normal, triumphant but also winded. I knew better than to bother him for anything less than an emergency at a moment like that, but it was hard not to feel his gravitational pull drawing me in once again after what I had just witnessed. Absorbed in the afterglow of the moment, I matched strides with him as we worked our way back through the maze towards his dressing room.

Up ahead, Natalie was waiting in the doorway, right leg bouncing away while she worked over whoever was on the other end of her cell phone. Noticing her there seemed to rouse Jordan out of whatever interior space he had been occupying since coming off the stage. He stopped twenty feet short of the door and turned to me. His face and arms still shone with sweat; his hair was matted in glistening curls. He found my eyes and virtually pinned me to the wall with his.

"We need to talk."

I liked working for someone who didn't beat around the bush, but this particular combination of intensity and directness was unsettling.

"Okay."

Toweling off his forehead again, expression inscrutable as ever, he said "Tim, you've been just what I needed these past three months and I hope it's been a good experience for you."

I didn't care for his use of the past tense in the latter sentence, but was too off-balance to do more than roll with it. "Sure. Sure, it's been great. I've learned a lot."

"Whatever else is going on, I know you have a good heart. I know it. I chose to trust you once, and I'm going to choose to do that again. I'm going to tell you about Maya."

My throat just about closed up. "Wha –"

He motioned gently at my chest. "Don't."

So, I didn't. I just stood there, glancing all around at the walls, the ceiling, Natalie waiting down the hall, anywhere but into Jordan's face.

"Shit." I swallowed hard. "You saw me?"

"No." A small, sheepish grin. "I didn't see you. But Ray, you know, he did four years in special forces. He doesn't miss much."

I nodded, and looked around at the stark white walls, and down at the scuffed concrete floor, and generally felt like a microscopic piece of hamster pellet. "I'm sorry. I'm really sorry. I just –"

"I know you are. But it's my fault, too. By now we should have had this conversation already. I've been thinking about telling you for a while. And of course you're wondering about the schedule, that's totally natural. I just didn't handle this very well."

"I didn't either."

"I don't know. A cab – that was pretty resourceful."

He chuckled. I didn't. I was too busy being stunned at how calm he was.

"So anyway, I want to tell you the whole story. It's just – it's a long story, and this isn't the time or the place. I need to get through these shows first, and when we get back to California we'll take an afternoon, sit down together someplace quiet, and square up on all this. Is that cool?"

I nodded, almost certainly more vigorously than necessary.

"Cool." He glanced down the hall at Natalie again. "Oh, and the other thing – I called Jessica Turner back this afternoon, before we headed over here."

"You did?"

"Yeah. I wanted to tell her about a decision I made today."

16

CITIZEN CELEBRITY
Jordan Lee Puts His Money Where His Mouth Is
By Jessica Turner
Special to the Los Angeles Times Magazine

Jordan Lee — singer, songwriter, activist, kung pao connoisseur and citizen of the world — does not like to be interrupted.

This is worth mentioning because interruptions — and they are plentiful in a life spent mostly on the road — seem to be the only external stimuli that get under his skin at all. The lead singer of iconic Bay Area rock band Stormseye is polite, unassuming, idealistic, observant, quick-witted, determined, flexible, resolutely down to earth and startlingly well-read. In a day spent in his company you're as likely to end up talking about where in the imagination poetry comes from (the remnants of dreams) and how Chinese spices spread across the globe (Marco Polo had help) as you are either the music for which he is famous or the environmental causes for which he so passionately advocates.

His essential modesty is at odds with the central reality of his life, which is that any time he appears in a public place, heads swivel with almost comic effect. The deep-set blue eyes, the chiseled cheekbones, the dark, flowing hair — whether they actually recognize him or not, people seem naturally drawn to Jordan Lee. And why not? It's not every day you comes across someone who looks as if he could pull off a GQ cover shoot on five minutes' notice any day of the week. The man has one of those faces that through history has opened movies, advanced political careers and on occasion launched a thousand ships or so.

It's easy to imagine Lee scoffing at the above paragraph, though. After spending most of his adult life leading one of the most successful bands ever to emerge from the Bay Area's fertile music scene, he appears focused today on two things and two things alone:

completing Stormseye's hugely successful reunion tour, and advancing his role as perhaps California's most committed celebrity activist. Any more material or personal concerns, he dismisses or diverts with a natural charm that's as difficult to penetrate as any politician's armor of spin.

The Evangelist

As comfortable with silence as conversation, Lee becomes fully animated only when talking about one of two subjects: music, and the environment. "Have you been to Yosemite?" he asks within five minutes of our first meeting. The question carries the same tone of implied significance that a Muslim might use asking a co-religionist if he has gone on pilgrimage to Mecca. Nature is Jordan Lee's temple, and he its evangelist.

He waxes rhapsodic about Bridalveil Falls until I assure him that I've seen it. He then discovers I've only visited the valley floor and extracts my promise to hike up to Nevada and Vernal Falls next time. Conversation from there turns into a travelogue of natural beauty in America, from Joshua Tree National Monument to Niagara Falls to the Louisiana bayous to the Continental Divide.

As an activist, Jordan Lee has repeatedly put his money where his mouth is. State and federal election records show he has donated more than $3 million to a variety of environmentally-focused campaigns and candidates over the past six years. National groups like the Sierra Club, Natural Resources Defense Council, the Audubon Society and the Wilderness Society all acknowledge him as a major donor and he appears frequently at fundraising events and rallies associated with their "educational" (i.e. lobbying) efforts. He declines to reveal how much he's donated directly to these groups, saying only, when the $3 million he's known to have given to various campaigns is referenced, "more than that."

As engaged as he is politically, Lee dismisses any suggestion that he might one day throw his own hat into the electoral ring. Asked if he'd ever consider running for office, he first laughs at the very thought, then responds "I already have a job, and I like it, and people seem to think I'm pretty good at it. Plus I know just enough about how the system works to understand that the one thing it demands from everyone on the inside is compromise. And I won't. So I work from the outside."

"Obscene"

As the conversation turns to Lee's latest cause celebrité, the Clean Futures ballot initiative sponsored by the California Climate Change Coalition, he edges forward as if about to leap out of his seat. As I play devil's advocate with him, his expression grows fierce.

How do we balance human needs with environmental needs? How do you sell this idea to an auto worker who might lose their job if it's enacted? "That's one of the biggest lies being told about this initiative. It will create jobs, not eliminate them. There are whole new industries growing up around clean technology, hundreds of new jobs being created every day as people wake up and realize we're going to have to change how we live and do business in this fragile world."

But that means job losses in the old, "dirty" industries. "It does. People will have to adapt and no one's saying it's always going to be easy or smooth. But there will be new jobs in new industries, absolutely there will be, and in the end there's no other choice. I mean, what use is a job if our coasts flood and our crops die?"

What about the debate over whether global warming is a man-made threat or simply an inevitable cyclical phenomenon? "There is no debate. There's overwhelming scientific evidence that global warming is both real and driven by human activity, especially burning carbon-based fossil fuels. The only scientists out there with political agendas are the handful on the fringes who're still grasping for some way to deny that that's the case."

Lee is at his most passionate when talking about these holdouts, the cadre of scientists and political figures on the right who continue to maintain that global warming is a fiction invented by liberals and environmentalists to advance their agenda.

"If we can agree – and I hope we can – that denying the Holocaust, which killed six million Jews and thousands of other innocents, is obscene, then what should we call it when people try to deny a scientifically proven global phenomenon that could wipe out entire species, including our own? How can that be anything but obscene?"

*   *   *

The cover shot for the piece was a photo Natalie had supplied from a promotional shoot earlier that year for the *Pieces of the Night* album. In it, Jordan was wearing a brilliant maroon tee and blue jeans and squatting at the edge of a lake, left forearm resting on his thigh, right hand down for balance. The remarkable aspect of the photo is his tractor-beam focus on the camera, those striking eyes pulling all attention inward towards them until finally, sometime later, you register that his hand is actually *in* the water, his fingers half hidden under the surface. There is a shamanistic intensity to the shot, as if he's drawing some form of primitive spiritual power from the lake, the earth, nature itself.

The middle section of the profile was all about the musical portion of Jordan's life, encapsulating the band's history, giving a quick overview of the new album and tour, and – for the most part, anyway – debunking previous media references to Stormseye as a quote-unquote nostalgia act. "By all appearances this band still has legs, even if they might wobble occasionally." *Gee, thanks.*

Sitting at my hotel room desk in my boxers reading the very end of the piece on my laptop screen was where I experienced my first deep pangs of sympathy for Natalie. It had to be tough, trying over and over to "handle" a boss who not only refused to be handled, but consistently, repeatedly, stubbornly did whatever the hell he wanted.

*   *   *

Public Face, Private Life

Lee's entourage of family and business associates is protective. Contacted for this article and informed he was in full cooperation with it, his parents, divorced and both living in the Los Angeles area, nonetheless declined comment. His sister did not return phone messages, nor did his business manager. Lee's peers acknowledge his guardedness. "Jordan had some bad experiences with the press early on and I think he just decided he needed to control the message," commented a music-industry peer who did not want to be identified.

Indeed, Lee faced intense tabloid scrutiny early on in his career when, as a rising figure in the music world, he dated first actress Winona Ryder and then Belgian supermodel/Bond girl Aurelié – both of whom also declined comment for this article. Asked about his history with the tabloids, Lee notes wryly that "in England they have the Royal Family to entertain them. Here in the states we keep trying to make up our own version, whether it's political dynasties or actors or people who are famous just for being famous." Pressed further, he says simply "My family doesn't want to be part of all this," meaning media attention.

Asked if he's seeing anyone special right now, Lee turns the question around: "Are you?" Reminded that he's the one who's the subject of this profile, he grins and says simply "Fair's fair." The subject drops.

"Seed Money"

When the conversation rolls back around to Lee's generous giving, he reveals an undercurrent of – guilt? noblesse oblige? – behind his actions. "I think when you've been as blessed as someone like me, you have an obligation to give back. Money – it isn't power, exactly, but it gives you a chance to try to influence the world for the better, and that's what I want to do."

Why the environment? His response is passionate yet curiously vague: "I think a lot of people in my position feel like they want to concentrate their efforts on one area to the point where they can maybe make some kind of noticeable difference. There are so many needs in the world and if you spread yourself thin I'm not sure you can have the same effect as if you focus on one area, one issue, and try to change things. For me, it's the environment. For someone else it might be hunger or poverty or AIDS."

Lee is surprisingly pragmatic about what it takes to create change. "I'm just a rock singer. It's hard for the average person to take someone like me seriously, and I don't blame them. I'm not an expert on anything that goes on outside a recording studio or a stage. My name and face might change a few people's minds, but that's not enough."

Several days after our initial interview concludes, Lee calls back from his New York City hotel room to put the exclamation point on this particular thread of our conversation. It seems he's found a more concrete way to try to accomplish his goals.

"I've decided to create a campaign committee – they call it an independent expenditure committee – to promote causes I believe in. The first one is going to be the Clean Futures initiative. I'm going to accept donations from anyone who wants to

contribute, but the initial seed money is going to come from me."
    Seed money?
    "Twenty million dollars."

17

The profile hit the streets the morning of the band's last show at the Garden. By the time we loaded into the bus that afternoon, it seemed just about everyone in and around the band knew about it, even those who had never seen, let alone read, a hard copy edition of the *Los Angeles Times Magazine*. If I had to suggest one single, pervasive effect that the proliferation of laptops and smartphones has had on society, it would be this: gossip now travels at the speed of ten kilobytes of electronic text. If alternative energy research was carried out with the same degree of ruthless efficiency as the dissemination of "news" about Jennifer Aniston and the Kardashians, climate change would be a blip in humanity's rear-view mirror by now.

The funny part – if you could call it that – was that within the insular tribe of band and crew, people seemed more uncomfortable than if Jordan had been caught, say, wasted out of his gourd running down Park Avenue in his jockeys screaming out the lyrics to "Mandy." Under the unwritten code of the rock and roll band on tour, it was perfectly acceptable to sit around backstage drinking, smoking, leering at women and bitching about life on the road, but actually putting yourself out there, making a serious attempt at grappling with real issues in the everyday world, not to mention throwing ungodly sums of cash at them? Not cool. The bubble wasn't just to keep everyone else out; it was to keep you in. It's like Stewart Copeland said in the documentary he put together about his experiences as drummer for the Police – "Pretty soon the real world that most people live in just seems like wind rushing past the car window. If you grab hold of anything, you'll lose an arm." People looked at Jordan as if by opening himself up to the world he'd somehow endangered them all.

Jordan, for his, part, seemed to do his best to stay out of everyone's way all day. I didn't bother calling his paperweight of a cell phone, and he didn't call me, which made me wonder if he'd really meant what he'd said the other night about telling me everything. This new cone of silence felt like it could be one of those passive-aggressive deals where the boss reminds the help who's in charge; I had plenty of experience with those.

From the outside, I imagine the last New York show probably appeared pretty similar to the first two. They played strong, they played hard, they played an extra-long set with four relatively rare tunes added to spice things up. Nicky, Wayne and Seth were each up to their usual instrumental heroics, and Jordan sang with passion. But someone like me who'd seen more than fifty shows over the past three months could see something was missing. The individual members were running hot, but they weren't in that unconscious groove with each other. They were out of sync and missing notes and there was one near train-wreck on an obscure album cut they hadn't practiced enough before adding it to the set.

None of which put a damper on the after-party. The band had been on the road for almost six months, with no break of more than two days for the past two months, and now they had a four-day breather before finishing up back home in California. So they did what any sensible billion-dollar musical juggernaut would do – they booked the entire 22nd floor of the Ritz for the night.

Moving down the hallway, visitors found suite after suite with its doors thrown open, fresh flowers everywhere, catering staff standing at the ready with champagne and hors d'oevres, every grand light fixture in every room on full, the better to accent the artwork, the drapes, the plush wing-back chairs, every luxurious appointment. A catering table and full bar had been set up in the living-dining area of the Royal Suite, which was, at over 1500 square feet, the size of a small house.

Into this opulent setting poured the band, staff, and a hundred or so specially invited guests. In one room Lady Gaga could be found lecturing a well-known national promoter while surrounded by an entourage the size of a small European nation. In another, Don Henley was talking bio-fuels with the violin player from the Dave Matthews Band. In yet a third, Bruce Springsteen and Patti Scialfa sat on a love seat with an acoustic guitar, playing Woody Guthrie songs for a puzzled-looking Nicky Frost. Executives from the band's label swapped cell numbers and BMW specs with managers, agents, publicists and big-name rock journalists. Groupies, unless they were lucky enough to get waved in by a band member, were turned back at the elevator. From midnight until check-out time the next day, the 22nd floor was Stormseye's own private kingdom, with the five in the band its royal court.

That said, when Natalie, Ray and I first emerged from the elevator and moved down the hallway clustered around Jordan, I could sense certain people shrinking from us, feel the murmur of disapproval running underneath it all: *The code, man. You broke the code. Hands and feet inside the bus at all times.*

* * *

An hour into the proceedings, Jordan had been diverted into one of the secondary suites where a stylishly disheveled A&R guy was haranguing him with a theory that global warming was actually caused by the excess of natural gases produced by organic farming. Natalie was huddled in a corner of the Royal Suite with Jim Dowland and Nicky's manager, talking about reserving post-tour studio time in LA. Ray was down the hall chatting with the security team guarding the elevator. And I was standing ten feet from the bar, trusty Stoli in hand, deep in a daydream of Terry waiting for me at home in Santa Rosa, when Seth Lamiroult came wandering up smelling like he'd just emerged from the deeply forested confines of a Humboldt county pot farm.

"Hey man."

"Hey, Seth," I said, speculating briefly on whether there was enough second-hand smoke clinging to him to set off the sprinklers overhead. "Good show."

"Yeah man." There was a long pause, during which Seth seemed to be trying hard to focus on the elaborately-framed 18th century oil landscape hanging on the side wall. A fortyish blonde knockout in a spangly black cocktail dress that barely covered her hips strutted by and smiled at Seth, who didn't even seem to register her presence. Then, without warning, he turned to me.

"So, Jordan said you worked for the attorney general."

Of all the – "Yeah."

"So, I wanted to ask you a question."

"Sure."

"What's up with the ferret law?"

"The ferret law?"

"Yeah. California's the only state in the country where they won't let you keep a ferret."

Don't laugh. Don't laugh. Don't laugh.

"A ferret?"

"Yeah, a ferret. This chick gave me one a couple years ago. I keep him in a pen in my side yard in Malibu. Cute little bugger, domesticated as hell, tame as any dog or cat. But if Animal Control ever found out about Francisco, they'd lock him up and fine the crap outta me."

I clenched my jaw as hard as I could without actually grinding my teeth, but in the end my will power simply failed.

"Francisco?"

He stared at me, eyes boring in, pupils dilated to pinpoints, breath like a walking greenhouse. "Yeah."

"Francisco – the ferret?"

"Yeah, Francisco the fucking ferret! What the fuck is wrong with you?"

"Nothing. Nothing. I'll have to check into that and get back to you."

*　*　*

It was hard not to miss the fact that within minutes of their arrival the band had once again scattered in five different directions, each adopting one of the suites as their personal staging area. I happened to poke my head into Jordan's chosen domain just as he was finishing up with the band's A&R rep and his plastic-surgery-addicted wife, and I was working on my third double. It was an all-too-familiar feeling now, three sheets to the wind with no idea what's going on other than I'm at Jordan Lee's side and we're traveling at high speed toward parts unknown. I hung back until his company moved off.

"So."

He turned and offered me a lopsided grin, sipping from what looked like a whiskey and tonic, but was more than likely a hundred percent ginger ale. "So."

"I don't seem to remember briefing you about independent expenditure committees."

"Me neither," he agreed.

"Gene?"

"Gene."

"You know, he's working for a good cause and everything, but he's looking out for number one. He always does."

"That's alright. So am I. Our interests just happen to match up here."

"Twenty million?"

"Twenty million."

I was having a lot of repetitive conversations. Maybe it was the vodka. I decided the solution was to drink faster.

"'S a lot of money."

Jordan looked at me with eyes that were simultaneously skeptical and sympathetic. "Not for me."

"Why?"

"Why isn't it a lot of money for me?"

"No, why suddenly throw twenty million at this thing?"

Jordan just looked at me for a minute. I was being a pain in the ass, and I knew it, but I had a good buzz on now and my inhibitions were nothing but white noise in the background.

"Because it has to win."

Has to? I stared at him for a minute, but he didn't flinch, or do much of anything but stand there looking back at me with those ocean-blue eyes of his. "What's Gene say about the polling numbers?"

"He sounds bummed. Says it feels like the momentum they picked up over the summer's faded away."

"So they stalled out and they need a booster shot. And you're it."

"He said if we don't do something soon the whole thing could go down."

"Hey!" We both turned as Natalie squeezed through the crowd in the doorway to reach us. "I was looking all over for you guys Jordan there's a guy back in the main suite big guy with a goatee and suspenders says he's with Arista and wants to talk to you about singing on a track for the new Santana album I told him I'd send you his way as soon as I found you."

* * *

As Jordan headed out into the hallway, I decided in my infinitely foggy logic that before I went home to Santa Rosa, I needed to clear up the whole Natalie thing once and for all. It's the sort of decision you make with absolute certainty after a few stiff belts, that you can't walk yourself through the next morning without grimacing. And while it was technically morning, I had not in fact slept, and was in fact both half-drunk and wholly irritated, so I went right after it. Or rather, her.

"So, all business again tonight, or are we allowed to have some fun?"

"What?"

"C'mon, I wanna hear about your cat."

"What?"

"What is it with you people and pets, anyway?"

Now she just stared at me.

I went at her again, and then again, and for a minute I thought maybe she was just going to walk off and leave me standing there alone among the velvet draperies and brass lamps, but instead she took a long look at the empty hi-ball glass in my hand and did the verbal equivalent of whacking me on the nose with a newspaper.

"Tim. I'm seeing someone."

I was speechless, albeit not for the reason she probably assumed. *Finally! Somebody tells me something!*

"You're a nice guy and everything and I like working with you, it's just – I'm sorry."

I laughed – ruefully, to be sure, but I laughed. "No, s'alright, really. You don't have to – that was – I'm just stupid sometimes. It's not like I didn't get enough hints."

She looked down at her drink and tried to smile. I could tell it was an effort, and her compassion, rather than stinging, actually made it easier.

"I mean, I kind of thought you guys might have something going on."

Natalie's eyes went big. "You did?"

"Yeah, I was just, I don't know, in denial. I guess I just needed to hear you say it, and now you did, so – it's fine. Really. Do you want to go find him?"

"I'll check on him in a minute. The thing is, Tim, we aren't public about it yet, not with anyone. It's just – kind of one of those awkward workplace things, you know? In fact, I'd really appreciate it you wouldn't let on that you know. Not yet. I just don't want him to feel uncomfortable about people around us knowing."

"Sure. I mean, whatever. Sure."

"Okay. Well –" She reached over and gave my arm a quick squeeze. A quick, *sisterly* squeeze. "I'd better get a move on."

"No problem."

Which wasn't exactly true just yet, but at least I wanted it to be. That had to count for something.

*   *   *

I trailed from room to room for the rest of the night, swimming in and out of a series of disjointed conversations and spending more and more time just hanging out in corners, watching. I almost went downstairs to bed a couple of times, but there was something about the moment, the time and place, that I wanted to imprint on my brain. The Ritz at three a.m., surrounded by rock and roll royalty. There was an aspect of pure spectacle about it that made you appreciate why people buy tabloid magazines. All most of those people wanted was to feel like they were part of the "in" crowd for once, to experience a little glamour in their otherwise unremarkable lives. And there I was with a free all-access pass.

By four the "A" list guests had all faded away into the night, leaving the Royal Suite empty of all but the hardest of the hardcore. Glen had disappeared some time before, as had Natalie. When Ray headed out with a wave, it left me, Jordan, Wayne, Nicky, Seth, a trio of crew members and three or four women of dubious sobriety and intentions. Nicky had the center seat, a high-backed Queen Anne of plush golden velour, with the rest of us splayed out on a pulled-together, helter-skelter scattering of equally fabulous couches and chairs, a scene that was half Rockefeller, half Andy Warhol and all rock and roll.

"What this band needs," Nicky was explaining from his throne in a loud and slurry voice, "is more songs about tits."

This set off a round of guffaws from the guys in the crew. Seth lifted his head from the corner of one of the couches long enough to demand five from Bill the road manager, who grinned sheepishly and gave it up.

"I know." Here Nicky paused for another swig. "I know. We've got this repuTAtion now of being all SERious and acting like EVerything we say MATTERS so goddamned much." He was too far gone to even try to be subtle anymore; he was looking right at Jordan. "But come on. I mean, COME ON. It's jus' music. All those people out there just hear someone singing about something besides getting laid and all of a sudden they think –" now he was actually pointing an accusing finger at Jordan "– he's Robert Fucking Kennedy!"

Wayne was staring blankly at the large plant next to him as if he might need to throw up in it at any moment.

"But we're a band. We play some songs, sell some CDs, an' tickets, an' hats an' hoodies an' t-shirts. That's it. That's all. It's ENTERTAINMENT, baby. And that," he continued, stabbing at the air with his finger again, "means tits. LOTS of 'em. In every song. From now on. Tits tits tits tits tits."

Wayne stood up and, without a word, headed for the door.

"Hey! Hey! I'm FUCKING TALKING HERE! Hey! DON' LEAVE!"

Wayne turned in the doorway and let his eyes scan across the entire silent group for a moment, his grim expression framed with incongruously cheery red curls. His gaze rested briefly on Jordan, who sat watching the scene with a mild expression, as if from a great distance.

"Fine. No one else's gonna say it, so I will. Nicky, you're an asshole, and you need to shut your goddamned mouth." As Wayne disappeared down the hallway, his final outburst reached everyone in the room: "I'm done with this fucking nuthouse!"

It was time to go home.

18

One summer day a year or two before Terry kissed me down by the creek, I found myself locked away in one of those endless late-August afternoons when even the most truant kid in town starts to think going back to school might not be so bad. Every conceivable form of entertainment had been tapped out in the preceding weeks: Terry was out of town with her family, my other two reliable neighborhood pals were at summer camp in the Sierras for a week, the creek had run dry for the season, I had no money left to buy candy or baseball cards or comics down at the Seven-Eleven, I'd finished my sixth book of the summer the night before, there was nothing on TV, the Giants had a night game in St. Louis that wouldn't start for an hour yet, and Dad (the last resort himself) was napping in his room. Lying flat on my back on our living room couch, I felt as though the crushing weight of my boredom cast a shadow not just over the afternoon but over my entire life.

When picking at the little burrs of couch-fibre sprouting up all around me had finally lost its appeal, I got up and wandered into my father's office, which was tucked in a cozy corner along the far left as you faced the back yard from our family room. The room was three walls of floor-to-ceiling shelves – store-bought, not built-ins – plus, under the single line of casement windows, a huge old roll-top desk Dad had picked up at a garage sale for fifty bucks. The roll-top wouldn't close, but since the desk surface was rarely clear enough to even attempt it, that seemed like a minor defect.

I fell into dad's desk chair – another garage sale purchase, and a decent one at that, the thing had plush armrests and a nice springy feel to the cushion and tilt – and studied the scene. Electric typewriter, coffee cup half-full of cold inky muck, the last two issues of *Noise*, a stack of CDs (which Dad hated, being a vinyl purist) and a matching one of LPs, and snowdrifts of paper pushed up against the cubbyholed back of the desk.

Tucked away behind the coffee cup I spied Dad's hand-held tape recorder, and suddenly an idea sprang to life. *Entertainment! Yes!* Grabbing it, I headed back out through the family room and out the sliding glass door to the back deck, where we kept a small portable AM-FM radio so we could listen to games out in the back yard. Sure enough, the Giants' pregame show was about to start – twenty minutes of interviews mixed in with ads, followed by twenty minutes of scoreboard roundups, commentary, the reading of lineups, the singing of the Star-Spangled Banner, and game time.

Today's interview was with some guy on the Cardinals who'd been in the Giants' minor league system years before – nobody, in other words. The perfect scenario. I hit record and taped the entire sequence, twenty minutes' worth, planning to go back and tape over the player's responses with my own brilliant anecdotes about my career in the Giants' farm system and eventual rise to the majors. Dad would laugh his head off.

The interview had finished and I was almost done rewinding when Dad wrenched open the sliding glass door and stumbled out onto the deck with an ashen expression. "What did you do?" he blurted.

I had seen my dad frustrated and even angry a few times, but never like this – at least, not with me. His face was so rent with concern that guilt overwhelmed me before I even knew what I was guilty of. He advanced and pulled the tape recorder from my frozen hands, popped the eject button, looked at the cassette for a minute, put it back in and hit play. The tail end of a Chevrolet ad came through, followed by the deep, sonorous, friendly voice of Lon Simmons introducing his guest.

"Oh no, buddy, what did you *do*?"

"I was – I was making a tape –"

"How long?" He'd interrupted me. He *never* interrupted me. That was when I started to get scared.

"Wh-what?"

"How long did you tape?" He looked like he might cry, which scared me even more.

I looked down at the deck, found a knothole, and stared at it until the words came. "Twenty minutes."

"Oh, no." I could hear him breathing loud and fast as the tape whizzed forward now, working its way back toward the end of what I'd taped. He hit play a couple of times, getting more ads, more Lon Simmons, a snippet of the interviewee, and then finally, his own voice:

"—anks, man. I really appreciate your time. This should run in about two weeks."

"Cool. Take it easy. And come see us again next time we're out there."

"I wouldn't miss it."

The conversation ended with a click and then the tape was rolling dead air.

In the silence that followed I slowly, cautiously looked up and found my Dad with eyes hollow, cheeks sagging, mouth open in a wordless cry. It was the saddest face I had ever seen, and it terrified me. I had to say something, anything, to break the moment open and get past it.

"Wha – who –"

"Stevie Ray Vaughan," he said.

"Oh," I said, knowing he was one of my Dad's favorites, but unable to call up a memory of either the man or his music. "I'm sorry." This felt utterly insufficient, but I didn't know what else to say. "I'm sorry, Dad."

"I know," he said, a hitch in his voice. He took another big, lurching breath and grimaced hard, like I'd stuck him with a knitting needle. "I know you are."

"Can you – can you call him back?"

"No. No, I can't."

I couldn't make sense of this. "Are you sure?"

"Tim. He was in an accident day before yesterday. He was riding in a helicopter after a concert, out in Wisconsin. It crashed. He's dead."

The finality of that statement settled over both of us. In the stillness of the moment, and indeed ever since, I wondered if a greater crime could exist than stealing words from a dead man's mouth.

* * *

That particular tape recorder stopped working years ago, of course, and was replaced by a newer, smaller, better one, but the effect of finding the current edition amongst the scattering of papers that covered the surface of my father's desk like leaves on the forest floor was the same. It seemed that every single thing I had touched since returning that afternoon to the house that I had grown up in had hit me with a static shock of unbidden memories.

I put the recorder down and rummaged a bit more, not looking for anything, just feeling my way through the piles, glancing at names and notes and receipts and CD cases. One buried lump turned out to be an old lighter my dad had used for years, one of those old-school, flip-top, refillable brushed-steel jobs. I had hated everything about his smoking for the past ten years, except for this. This one small avatar somehow felt more like a part of the man himself than of the habit that had poisoned him. I picked it up and flipped it open and shut, open and shut like the guys in those old movies, James Dean or Steve McQueen or Paul Newman, back before the salad dressing took over.

After a minute, I slipped it into my pocket and kept going. I'd been at it for three hours, now bumping around the study in the early-evening twilight, when Terry got home from class. I heard the front door open and shut and by the time I got up out of my dad's chair she was yelling "Honey, I'm home!" in her most sarcastic tones and giggling her way down the hall. I ducked out of the study and met her by the kitchen for a hug that seemed to go on for hours – or maybe I just wanted it to. After months on the road and coming home to a house full of ghosts, I was wrung out, as unsteady as a sailor stepping onto dry land at the end of an around-the-world odyssey. I held onto her as long as I possibly could, drinking in the warmth of her body pressed against mine, the subtle scent of strawberry in her smooth, dark hair.

As we settled onto the couch moments later with drinks in hand, I took a minute to study her face. It had been not just months but years since I had spent an evening alone with Terry, just the two of us. She had high, strong, very Spanish cheekbones, a pert little nose and chin, great teeth – I'd had braces for two years, myself – and dark, carefully-plucked eyebrows that danced above her coffee-colored eyes. For months now I'd felt like my life was spinning out of control. Five minutes with Terry, watching her watch me, seeing her smile and laugh just because we were together again, and it all had a center again, a focal point from which I could sort through everything that had come before.

"So, what class did you have?"

"EDMS 471 – Teaching Social Studies in a Multicultural Society."

"That actually almost sounds interesting. Is your professor cute?"

"She's fifty-nine, has bad breath and doesn't dye her roots."

"Perfect!"

"Shut up."

I sipped at my drink – I was making do with Popov from the neighborhood Safeway until we hit the road again – and watched her face for a minute. The slanting, dappled early evening light played across the soft curves of her nose and cheeks as if she had stepped in front of a movie projector. She held my eyes for a minute and then looked down.

"So what've you been up to since you got in?"

"Just sitting at his desk, looking through some of his stuff."

"I didn't touch anything in there."

"I know. Thanks." Outside, a little breeze was playing in the lower branches of the oak by the patio. "It's so weird being in there. It still smells like him."

"I know." She sipped at her drink – ninety-seven percent Diet Pepsi with a splash of rum – and tucked her legs up under herself in the chair. She was wearing fashion-cut jeans and a pale green blouse that made the olive tone of her neck pop that much more.

We chatted for an hour, catching up with news about some old high school friends and the latest from her dad, who had left the family behind fifteen years before for a new life in Phoenix, only to fall on hard times after a second divorce. When our stomachs began growling too loudly to ignore we got busy in the kitchen, throwing together some shrimp quesadillas and rice with tomatoes and green peppers. I put some Van Morrison on and smiled inwardly as "Brown-Eyed Girl" played in the background over dinner.

* * *

While we did the dishes, I filled Terry in about all that had happened in New York. She was fascinated to hear about Maya Baptiste – what I knew, anyway – and chagrined about the band's internal chaos. It felt so good to be unhurried and relaxed and back in a familiar place that I wouldn't have to leave for three entire days that I just rolled with it and we talked and talked until we ended up sitting cross-legged on my bedroom floor sometime after eleven, looking through my old yearbooks and laughing at pictures of people we'd known in high school.

After I'd leaned my head back on the bed and yawned for the third time, Terry said "Hey, I better let you get some sleep," and stood up.

As I levered myself up from the floor, she stretched like a cat, arms high above, then dropped her forearms back behind her head and played with her hair for a minute. By the time I realized I was staring at her chest, she'd caught me and we both looked away sharply.

"I made the bed up in your dad's room. Is it – I mean, did you want to sleep in there or in here?"

"Oh. Yeah." And suddenly everything that had been so easy and carefree all evening felt awkward. I looked at the neatly made single bed under the sloping, gabled roof, into which I had tumbled with Julie DeFrancesco eleven years before, and swallowed hard. "Where've you –?"

She smiled. "In here. I hope you don't mind, but it just felt a lot homier to me than your dad's room. I don't know if I could've gotten comfortable in there when I was living here alone."

"No, it's fine. I'm glad." My desk looked the same, three single red drawers across the top, the superstructure resting on sawhorses painted blue, a row of books across the back. "Do you study up here, too?"

"Sometimes at night. Mostly on the patio, though, or at the table downstairs."

"Yeah." *Following in my footsteps.*

She worked her hands together, glancing around, suddenly as fidgety outwardly as I was feeling inwardly. "Tim, I just – I don't know how to thank you."

"You just did."

"No, I mean, I was a wreck at first, and it meant a lot to me to be able to hunker down for a while someplace that felt safe and familiar."

"Of course." I moved in and gave her a hug. She sighed and let her head rest against my shoulder for a minute. "Of course, Ter."

We stayed like that, standing close, arms around each other, her head resting on my shoulder, her breath a warm tickle on the side of my neck, for so long that I lost all track of everything – time, the thread of our conversation, even where we were. I just let that feeling – that cozy, comfortable, *right* feeling – seep through every pore.

After a while I awakened from whatever reverie I'd slipped into with the realization that I didn't feel her breath on my neck any more. I looked down and she was looking up at me with eyes full of questions that I couldn't answer.

I hesitated for a split-second as all the old warnings and fears rose to the surface again – and then I told them all to shut up, and kissed her. It started out timid, friendly, almost chaste. Our lips brushed, brushed again and then held. And shifted. And pressed. And opened. And explored. And then explored some more.

And then we both jolted backward as if hit by lightning and stumbled apart.

Terry's hand was at her mouth, which hung partway open. Her eyes were wide and shiny. My hand was outstretched in a silent plea for – Forgiveness? Sympathy? Another bite of the apple? And then, without a word, she turned for the door.

I followed her downstairs in silence, neither of us exactly hurrying, both in some sort of shock. She headed for the back of the house, into the living room and up to the sliding glass door that led onto the back patio, where she stood, nose almost pressed against the glass, staring out into the night.

I stopped ten feet behind her. "Did that – oh Jesus, was that okay?"

"I don't know what that was."

"It – I – it just felt right."

"And?"

"And what?"

"And what comes after that?"

I didn't know how to respond, so I didn't. So she tried again.

"Where does that take us? What do you want?"

"I – I don't know. I wasn't planning it all out in my head, Ter, it just kind of happened."

"Uh-huh."

"Are – are you mad?"

There was a long silence. And then:

"Yeah." She turned around with tears in her eyes and stood, arms crossed in front, holding herself tight. "Yeah, I'm mad. Mostly I'm mad at myself for letting – no, wanting that to happen. I'm mad that I never found a way to quit feeling like that about you. Not when we were fifteen and you used to tease me, tell me I'd better start dressing like a girl if I ever wanted to get a date. Not in college, when I tried to change everything about myself, but I could never change that one thing. Not even when I got married to someone else. Shit, Tim, I even wanted you then. Even when I was sleeping with another man, I wanted it to be you. Shit!"

I was miles beyond stunned. I had been preparing myself to take the fall, to apologize and try to make a joke so we could get past what had just happened and get back to our old familiar comfort zone. Wherever that was now.

"When…?"

"I don't even know when it happened, okay?" A great bulbous tear broke free and ran down her right cheek, leaving a glistening trail. "We were friends all those years and it was always good and it was always enough. It wasn't like I just woke up one day and said hey, I think it's about time Tim and I hooked up. You know? It wasn't like that at all. It just built up little by little. For a long time it was off in the distance somewhere, and then one day it was all around me, everywhere I looked."

"I – God, Terry, that's – I felt guilty all this time because I didn't try to stop you from marrying him, and then even guiltier the last few months because I was actually glad it didn't work out. I was actually *glad* my best friend's heart got broken. That is so messed up."

She nodded and took a long, ragged breath, her arms still tight in front of her like a shield, whether against me or against everything inside her that wanted to come flooding out.

"So – you started feeling that way, and then…?"

"And then nothing. And then I played it safe and you played it safe and we kept on like always, and then one day I met Michael and it was good for a while and then it wasn't anymore and then I divorced him, and here we are. Here we fucking are, Tim."

I had no idea what to say. Time passed and Terry finally turned away again, staring out into the darkness, our patio furniture reduced to dim outlines in the glow from the house. I stayed quiet until I couldn't stand the silence between us a moment longer.

"So what do we do now?"

She wheeled and shook her finger at me, infuriated, scolding. "No, see, I'm not gonna do that. I'm not gonna do that anymore. *You* kissed *me*. What do *you* want?"

"I –" My mind was a blank. I wanted to be honest and the honest truth in that moment was that I had no answer. All I knew was that I loved her more than I ever had before, more than I had even half an hour ago, and that the idea of our friendship unraveling terrified me beyond all reason. Finally, words dribbled out. "I don't know. I don't know what I want."

"Exactly."

"What? What do you mean?"

"I mean this is exactly what the problem is, Tim. You're all about that initial impulse, the opening scene. You're great at that part, all sweet and witty and everything. And then when the moment passes and the hard work starts, when you have to follow through and deal with the nitty gritty stuff that comes after, you check out.

"I married Michael. I'm not saying it was the smartest thing I ever did. But I made a decision, I made a commitment, and I followed through. I fought for it, I worked at it as long and hard as I could, and when the time came, I walked away. I didn't let him talk me into sticking around and hanging on and trying to forgive something that was unforgivable. The minute I understood that what I had could never be what I'd wanted it to be, I was done. And I finished it.

"That's what you have to figure out how to do, Tim – finish things. I thought maybe when you left the job with Cassini that you were turning the corner, that you were gonna start getting it together. But you're still stuck in neutral. Everything going on with you right now – your dad, the house, your job, you and me – it's all loose ends. None of it's finished. And you want me to stand there in the middle of it all with you and hold your hand while you scratch your head and feel sorry for yourself and put off making any decisions a little longer. And I can't do that anymore. I just can't."

I could feel my own eyes starting to well up and it just made me angrier. "So what the hell am I supposed to do?"

"Figure out what you want. And then go get it."

"Just like that?"

"Just like that."

19

Nothing stings quite like the truths you don't want to hear – which meant Terry's words stung a lot. She packed a small bag and left a few minutes later to go stay at a friend's for a couple of days, saying she'd be back before I left. I puttered around the house for two days waiting, sifting through my dad's papers, trying to bring some order to the chaos of clips and notes and research. It was lonely work and I still didn't know what I meant to do with it all when I was done. I wasn't really expecting it to come to anything, but I also knew I couldn't simply throw away the most tangible of all my dad's legacies.

Terry returned an hour before I had to leave for the airport to meet up with the band again in San Diego. We talked a little while I finished packing, but it was dodgy stuff, the small talk you make with someone you just met instead of someone you'd been sharing your innermost thoughts with for a couple of decades. All in all, though, it still felt like a kind thing for her to do, to come back and say goodbye before I hit the road again. We didn't talk about whether she'd still be living at the house when I got back in two weeks. We didn't touch the subject of our own undefined connection. We just hung out, however uncomfortably, smoothing little verbal band-aids onto each other's wounds. At the end, she hugged me in the driveway and waved as I backed my rental car into the street and hit the road again.

For the first time in about fifty plane rides, I left the iPod quiet and undisturbed in my bag. I thought about ordering a drink, and didn't do that either. I had just gotten my ass kicked, and the thing was, as the immediate pain had faded to a kind of dull ache, I had come around to accept that it had needed kicking. *Oh hell, just say it. She was right. Damn it.* Whether I would or could ever admit it to her face, she was right. Everywhere I looked around me, there was unfinished business, and the only person who could fix that was me.

* * *

It was obvious that the band had unfinished business of its own. They played good shows in San Diego and LA – whatever came between them offstage, when the music started, they were professionals and they played like it – but there was an unresolved tension lurking around every corner now, filling in the space between every note. Without explanation, the gang vocals were always done at separate mikes now, instead of Jordan, Nicky and Glen sometimes gathering around a single one. There was a little gag Nicky and Jordan would do during "Road Dog" where Jordan would try to hold him steady as he swayed every which way while playing a solo; now he just stood and played while Jordan used the break to grab a bottle of water off Seth's drum riser. The after-shows had been ceded to Nicky and Seth; Wayne didn't make a single one and Jordan and Glen split early every time.

From an outsider's perspective it probably looked like a typical scene near the end of a long tour, where everybody's tired and ready to get off the road for a while and let the batteries recharge. From my vantage point, though, with all that I had witnessed, it looked like a rocket barreling through the upper atmosphere, aglow with the scorching heat of re-entry and headed for an uncertain fate below.

The tour's four-day stop in Los Angeles gave me a chance to collect my mail from the post office and drop by the apartment, which now felt so alien and empty of life that it began to spook me after only an hour. After confirming they had room for me back at the band's hotel, I scooped up the unpaid bills, grabbed a couple of shirts from the closet and headed for the door. Turning around to take a last look, it hit me: *I don't live here anymore.*

I knew immediately that this was true, that I would only ever come back here again to clean the place out and ship a few boxes of things north to Santa Rosa. And knowing that, I remembered the one item I needed to take with me now, rather than later. The picture of me and Dad from the front hall table fit snugly into the padded center section of my laptop shoulder bag. And then I was out of there, feeling a little unhinged and a lot better. I had made a decision, and I knew it was the right one, and with every step that took me farther from the way station I had occupied for eighteen months, I felt stronger.

* * *

As Frank Cassini's Republican opponent in the general election, Darcy Kendrick had supplied me with a whole other set of rationalizations for working on Frank's campaign.

First and foremost, she was loopy as a cardinal drunk on mulberries, a spittle-spraying ideologue of the first order. Liberals were "Godless America-haters"; the Democratic Speaker of the Assembly was "a pimp for welfare queens." She didn't just want a fence on the border with Mexico, she wanted a new Berlin Wall, electrified with guard towers every half mile manned by snipers with scopes. When a reporter had e-mailed her a request for comment on a bill clarifying language in the labor code barring discrimination on the basis of sexual orientation, he had gotten back a quote from Leviticus leading off a note that proceeded to refer to the bill's author as "pro-sodomy" and "pro-bestiality." And anyone foolish enough to favor any form of conservation over unfettered exploitation of natural resources was not just a "tree-hugger," but an "eco-freak."

Kendrick had in fact managed to alienate so many members of her own party structure with her name-calling that they'd actually drafted an equally conservative but considerably more rational state Senator to run against her in the primary. His challenge hadn't lasted long, though, as he'd been taken down by a series of borderline-slanderous third-party attack ads funded by Kendrick supporters.

In the end, the two chief assets Darcy Kendrick had to offer her party – besides a penchant for making headlines with her comments – were her gender and her base in the party's one solid urban stronghold, Orange County. The thing most outsiders don't appreciate about California is that the biggest socio-cultural-political divide in the state isn't north versus south or rich versus poor or even coast versus inland; it's urban versus rural. With 55 members of Congress and 120 state legislators, California does include a handful of rural Democrats and urban Republicans – the former skirting the more urbanized areas of the Central Valley, the latter finding purchase in Orange County and parts of San Diego – but for the most part it's a state divided into city Dems and country Reeps, with moderates of either party an endangered species.

Whatever Frank Cassini's faults – and Lord knows I was acutely aware of those by the end of my first month working for him – he did appear to believe that women could be trusted with control over their own bodies, he did not appear to believe that gay people were compulsive pedophiles, and he wasn't in favor of leaving people in need of emergency health care to bleed to death in the street if they couldn't produce the right form of identification. He was, in short, not Darcy Kendrick. It would have been nice if he had more than that to recommend him, but as in any relationship, sometimes you demand, and sometimes you settle.

* * *

The day of Stormseye's last show in LA – the third of three sold-out nights at Staples – I got a call from Gene Ostrowitz. I was considerably irritated with him after the way he'd worked around me again and again, but I still believed in what he was trying to do and decided I had nothing to lose by meeting him for coffee.

My price for Gene's misbehavior was to make him dance a little while I played dumb. We were sitting at a window table at the Starbuck's at Santa Monica and Bundy in West LA, Gene with a double-latte half-caff with whipped cream, me with a mocha with an extra packet of sugar mixed in. As Paul McCartney sang about vintage clothes, I let myself be entertained by Gene's impish manner, though if we were talking wood nymphs, he was definitely in the white birch family, skinny and pale with wispy gray-blond hair worn in one big swirl.

"So, where do you think Jordan got the idea to start an independent expenditure committee?"

Gene looked down at his cup immediately, but it was useless. I could see his lips pursing, trying to hold back the grin that was dying to come out. "You know," he said, looking away now, choosing his words, the corners of his mouth twitching. "He's a smart guy, very curious, wants to understand how everything works. Everything." He adjusted his round wire-rimmed glasses – very Lennonesque – and looked at me again, letting go of the façade now. "So, yeah, I might have mentioned independent expenditure committees to him, and he might have asked me a few questions about how they work."

"Really," I said.

"Oh hell, he must have grilled me for half an hour! The man is insatiable!" Gene's chortling was loud enough to turn heads two tables away.

I shook my head and grinned a little in spite of myself. "That's what I figured."

"He just caught me totally off guard, wanting to go that high." My brow must have furrowed, because he went on. "I just told him how to do it; I never suggested a number. I though he might go for two, three, maybe five million if I got lucky. Twenty million? I just about dropped the phone in my martini!"

I tried not to let my expression show how bizarre this seemed. One minute Jordan's on all fours in a graveyard talking to a ghost, the next he's shoveling twenty million dollars out the door without even being asked.

"Look, Tim, I should have brought you in on this, I know I should have, and I apologize, but I was starting to get a little desperate. Jordan was the best play I could see to get this thing back on track, but I'm just not sure right now if any amount of money is going to be enough to get us over the top." The glow that normally animated Gene's eyes had faded.

"What're the numbers looking like?"

"Last night's tracking poll was still forty-eight percent. That means after pounding the mailboxes all summer and going on cable three weeks ago, we've moved four percent. I've got a bad feeling, like all we're doing now is preaching to the choir. Yeah, we've got two-thirds of the Dems behind it in a solid blue state, but turnout always skews a little conservative on election day and if we don't hit at least fifty-two in the tracking polls by then, we're probably dead. And if the CCCC's first big-deal gig goes down, it could take the whole organization down with it."

I could appreciate it better it now – the desperation behind Gene's actions. He had gambled everything on the initiative and now it was sinking underneath him.

"How about the splits?" I asked. "What're they looking like?"

"What you'd expect. Strong in the Bay Area and LA County, strong in the upper education bracket and liberal-identifying pockets in urban areas. Some appeal to tech-savvy moderates in San Jose and San Diego and a couple of the North Coast counties that're stacked with ex-hippies."

"The usual suspects."

"Exactly. And that's exactly the crowd your boy Jordan already appeals to. We can spend all the cash in the world, but as long as the average voter sees this as just another lefty Hollywood Democratic circle jerk, we'll never pull the moderates and independents we need to win. They aren't listening right now, and even twenty million bucks probably isn't going to change that."

We sat there quiet for a long moment, silently contemplating this all-too-likely scenario. Gene's dour analysis reflected everything I thought I knew about the normal behavior of the California electorate; I couldn't argue with any of it. *It's political common sense, the exact same set of calculations Frank would have gone through when – when –*

Without warning, fireworks went off in my head. The epiphany came all at once, like a massive headrush that takes the whole world to grey speckles for a minute before everything comes back, suddenly crystal clear. For the first time in months, I knew exactly what to do – where to go, how to get there and what would happen next. And if it all worked out the way I already felt sure it would – oh, the irony. Oh, delicious. Instant karma.

"Thanks, Frank."

Gene looked up, startled. "What?"

"No, it's just that, Frank did us a favor, holding out, staying neutral all this time. He's positioned himself as the rational, feet-firmly-on-the-ground moderate in his race, in contrast with the raving extremist on the other side.

He's his own man, not a captive of anyone's dogma. An independent-minded leader who won't be badgered or bullied by the ideological purists in his own party, who reaches his own conclusions in his own good time."

Gene was baffled. "Well, sure, whatever you say Timmo, that's all fine and dandy, but how does it help us? The man's made himself irrelevant; he won't even talk to us."

"Oh, he's relevant. And he *will* talk to us. I just need forty-eight hours. And then not only will he talk to us, he'll come knocking at our door."

20

Two days later I was standing by the window of the second-largest suite on the top floor of the Sacramento Hyatt Regency, looking out over the expanse of Capitol Park. The oaks and maples were starting to turn, the rippling blanket of deep summer green being infiltrated by a mosaic of orange and yellow pastels. Above, the late afternoon sun was dodging billowing grey clouds, creating intermittent columns of light as the front edge of an early-season storm began to assert itself.

Behind me, Jordan was throwing the last few things in his bag on the king-size bed as CNN chattered in the background. At three fifty-nine there was a knock at the door. Three firm raps, then an expectant silence. Jordan went for the TV while I went to get the door.

Standing in the doorway, in khakis and a white polo shirt with a modest anchor logo at the left breast, was California Attorney General Francis J. Cassini. I supposed this was his clumsy version of dressing down for a private Saturday afternoon tete-a-tete with a rock star. His hair was still sternly parted, though, and the heavy scowl he wore overwhelmed whatever softening effect his clothing choices might have had.

"Green."

"Sir," I replied reflexively. "Come in."

He glanced down the hall to his left, then brushed past me into the room. Sticking my head out the door for a minute before closing it, I saw Officer Bob waiting at the end of the hall, leaning against the wall near the elevators. I gave him a quick nod and caught a glimmer of amusement on his face as he returned it.

Back inside, I found Jordan and Frank finishing their handshake and settling into a pair of plush armchairs sitting at ninety degrees to one another near the window. I didn't even try to sit, knowing I'd just fidget. I picked a spot in the middle of the room, shading closer to Jordan's side of the small coffee table in front of them, and stood. Feet slightly apart, hands loose at my sides, a gunslinger at the ready.

"I've heard a lot about you," said Jordan, only partially successful in suppressing a wry smile.

Frank looked at him, then over at me, then back at him. "Don't believe everything you hear. I'm in a tough business."

"Yes you are. A lot of scrutiny. Lots of pressure, I'm sure."

"You bet."

"How's the campaign going?"

Frank shot me a quick look: *What the hell is going on here?* He knew we hadn't asked him over for coffee and small talk. But with deep pockets the size of Jordan's in the room, he wasn't about to be rude – yet.

"It's good. Polls look solid, we're making inroads here in the Valley, good events the last couple of weeks and our TV buy's ramping up again this week. We'll be full bore from here to the finish line."

"Very cool. You've been looking forward to this for a while, haven't you?"

"The Senate? Of course. Who wouldn't want to be a United States Senator?"

Jordan just smiled. "There's something we'd like to show you."

Frank's eyes moved from Jordan to me again and narrowed, even as Jordan rose and moved to the huge armoire that held the TV and DVD player. "What is this?"

I didn't respond. Jordan continued fiddling with buttons while he answered. "You know I started an independent expenditure committee to support the Clean Futures initiative?"

Frank was watching Jordan's back now as he got the TV on and found the DVD remote. "Sure."

Jordan turned and walked back over to us, remote in hand. "We wanted to show you one of our new commercials."

The screen came alive and a sequence of bold color images of iconic California scenery faded in and out – Yosemite, the Golden Gate, Mission Beach, Lake Tahoe, Death Valley, a grove of North Coast redwoods. A narrator's voice intoned words I had been scribbling on a legal pad just two days ago, waxing philosophical about the bounty of natural beauty that was the legacy of all Californians, all Americans. Ten seconds in we cut to flash-card speed contrasting shots, black and white images of Arctic ice sheets breaking up and coastal flood simulations running, played off clean color shots of hybrid cars rolling off assembly lines. No canned narration here, though; the voiceover was of a woman exhorting a cheering crowd to "safeguard our environment and win our independence from fossil fuels."

With eight seconds to go, the images faded into a reveal of the woman speaking – Green Party Senate candidate Elaine Supchek – standing on the Capitol steps firing up a crowd with a rousing call to pass the Clean Futures initiative on November 7.

As the screen faded to black, Jordan clicked the TV off and set the remote down on the table between him and Frank. Cassini stared at him for a second, then focused in on me.

"Christ, Green. Chambers said you told her you had something for me that was make-or-break. And this is all you've got? The enviro party candidate backs the big enviro initiative? Dog bites man. So what."

Jordan glanced at me, saw I was ready, and backed off from the response that was clearly on his lips. I appreciated it. The moment was one I'd long since given up on ever happening, and now that it was here I didn't want to surrender it to anyone, not even the man who had made it all possible.

"We're not talking about a few slots on late-night cable."

Frank's irritation grew as he shifted his gaze to me again and held. "You're gonna buy network time? For this?"

I took a deep breath and let fly. "All the networks, and heavy cable coverage, statewide. Every market. News adjacencies, top thirty dramas, *Ellen*, *Wheel of Fortune*, *Good Morning America*, *The Today Show*, *The Tonight Show*, *The Daily Show* – you name it. Plus complementary Internet buys on every major news site, blog and forum out there. Saturation."

I had seen Frank Cassini in a hundred contexts, private, public, before cameras and behind them, in cars, planes, restrooms and alleyways. I had never seen him speechless, until that moment. And I wasn't even done yet.

"For fifteen days straight, starting Tuesday."

Cassini looked at Jordan – who smiled gently as if to say *Uh-huh, what he said* and kept quiet – and then back at me. His expression was tight and steely as ever, but there was a little tremor developing at his left temple.

"That's gonna cost you a lot more than twenty million."

Jordan smiled patiently. "That was kind of a – downpayment. I put another forty million in the committee account this morning."

Cassini blinked, blinked again, then refocused on me, his face beginning to redden.

"She can't win, you know."

"No," I agreed. "She can't. Not even with a sixty million dollar saturation media buy. She's too far left to pull from the middle. The only votes she could really hope to pick up in substantial numbers are liberal Democrats. The ones who thought they didn't have any choice other than to settle for a candidate who hasn't endorsed the most important environmental initiative so far this century."

Frank was staring at me in a way that would undoubtedly have frightened me six months before, face darkened, eyes burning, pupils dilated. In the moment, though, I felt bulletproof, invulnerable. Even when he bolted up out of his chair and took a single, lunging step in my direction.

"You little son of a bitch," he hissed.

Before I could respond Jordan was out of his chair and easing between us. It didn't matter; I was in the zone.

"Maybe so. Maybe so, Frank. But at least I'm my own son of a bitch now."

Frank shot a glance at Jordan, waiting quietly between us, and then seemed to catch himself. Stepping back, he adjusted his belt and took a deep breath as the struggle for control rippled across his face in waves. After a moment he came back at us again.

"So what's the play here? Take me down and you get six years of Darcy Kendrick. How's that gonna help you?"

"It isn't."

This nearly cost him his composure all over again as he strained to fit this response into his calculus of how the world worked. I let him grasp for purchase a little longer before poking him again.

"You know what I admire about Darcy Kendrick, though?"

He couldn't possibly imagine.

"She might be a self-righteous, bigoted, fear-mongering, to-the-right-of-Genghis-Khan looney tune. But at least she's honest. She says what she believes, and she believes what she says."

Frank's face was approaching a shade of maroon I'd never witnessed on a human being before – not blotchy; solid. Neon, almost.

"Don't... you... fucking... patronize... me."

"I'm not, Frank. Just a little straight talk. By the time we're done, you might even thank me for it."

The battle went on inside Cassini for a moment longer before the supremely pragmatic political animal that ruled his core assumed control once more. He strode around Jordan to the window, staring out into the darkening afternoon, doing his best Macarthur, ignoring the vivid flush now gradually turning blotchy again all over his neck. After a long moment he spoke, his tight, clipped sentences now directed at the window.

"What do you want?"

Jordan's turn. "We want the initiative to pass."

"Well, sixty million's gonna help."

"Yeah, but it's still an uphill fight. See, Tim and I talked about it and we agree with you – there are definitely folks who'd move a lot more votes by speaking up for the initiative than Elaine Supchek. The good news is, no one's actually talked to her or even seen this version of the ad yet. We just grabbed some video from one of her speeches and dubbed it in."

Frank turned, furrows cutting deep across his forehead, and stared as

Jordan finished his thought.

"Which means, we could still substitute in a more effective spokesperson. You know, someone with a higher profile. Mainstream. Moderate. Pragmatic."

"What – what're –" You could see he recognized where it was going now; he just couldn't accept it. Floundering, he glanced over at me again, and that was all I needed.

"Endorse it."

"That's – I can't – I'll –"

"Endorse it, Frank. You'll be a hero to the liberal wing of the party and you'll get a hell of a lot more airtime out of it than the Chamber of Commerce is ever going to buy you."

I let the wheels turn a minute longer before hitting him again.

"It's not complicated, Frank. Endorse it and you win. Don't and anything can happen."

He was staring at me with real fury in his eyes now. Something new had gotten under his skin.

"I'm still the Attorney General of the State of California. A little fucking respect."

I'd somehow forgotten – before he walked in the door that afternoon I'd never called him by his first name, at least to his face.

"Fair enough," I said, stretching out the pause. "Sir."

And that was the end of our conversation. After that Frank wouldn't even make eye contact with me, staying focused entirely on Jordan.

"I want a two-way street. I endorse it, you endorse me."

I was still wired enough on adrenalin that I might have blown the whole deal up over this petty gamesmanship if Jordan had left me the opening. But he never hesitated. "Done. If you want me to do it at a rally or something, I'm headed to Vegas today, but I'll be in Oakland for a week starting tomorrow."

Jordan held out his hand. Frank stared at it for a full second before signaling his defeat with a hard sigh. "Fine. Fine," he said as they shook. "I'll get back to you about the announcement. I'm in and out of the Bay Area every couple of days from here on. How do we put the ad together?"

"You'll need to publicly endorse the initiative, and we'll need to have someone there to film it. We'll take it from there."

"Do I get approval on the ad?"

"You know how this works better than I do. I'm running an independent expenditure committee. We're not supposed to coordinate with any candidate or campaign operation."

"Yeah, right," he snorted.

"You have my word," said Jordan. "Follow through on this, and we'll make you look good."

At that, he grimaced, turned sharply on one heel and would have walked right out the door if Jordan hadn't called to him. "Frank?"

With the door cracked open, handle in his grasp, he turned back, jaw like a vise, still avoiding eye contact with me.

"Just one more thing. Remember that fundraiser you had at Nia Lamar's place, back in July?" It took him a second, but I could tell by the way his eyes flitted to me that he did.

Jordan grabbed me by the shoulder and nodded sideways at me. "You really should've talked with him. A little respect. You know?"

Frank spun away without a word and pulled the door shut behind him, leaving us alone to consider its blank backside.

Jordan looked at me, shrugged and raised an eyebrow for effect. "I'm just saying."

21

Because Frank wasn't available to meet with us until four, we'd missed the band's flight to Vegas earlier in the day. Ray had tried to insist on staying behind with us, but once Jordan pointed out that I'd be with him all day and promised that we wouldn't leave the suite except to ride out to our charter at the airport, he relented and agreed to leave with the rest of the group.

Natalie had arranged for the concierge to slip us out a side door into the garage, where a van was waiting to shuttle us out to the airport. It was a different route than the driver was used to – we were catching a small charter out of tiny Sacramento Executive Airport, just south of downtown – but we managed to arrive on schedule at 5:15. With a 5:45 departure and ninety minutes of flying time we could just make the band's 8:00 show at the MGM Grand Arena.

After clearing security in the nondescript terminal – Executive is all general aviation, no regular airlines – we were ten steps through the doors and out onto the tarmac when Jordan stopped cold, ignoring the light rain that was just beginning to fall around us.

"You've gotta be kidding me."

The charter Natalie had arranged for us was a six-seat Lear. Pilots up front, then two portholes on each side for the four seats in the cabin. The entire plane was about forty feet long, and Jordan was clearly not happy about it. Let me tell you, a soul patch on a frowning man is not a pretty thing. It becomes a scar, a gun-barrel through which all negative emotion is projected. I tried to reason with him as we moved slowly across the tarmac toward the waiting jet, the breeze gusting a bit, pushing the rain in sideways at us.

"The next commercial flight out of Sac International isn't for an hour and a half, and it'd take that long or longer to drive to Oakland and try to catch something out of there. If we don't take this, you miss the show."

He gave me a brief, infinitely frustrated look and walked a little closer to the plane. Twenty feet away he stopped again. His hair was blowing forward in the breeze now, a wild mane of black curls shadowing his face. "What?"

"What do you mean, 'what'? Buddy Holly, Ritchie Valens, the Big Bopper. Lynyrd Skynyrd. Aaliyah. Bill Graham. Stevie Ray Vaughan. DJ A.M." He moved closer, eyes wide and fierce. "I don't need to keep going, do I?"

He didn't. The historical record did suggest that the ratio of small aircraft carrying musical luminaries crashing to the ground versus the same carrying regular civilians was abnormally high. But that was only because the stars' crashes all made headlines.

"Look, it's a 90-minute flight. High rollers charter these things in and out of Vegas every day. We'll go right over the top of this rain. These guys probably do this run ten times a week."

One of the pilots, a trim, athletic-looking Korean American fellow wearing a crisp blue dress shirt, popped his head out of the open cabin door and called to us. "Let's go! Daylight's wasting!"

I called back that we'd be right there and turned to Jordan, who was still staring at the plane through spinning whorls of hair. He took a deep breath, let it out, gave a resigned little shrug and got moving again. "Alright," he grumbled. "Alright."

* * *

Twenty minutes into the flight, the co-pilot who'd called us on board clambered out of the tiny cabin up front and came back to kneel between our seats. I folded the day's *LA Times* up in my lap to listen. He wasn't shouting, but he had to speak loudly to be heard over the shroud of white noise created by the combination of rushing air and twin jet engines powering away on either side inches from the cabin walls.

"The storm's a little stronger over the mountains and we're getting reports of a bumpy ride up ahead, so keep the seat belts fastened, alright?"

Jordan glanced at me, his unspoken accusation all too clear, then spoke to the co-pilot. "Can you get around it?"

"No, it's a broad front. It wasn't looking too bad an hour ago, but the wind speed and moisture content picked up when it hit the Sierras. We see that sometimes in the spring and fall. We'll climb, stay on top of it as much as we can. It's just gonna be a little bumpy for the next half hour or so."

We nodded like the helpless hostages we were and watched the co-pilot maneuver back into his tight perch. Before he'd cleared the doorway we could already feel the plane beginning to climb. The thing was so small you felt the lift and fall of every maneuver as if you were lying flat on a hang-glider. The last flashes of sunshine we'd caught on our climb to cruising altitude had disappeared behind thick cloud cover ten minutes ago; we were now barreling through grey soup at 450 miles an hour, over 10,000-foot peaks, into the middle of a storm. My neck began to tingle, my palms to sweat. *I put us here. The meeting with Frank, missing the band's flight, all of it. I put us here.*

A minute later we felt a bump, like a ripple, a belch of unstable air vibrating through the windpipe of the plane. Then another, and another, and pretty soon the entire plane was vibrating more or less constantly. We jolted downward sharply, then back up almost as sharply. The vibrations became more intense and more irregular. It was like riding through the sky inside a blender on frappe.

I became aware my hands were clamped onto my armrests like a lifejacket. I looked over at Jordan and his eyes were closed in concentration. After a minute he opened them, caught my eye and gave me an appraising look. In the space of five minutes of turbulence, we had reversed roles; he was now the calm one again.

"Nothing to do now but ride it out," he said, leaning in towards me, his voice vibrating along with the plane. "But if you start singing 'American Pie' I'm gonna have to climb over there and cram that newspaper in your mouth."

I closed my eyes, shook my head and smiled.

Then, without warning, we were becalmed. The air turned smooth, our altitude held steady, and the vibrations eased off. I relaxed my grip and peered out into the murky grey sky, weighing my hope that we'd cleared the storm against the knowledge that we might only have entered its eye.

I took three smooth, steady breaths – and then had the wind nearly knocked out of me as the plane pulled up hard for a moment, as if riding up the face of a wave, then crested it and dropped. And again. And again. And again. And then we could see through a gap in the curtain that the pilots were yelling at each other, but the wind noise and engine thrum and vibrations made it impossible to catch what they were saying.

We began to descend. *Changing altitude? Sure, that's what they always do when they get too much turbulence. But didn't he say they were going to try to stay on top of the storm?*

As our downward slide continued and seemed to actually accelerate, I realized the steady background hum of the jet engines had eased off a notch and become noticeably out of balance, mono instead of stereo, as if – *Oh. Oh. My. God.*

As if only one of the engines was still running.

* * *

Whether climbing or descending, there comes a point in any normal change of altitude on any normal flight where your equilibrium adjusts to the plane's movement. From that point you only notice another change in direction; after you've been ascending for a while, just leveling off actually feels like you're falling. The reverse also holds; after you've been descending for a while, leveling off actually feels like you're climbing.

This observation only occurred to me later; in the present, I went through a process of rallying hope over and over again, as we descended, then seemed to pull up out of it. At first the winds buffeted us even harder as we moved through the heaviest clouds; just as the side-to-side motion settled, the cloud thickness eased up and sheets of wet blowing snow invaded every inch of space outside our porthole windows. Peering out was like looking at a shaken snow-globe from the inside.

From there, our ride seemed to ease into a steady, almost reassuring pattern of drop-level-climb, drop-level-climb. I believed every second of the way that our pilots had it under control, that we were about to level off for good at a lower altitude, that we'd be on the ground in Las Vegas in an hour, laughing about our little rollercoaster ride in the sky in the limo on the way to the arena and the show.

I forced myself to believe it, right up until I felt the solid, purposeful ka-thunk of the landing gear deploying, caught a fleeting glimpse through the blowing snow of a jagged wall of rock, and saw the co-pilot turn in his seat, yelling and waving frantically for us to get down.

Then instinct took over as I reached over to press Jordan forward into the braced crash position I'd seen on the front of a hundred airline safety cards that summer, and began mumbling something incoherent that nonetheless felt suspiciously like a prayer.

What I remember of the crash itself is mostly the noise. Our ears had already been assaulted for forty-five minutes by the sound of the engines, the wind, the vibrations from the turbulence. The noise on impact made what had come before feel like a five-year-old blowing on a party favor. It was a thousand decibels of electric guitar feedback, it was a hundred cluster bombs exploding all around us, it was the singular bludgeoning cry of Armageddon.

And then, somehow, we were still moving, the noise changing, becoming less enveloping but sharper and shriller, metal grinding against a series of unyielding surfaces and, in turn, being rent and torn.

A bone-rattling jolt.

Then another.

Then a final, thundering impact.

And then a perfect stillness, like the end of the world, like death itself, and darkness everywhere.

IV.

MISTY MOUNTAIN HOP

Where would I be without my anger
at a world that's got to change?
Where would I be without these sins
made me who I am today?

– Mark Doyon
("My Mercurial Nature" by Arms of Kismet)

To live a pure unselfish life, one must count nothing
as one's own in the midst of abundance.

– Buddha

22

The summer before I left for college, Dad and I fought.

I don't mean to make it sound like there was a single issue or incident or item that we fought over. That would have been easy by comparison. No, we fought like Republicans and Democrats, like rock and disco, like fathers and sons. We were locked in perpetual combat over the one thing that seemed to matter: winning. Every sentence that came out of his mouth irritated me. He was a slovenly, overweight, controlling know-it-all, a hopelessly strange and embarrassing man whose very contentment with his station in life felt like an affront. How dare he be content, living here in the same boring, outdated house we'd occupied for fourteen years, pecking away at the same tired, meaningless job like a timid old worker bee.

The worst was when he'd make me go to the grocery store with him. As we'd make our halting way up and down the aisles, every stranger's glance felt like an accusation. *What a slob. What a loser. That poor kid, how humiliating.* And the way he'd strike up a conversation with anyone, leaning on our cart chatting about mangoes with the produce clerks, comparing flavors of tea with the blue-haired ladies on aisle nine. It was some exponential multiple of mortifying.

What did we fight about that summer? What *didn't* we fight about. He let the house get too warm on hot days. He didn't let me use the car every time I wanted it. He kept trying to get me to talk about college when the thing I was looking forward to most about it was that he wouldn't be there. But the biggest thing was the one we never spoke of. He didn't *get* me. He didn't understand what it felt like to be inside my skin, almost eighteen and about to move a hundred miles away from everyone and everything I'd ever known, relieved to be finished forever with the brutal social Darwinist experiment that is high school, giddy over the onrushing freedom and rebirth represented by college, and bitterly, secretly, consumingly terrified of leaving all that I had ever known for a new town, a new life in which I would have no one but myself to blame for what I and only I knew were my myriad failings. I felt blessed and I felt cursed. Mostly, I felt like at any moment I might explode.

When I did, it was usually in the direction of the person sharing my cell in this purgatory between the wasteland of adolescence and the promised land of adulthood. *God, how could I have tolerated him all these years? He's so slow, so clueless, so out of touch. So completely, freakishly weird.* I wanted nothing to do with him, yet he was everywhere. And when I did escape him to spend a few hours working, or with friends, or locked away in my room, I found myself imagining life in Davis, out from under his oppressive wing, making my own decisions, managing my own class schedule and food and clothes and money and *oh my God how am I going to do all that I don't know how to do anything.*

We fought.

Dad had a habit of trying to defuse situations with humor. The more pointed a conversation became, the more likely he was to throw in a wry aside designed to break the tension and bring back some sense of perspective. That summer even his witticisms grated on me to the point where once, in August – I think we were arguing over who had finished the bread and put the empty bag back in the cupboard, like I had tons of spare time just lying around to deal with his insane pettiness – I cut him off midsentence and told him to just shut up. Just (for what it's worth) *please* shut up.

He didn't speak to me for two days.

That was the summer before I left for college.

* * *

I dream in slow motion and I wake up screaming.

Somewhere back among the hundred pre-show set-ups I'd wandered into and around over the course of that summer I'd heard snatches of this cover by Queens Of The Stone Age of an old Subhumans song, a keening, eerie chord-cruncher that one of the roadies (Denny?) clearly loved. It was hard not to think of it when the first sound I heard rising out of the darkness after the crash was one of the pilots screaming. It was a guttural noise, an exhalation of agony, followed by silence and fast, heavy breathing.

I slowly became conscious of two things: the world inside the plane was tilted hard to the left, and harsh, cold air was blowing in from two sides. I touched my hands together, then felt my legs, my face, my ears. Everything seemed, miraculously, to be where it belonged. As my eyes adjusted I realized it wasn't completely dark yet outside; the graying twilight would linger a little longer, though it was fading fast. But outside didn't feel "out" anymore. A sliver of gray sky was poking through the formerly solid roof above me and I could half-feel, half-smell the rush of sharp, cold mountain air swirling an acrid bouquet of frictioned metal and plastic all around me.

"Jordan!" I felt around and found my seatbelt clip. Groping into the semi-darkness to my left I found his arm and shoulder. He wasn't moving. I heard something shift up towards the front of the plane, then a hard thump, a muttered curse, and from somewhere near the source of the loud breathing there was light. At first it seemed to dance almost randomly around the confined space ahead of us that used to be the cockpit; then it shone directly in my face.

"Are you hurt?" called the same low, pinched voice that had cried out a moment before.

"I don't – I'm okay, I think I'm okay. But Jordan, he's –"

The light shifted to my left and I could see Jordan's head hanging forward, loose, hair falling all around his face. I reached for his chin and my hand came back damp and red.

"He's bleeding!"

"Check his pulse." I found his wrist and felt around for the right spot, trying to remember the CPR training I'd had in high school a decade before. My efforts were interrupted by the sounds of a struggle up front, the light dancing all around again, followed by a loud thump and an even louder grunt.

"Yeah! It's there. It's good."

"Check –" another gasping grunt "check his head and neck. Carefully."

I reached over with both hands and cradled his head, running my fingers all over his neck and scalp. Near the top of his head I found a sizable knot. The second I touched it, he jerked away from me and groaned.

"He's got a cut on his head, but it doesn't seem too bad. I think he's waking up!"

"Alright. Don't move. Stay right there."

"Okay." My eyes were finally starting to adjust and focus in the dingy half-light. "Jordan?"

"Mmmm."

"Jordan, wake up. You hit your head, you're alright." I gave one of those million dollar cheekbones a gentle slap.

"Hey –" Now his head came up. There was another thump, another wheezing curse from ahead of us and then the light was full on us again. The co-pilot from the right-hand seat – the one who'd come back and spoken to us before – shuffled back towards us, keeping all his weight left, using one hand to brace himself and the other to hold his flashlight.

"What?" said Jordan, as if I'd just asked him a question and he hadn't heard me.

"We're down. We crashed."

"Oh." It was like he was stoned, which I'd never seen him be, which just added another needle to the bundle of them stabbing at my stomach lining.

Suddenly a hand closed hard on my shoulder. "We need to get out. Fuel's leaking. Get him out of his seat. I'll try the door." As the flashlight in his other hand moved over to illuminate the door we'd entered through, which hinged up and sealed with the fuselage wall, he released my shoulder, reached for something tucked into his belt and thrust a second flashlight into my chest.

As he braced and lowered himself awkwardly down the slope of the canting floor to the door, I found Jordan's seat belt clip and undid it. When I put the light on his face again his eyes were big and confused. "What –?"

"He's opening the door. We're just staying here for a second until it's open. Hang in there."

After a few click and clacks, the pilot gave another loud grunt and threw himself against the door once, twice. The third time the door gave with a loud creaking sound that provided a shivering reminder of the symphony of metallic agony that had enveloped us a few moments before. The top end levered down and hit the ground with a soft thud.

"Come on!"

"Let's go." I wrenched myself up out of my seat and leaned over Jordan, pulling him partway to his feet. "Gotta move, man."

"Okay. Okay." He had an arm around me, hand clinging to the crook of my neck on the far side as we slide-stumbled down the short interior slope to the door. It wouldn't open all the way because of the fuselage's leftward cant, so we ended up crawling out on all fours.

It took me a second to register the feel of snow underneath, the cold styrofoam crunchiness of it under hand, knee and foot. The pilot was on his knees a couple of feet in front of us, pointing his flashlight off through the falling snow, ahead and to our left. It seemed to have eased up a bit as twilight faded into night; I could actually see some shapes fifty feet or so away in the flashlight beam. "Treeline," he instructed. "Go to the treeline, right there, ten o'clock from the plane. Stay there. Turn your flashlight off when you get there. Don't turn it on again until you hear me yell. I'm going to use it to find you. Stay together. Five minutes, okay?"

I nodded and brought Jordan up to his feet with me as I stood. The snow was just thick enough to cover smaller obstacles without forming a solid layer over the larger ones yet. I stumbled over softball-sized rocks hidden underneath several times on our traverse, which started out flat but turned into a mild incline the closer we got to the trees. Shining my beam deeper into the trees as we reached the edge, I could see they thickened up steadily beyond the open area we had landed in.

The worst moment – at least as bad as the crash itself – was when I shut off the flashlight. Without even that comfort, all that was left was the cold, the darkness and a sense of complete isolation surrounding us. My hands were wet, my shoes were soaked through and my knees were bruised and damp from our crawling exit. We were partially shielded from the wind at the edge of the trees, but every billowing gust still cut right through my cotton shirt. Worse, Jordan was silent as a golem standing next to me, like a doll whose batteries have run out.

"Jordan?"

"Hmm?" His voice was quiet, dreamy.

"You okay?"

"Sure. Sure. Just – sleepy."

He started to sit down and I wrenched him back to his feet.

"NO! Gotta stay awake, buddy. Gotta stay with me here."

"Okay. Okay."

* * *

While we waited, I powered on my phone, knowing what I'd likely find, but needing to confirm it anyway. Plenty of battery power; no signal whatsoever. There probably wasn't a cell tower for a hundred miles and if there was, I was sure it would have been blocked out by the peaks I could feel more than see surrounding us. The darkness had fully taken hold now; we were utterly alone.

What seemed like half an eternity later, I heard a far-off voice call out and clicked on my flashlight. After a minute I could see the other flashlight's beam jerking along low to the ground, making slow, steady progress toward us. So slow that I figured he must be hauling gear of some kind from the plane. Checking Jordan to make sure he wasn't going to pass out on me – he did seem a little more awake, if not entirely lucid yet – I stumbled out of our temporary cover to try to meet the pilot halfway and give him a hand.

As I approached, I realized he was only carrying one thing, a small shoulder bag with a red cross on it, yet he was still crawling, the snow obscuring his hands at the deepest points. He'd tied three thin blankets onto one of the backpack straps so that they trailed behind him like a cape.

"Here, let me help. Can you walk?"

"No. Foot."

I shifted my flashlight beam to take a look where his feet were poking out from under the trailing blankets and regretted it. It didn't take a medical degree to know that human limbs were not designed to operate at the angle his right foot had assumed.

We agreed he'd try to stand on his good foot and he did, though the cry he let out once we got to vertical was so sharp I had to stifle a groan of my own. We moved gingerly from there, the backpack now on my back, his flashlight off now, mine alternately lighting our path and shining ahead to find Jordan in the darkness. As we shuffled along, the pilot filled me in with a series of breathless bursts.

"Lost an engine. Decided to try for Bishop. Storm kicked us around. Lost too much altitude. Tried to divert to Fresno. Too late."

"Do you have any idea where we are?"

He did the last thing I expected at a time like that; he laughed, a gritty, agonized, not even remotely-funny sound.

"Helms Meadow. Garrett – the pilot – knows this area. When we got down to a thousand feet. Recognized the lake at the other end of the valley. Brought us in here. Only straight, flat patch of ground for miles."

I looked back in the direction of the plane, shocked that in all the chaos I had actually forgotten there was a second pilot up front. "Garrett? Is he behind you?"

He held us up a second, taking three deep breaths with his head down before speaking again. "No. Last impact was on his side. Never had a chance."

I shivered, but not from the cold. We started moving again.

"I'm Tim Green."

"Henry. Henry Hong Sun."

A minute later we reached Jordan, who seemed to have returned most of the way from whatever netherworld he'd been lost in before. He reached out and helped me lower Henry to the ground. As we maneuvered one of the blankets under him and settled him to the earth, he cried out again. When I thought about everything he had already done – getting us out and away from the plane, going back inside for the first aid kit and crawling halfway to the trees with a shattered foot trailing behind – I tried to imagine myself doing it, and couldn't.

While he got his breathing back under control, I dug into the medical kit. There were large bandages, gauze, some kind of burn crème, and a small binder full of pocketed plastic sheets, each pocket filled with pills in individual dose packets. "Henry. Is there anything stronger than Advil in here?"

"No."

I opened two packets and handed him four tablets. Between swallows he told me the radio was out – they'd lost all power on impact – but the emergency beacon in the cockpit had been activated.

He was wearing a leather jacket, but Jordan and I were in shirtsleeves, anticipating a walk through the warm desert evening to a limo rather than stumbling across a snowy mountain meadow under the stars. First priority had to be warmth.

I asked Jordan to sit up close with Henry while I gathered wood, and left them huddled under the other two blankets. The forest behind us grew dense enough within a matter of yards to offer substantial cover from the elements, and another twenty yards in I came across a deadfall that the snow had barely dusted yet, a twisted mass of trunk and branches.

When I returned I asked Jordan to help me clear a small firepit in the crook of the treeline's elbow. We needed cover from the wind, but enough space to minimize our chances of catching the whole forest on fire. As I arranged the kindling of feathery pine branch tips in a dense pile and then hurriedly placed a series of medium-sized branches in an up-tilted formation around and over it, I caught Jordan staring at me.

"You know how to do this?"

"Ten years of camping. You never built a fire?"

"No." I didn't even have time to question this before he asked the next obvious question. "You got matches?"

"Nope." I reached into the pocket of my jeans, pulled out the lighter I'd absent-mindedly lifted from Dad's desk a week before, and flicked it. In the glow of the new flame I could see Jordan grinning like I'd just pulled a full-grown unicorn out of my pocket. A couple of minutes later, as I stood watching the fire's smokestack power a column of heat up through the falling blanket of snow, I brought the lighter up to my mouth and kissed it.

* * *

As the fire surged, then settled back to a steady crackle, Henry beckoned me over and told me the other thing he'd managed to do before leaving the plane – drag our bags out of the wreckage. "If there's anything in them we can use. They're thirty feet straight out from the door. Just don't stick around. Fuel all over the place."

Besides extra layers of clothes, I knew I had a couple of granola bars stashed away in the inside pocket of my bag. Arriving back at the plane, I took a minute to shine my flashlight beam up toward the front end and stopped in my tracks. After bumping along the uneven meadow floor for several hundred feet, the plane had to come to its final rest against a boulder the size of a compact car. The left side of the cockpit was simply gone, flattened like tinfoil against the stone. I shuddered and turned away.

Garrett, I thought, brushing off the light dusting of snow our bags had picked up. *His name was Garrett.*

Three quarters of the way back to our bonfire – which I found it at least marginally comforting to note was visible for several hundred yards even with the snow still falling – I remembered a conversation I'd had with Nicky Frost a month before, early one morning in the hallway of the St. Louis Hilton. I'd been moaning about a hangover and he'd reached into his pocket and tossed me a half-empty prescription bottle. I'd never taken any, never even opened the bottle, but I was pretty sure it was still kicking around the bottom of my toiletries kit.

Back at the fire, Jordan was kneeling next to Henry, who lay flat on his back grimacing, his right hand gripping his thigh hard as if to protect it from the pain trying to climb up his leg. I dug around in my bag for a minute, straightened up with the bottle in hand and shook out three tablets.

"Is there anything else we need to do?" I asked Henry.

"No. Just keep the fire going and stay here. We filed a flight plan. Radioed in every course change. Emergency beacon's working. They won't send search teams up now. Not at night in a storm. But as soon as they've got daylight, they should find us."

"Alright. Take these." I handed him the pills.

"What –?"

"Vicodin."

Henry Hong Sun had a nice smile.

* * *

The fire crackled. The wind whistled. Henry slept.

"You never built a fire?"

"No."

"Never went camping?"

Jordan shook his head, waves of dark hair now damp and stringy instead of frosted with snow. "Not like you. I was a city kid. No, not even that. I was a country club brat. If my parents wanted to go somewhere, they'd just buy property there."

My look was enough to keep him going.

"My dad's a developer. Speculated big in the '60s down around Newport Beach, Huntington Beach, Costa Mesa. Built like two thousand homes down there, most of 'em McMansions with ocean views. That's where I grew up."

"Costa Mesa."

"Yeah."

"Have you ever actually been to Yosemite?"

"Sure. Of course. But not 'til I was 22. Wayne took me up there with a couple of girls, made the fire, walked me through helping him get the tent set up. I didn't know how to do any of it. We were just taking a break, getting away from everything, you know, but it was so incredible that in one weekend I ended up writing three songs that made it onto the first album."

I didn't want to interrupt his flow, wanted to encourage him to keep riffing away like this as long as he was willing, but I couldn't help myself.

"Your dad. Is a developer."

"Yeah."

"Opposite side of the fence, wouldn't you say?"

Jordan shot me a brief, wry grin and stared off into the night. Eventually, he continued.

"It was a cold house. The sun was always out, the weather was always warm, but the house was cold. Everything had to be perfect all the time – the tables, the lamps, the paintings, even the magazines on the coffee table. It all had to 'show' like a house you were trying to sell that day. Sharon and I always felt like we were in the way, like we were supposed to just shut up and smile and be good little matching boy and girl accessories.

"I went to a prep school in Newport Beach. Grades were okay, nothing special. But I did pretty well on the SAT and that was enough for Dad to buy my way into Berkeley. Hell, for all I know your buddy Frank might have been one of the people he leaned on to make sure I got in. Anyway, I got there and started hanging out with my roommate – a scholarship kid from Antioch who played bass in a punk band – and realized the only things that had ever made me feel good about myself were music and writing.

"I'd written a couple of poems for English in high school. They weren't that great but I liked that feeling of playing with words, trying to find a way to express what you're feeling inside that makes it both yours and more than yours. I thought I'd be all embarrassed when we had to read them in front of the class, but I ended up digging it. And the girls…! Oh, the girls seriously dug it."

I smiled and waited. But this particular burst of revelation seemed to have run its course. After a couple of minutes I got up, hiked back into the trees, fetched a couple of more fallen branches, snapped them off to good sizes and tossed them on the fire.

The fire crackled. The wind whistled. Henry slept.

"You know when I knew you were alright?"

I looked down at Jordan. His eyes were boring in on me again, like they had the day he'd "interviewed" me. "No."

"When we were in the limo going from the studio to the ballpark in San Francisco, that first day. Before that, on the plane, I was just trying to help out a fellow traveler, you know? Keep you out of trouble and, after you told me about your dad, maybe cheer you up a little. But then in the car you were filling me in about what happened with Frank and the flight attendant and everything."

"Yeah…?" I still couldn't figure what he was getting at.

"You made a choice, man. You were stuck in the middle of a situation where you could either do what you were supposed to, or do what you knew in your gut was right. And you chose to do the right thing. People do that a lot when it's easy. You did it when it was hard. You did it when you knew it could cost you your job."

I glanced around at nothing, embarrassed and warm with a kind of deep affirmation I'd almost forgotten could exist. "Thanks."

There was a deeper truth to Jordan's words that made my scalp tingle with a burst of almost extra-sensory comprehension. That one decision had set so many things in motion – meeting Jordan, getting fired, getting hired, Natalie and Ray, hitting the road, Gene and Jessica, the initiative, leaning on Frank. All because I sat down instead of standing up. All because I listened to my gut. Gene had thought someone up there was trying to tell me something. Part of me continued to insist I was no one's chess piece, yet saying that everything that had happened was simply a random string of events felt like the most irrational argument of all. Reason only gets you so far; sometimes the only logical thing left to do is to give in to wonder.

After a minute more, I thought of something, smiled and glanced down at my still-damp shoes. "Remember how you were going to tell me about Maya when we got a minute?"

He chuckled ruefully. "I was imagining us in a couple of chairs on my deck in Oakland."

"Me too." I sat down next to him on the blanket and stared into the swirling, riotous depths of the fire. "But here we are."

"Yeah."

23

I was different then.

Music was one of my ways out of everything I grew up feeling – basically, that I was the equivalent of an Italian leather sofa, an expensive piece of furniture whose entire purpose was to sit there and look good and by all means shut the hell up. The other way was self-medication.

I met Nicky at a party my freshman year at Berkeley. He was in the band; I was in the crowd. By then I'd sung at some open-mike nights at coffeehouses, but I couldn't play guitar to save my life, and I was so distracted trying to keep track of the chords that I couldn't really do much with my voice. I knew if I ever wanted to get serious about music, I needed a partner.

Nicky's one of those guys who's never had a doubt in his life, or at least he manages to make you believe that. He started playing when he was thirteen. He and that guitar, man, they're like part of each other. And he was always clear about what he wanted – "I wanna be big, man. I wanna be so big they have to make up a new word for it."

Me? I just wanted to feel like someone was actually listening to me.

* * *

By the time we made our first album I was into weed, whiskey and 'ludes. The last night of our first tour – the one that broke us nationally, the album was gold by the end and we went back out on the road a month later headlining instead of opening – Seth herded us all into his and Glen's room after the show and pulled out a baggie full of coke. Must've been half an ounce. I didn't sleep for two days.

Things would calm down for a while when we got off the road – I'd come back to the Bay Area, spend some time alone, hang out with Sharon, who'd followed me up to Cal. Create little routines, have dinner with friends, go to local clubs. Get my land legs under me again. But by the time we finished the second album I was spending more and more time in LA, recording down there and hanging out on the Strip. I dated some actresses – you probably read about that, huh? Yeah. It was fun, but I was living in hotels, eating in restaurants, getting more and more disconnected from anything like a normal life. The next couple of albums and tours – three years, man – they're just one big blur.

And then we decided to record the fifth album, the one that became September Serenade, *in New York. We started in June and by the middle of August Wayne and his wife were separated, Seth had almost gotten arrested – twice – and Nicky'd started showing up for sessions three and four hours late day after day. Glen almost walked out a couple of times. Couldn't have blamed him if he had.*

I was just starting to think we were gonna have to call some kind of band meeting to get back on track when one night, Nicky and I were at this little club down in Greenwich Village, sitting with a couple of girls, drinking and acting stupid. At one a.m., after the main act we'd come in to see was packed up and gone, they had open mike time until closing. I remember I was feeling wiped out, just wanting to get out of there and away from all three of them so I could get some sleep, when someone started to sing.

It was a strange voice – high and delicate, with a little natural vibrato to it – but it had so much behind it. I don't know how to describe it; it's like the instrument was a little shaky, but the player was putting so much into the performance that you didn't even notice the technical flaws, you just believed *because she worked so hard to make you believe. She was singing a song about leaving home and looking back on her life, and it could have been total cliché, and some of the lyrics were a little flat that way, but she wasn't, she was flooding the mike with emotion, it was just pouring out of her like a confession she'd waited her entire life to give.*

Nicky kept talking, and I shushed him. He laughed and said "What the fuck?" I pointed to the stage and he gave me a look like I was hopeless and went back to chatting up the girls. I listened through that song and halfway through the next one before I got up and moved to an empty table away from the others so I could hear better.

She was kind of ordinary – brown eyes, brown hair, mousy and plain, a puffy peasant blouse on a small frame, jeans with the knees ripped out, sort of somber and intense – but what was coming out of her was completely extraordinary.

When she finished her last song I turned around and Nicky and the girls had moved up to the bar, getting in one last round before closing time. I caught Nick's eye and pointed at the stage. He rolled his eyes and turned away again.

She was closing the latches on her guitar case when I made it over to the stage.

Hey.

Hey, she said. Thanks for listening.

My pleasure. That was great.

She laughed like I would only say that if I had no idea what I was talking about. Not really, she said, but I'm working on it.

Her hair was shoulder-length with no styling, just brushed and left with natural waves in it, and she wore no jewelry and almost no makeup, just a little powder and eyeliner, but there was something intangible about her that just drew me in. She was so real, so present in the moment, completely unself-conscious, intensely aware of and engaged with everything around her. When you were near her the world felt sharper and more in focus, because you could tell that was the way she saw it. Two minutes standing around in a mostly empty club with her making musician small talk and I felt bigger, faster, stronger and full of an energy that came out of nowhere.

I asked if I could buy her a drink and she smiled and said it was too late, the bar stopped serving at quarter of. I asked if she wanted to go get a cup of coffee, then, and she said no, I've got class in the morning. I asked if she was hungry and she said no. I asked if I could give her a ride home and she laughed and said she lived around the corner.

And then she said, wait, I recognize you. You're in a band.

And I gave her my best "what can I say, you got me" grin and told her I was Jordan Lee from Stormseye.

And she looked at me standing there all cocky like "I'm a rock star, pretty sweet, huh?" and she said yeah, you guys are having a good run.

And I said, yeah, working on our fifth album. Booking an arena tour after it comes out in the spring. Probably do Europe next fall. Maybe Japan, too.

And she said well, have a nice trip, and walked away.

* * *

It had been a long time since a woman had treated me like that.

By the time the second album went platinum — and the first one along with it — our success had created a kind of aura around us. After a certain point, there was no such thing as "no" anymore; everywhere we went, anything we asked, the answer was always yes. Hell, just that night Nicky had wanted to go to some exclusive club uptown where we could walk right up to the door, past the line waiting to get in, and make the girls feel special. I'd been the one who wanted to go wander around Greenwich Village checking out the local music.

I went back the next night and asked around. That's Maya, a guy at the bar told me. She usually comes in on Tuesdays. Six nights later I was there early and alone. She came up the stairs from the little basement cave the club used for a green room and had just made it up onto the stage when she saw me sitting at a little table front and center. She looked away and kept moving, getting set up and adjusting the mike, but as she started the first song — same one as the week before, though she'd tinkered with the lyrics and they were definitely getting better — she looked down at me again and gave a little nod.

We sat in an all-night diner until four in the morning, sipping coffee, nibbling on fries, splitting a fruit salad. She was twenty-four, a grad student at Columbia. Journalism. Which she was committed to, but not all that excited about. To her, it was just a means to an end, a way to create a platform so that she could say the things she wanted to say, that she felt had to be said.

We talked about music. We talked about music a lot, about how it felt to sing in front of a crowd, about what it meant to us to connect with an audience, about what it means to be an artist in society today, about how undervalued art is in America unless everything that's original and meaningful and powerful about it has been dumbed down or stripped out. About how most people in America today either never learned how to think critically or are too tired or stressed or self-absorbed to bother, unless you count the tiny little fringe of old-school intellectual types who're still there, but who're mostly so fuckin' proud of how smart they are that no one cares what they think anymore.

It was amazing.

It was the first time in years, maybe in my life, that I was connecting with someone who seemed to care about the same things I did, who seemed to come at the world from the same place, who seemed to know what I was trying to say before I'd even figured out how to say it. Who understood me, at a gut level, from day one, hour one, minute one.

I invited her to come by the studio the next day after class. She watched us work on a song for four hours, the guys alternately curious and dismissive of the little hippie chick in the booth. At the end when everyone was clearing out I invited her to come in and check out the gear. After puttering around Seth's drum kit and strumming the acoustic Nick had left behind, she stepped up to the mike and sang the first verse of the tune we'd been working on that night, note for note, rising to meet the chorus, powering through it and then just stopping and standing there looking at me with this little grin that made me want to kiss her so bad. And then I looked back in the booth and our engineer was sitting in there staring at her through the glass, mouth open, catching flies.

We went out for a late dinner afterwards and that was it. Every night from then on the only question was whether we'd end up at Maya's little apartment down on 8th Street around Washington Square Park or over at the place I was renting for the summer at the Dakota. We spent every spare moment together and every moment that we did felt vital, like my life up to that point had all been in black and white and now all of a sudden everything was in technicolor. We were in tune on a scale I couldn't even comprehend, and every day it seemed to get better.

* * *

As for the recording, the guys settled down some as summer moved into fall and we all realized we had to finish by the end of October if we were gonna get the album mastered and pressed and packaged and promoted in time for the March release that was supposed to kick off our next tour.

I wrote half the songs that ended up on that album in August and September. We trashed about four we'd already started working on because the new ones were better. "Alive and Awake," "Cartwheeling," "If I'm Okay," "September Serenade" – those were all Maya songs. I'd get up in the middle of the night sometimes and work on them when the feelings were fresh and everything was quiet.

You want to say, you want to believe that love will change everything. That it will fix everything in you that's broken. It doesn't. It just sometimes helps you find answers that you couldn't get to on your own. It helps you step outside yourself and see the world from a different perspective.

Maya's perspective was all about purpose. Her dad worked construction, her mom stayed at home until the kids were in high school and then worked retail at a corner drug store near their place out in Brooklyn. They spent their entire lives just trying to get by, and they told their kids over and over that they wanted them to do more, to be more than that. I don't know how well it took on the others – she had two older brothers and a younger sister – but at twenty-four there was nothing more important to Maya than making a mark, somehow making a difference in the world. And it had nothing to do with ego.

Growing up in Brooklyn, she'd walked on concrete more than not all her life until junior high, when she got sent to summer camp for two weeks in the Adirondacks. She hiked around Mirror Lake, camped out at Saranac, saw Champlain and Placid, read about Emerson and the Philosophers Camp, climbed three of the Forty-Sixes, learned about the constitutional amendment that's preserved the whole area for the last hundred years.

She went back four or five times in high school. Somewhere in there she signed up for the Adirondack Council's youth advisory group. By the time she started at NYU, she was marching and tabling and petitioning and pamphletting like it was the Sixties all over again. And that could sound a little shallow, I guess, like it was just some trend she followed or dogma she swallowed whole, but it wasn't like that. Those mountains got into her soul. She found something out there that changed her life, a kind of peace and connection and belief in something bigger than herself. Whatever it was, it drove her to major in poli sci at NYU, and helped get her into Columbia on a pair of scholarships she won, one from the Brooklyn Rotary and the other from Audubon. There was nothing superficial about it. It was her identity. It was her purpose.

And on some level that I didn't recognize until much later, I was jealous of it.

* * *

I wasn't trying to change the world. I was trying to change myself, from nothing into something, from the kid no one wanted to hear from, to a man people would listen to.

And then everyone did start listening, and I got real good at putting up that front, the successful guy who has his act entirely together, and I even started to believe it a little. Until I met Maya, and realized just how full of crap I was. One day we were in Central Park – she loved to walk around the boat pond on the east side and watch the little model ships, even though I had to keep a hat and sunglasses on all the time or people would come up to me almost non-stop – and she asked me how many people Stormseye had played for that year. It took me a couple of more times around the pond to do the math.

So you sang to more than a million people this year.

Yeah. (Grinning like, "Pretty cool, huh?")

What did you teach them?

What?

What did you teach them?

What do you mean?

You had a million people focused on you. Young people mostly, not really sure what to do with their lives yet, looking up to you, wanting to believe in something. What did you give them to believe in?

Maya.

What?

We're just a band.

What's that supposed to mean?

We — I mean, the lyrics mean something to me, and sometimes people in the audience seem to get what I'm saying and that's awesome when it happens, that's what I love the most, but it doesn't always work that way. Sometimes I'm just up there helping them have a good time, you know, entertaining them.

And you're okay with that?

Why not? Sometimes people want to think and sometimes they just wanna rock out. I can't stand up there preaching at them. Nobody's gonna pay to see that.

No, they come to see you perform. But does that have to be all you do?

What do you mean?

Good songs are like the best drug ever invented. They affect your mood, they focus your mind on a time, a place, a feeling. They take you someplace new and make you want to be there. Getting people to imagine a new way of being, and to want to make that real — that's what I'm talking about. Inspiring them while you're entertaining them.

We'd go around and around like that for hours. We'd start up in the morning and then she'd go to class and I'd go to the studio and then we'd meet up at nine o'clock that night and start all over again. There she was, working her ass off to get to a place in life where she'd have access to an audience. And I already had one — a huge one — and my vision was so limited that all I could imagine myself doing with it was being a human jukebox.

* * *

As much as I wanted to get closer to Maya, she wanted to get closer to me, too. And that meant hanging around while I got high, or getting high with me. It never got too heavy — from early on we had an understanding that Stormseye wasn't going to be one of those junkie bands, we were going to draw the line somewhere. But it was still rock and roll, you know? There was just always something around if you wanted it, booze or weed or coke. I wasn't into any one of them more than the others, but I was usually into something. For most of my life up to that point, feeling normal meant feeling shitty about myself, so I tried to do it as little as possible.

And Maya went along. Never as far as I did, she'd usually stop after a few hits or a few glasses, but she didn't hate it and it let her fit in, so she went along.

When we finished recording, the rest of the band headed home, but I stayed in New York. We had a couple of months off before we'd have to start promoting the new album, and I didn't even want to think about leaving town. From that point on, the only time

Maya and I were apart was when she was in class or absolutely had to study.

The tighter we got, the more she pushed me. *You have a gift,* she'd say. *But it isn't your voice or your songs or your money. It's your audience, Jordan. Your gift is you have millions of people who care about what you have to say enough to pay for the chance to listen. And there are a hundred times that many people out there across the country who might listen if you gave them a reason to.* But it's not an obligation, she'd keep saying, *it's a choice. It's a choice you make every day about what kind of life you want to live and what kind of person you want to be. You're a good person, but this rock star fantasy you're living — is that all you want to be?*

I resisted for a long time, but at some point she just kind of overwhelmed me. There I was, I had this platform, and I was using a fraction of its potential. I was being a fraction of the person I could be, if I started caring about something outside of my own success, my own validation. Stormseye had done a few charity gigs here and there over the years when someone asked — usually the label or some other industry suit — but that winter was the first time I ever reached out on my own. I sang at a couple of fundraisers for local groups around NYC, and they were great gigs, small-time stuff next to what I'd gotten used to, but I felt really good afterwards. It felt different, knowing I wasn't doing it just for the money or the applause, but it felt right. I felt right.

And then I went out west to spend Christmas with Sharon and Rick and the kids — Adam had just been born, he was maybe eight weeks old — while Maya spent the holidays with her family, and when I got back, everything had changed. Somehow turning the page on the calendar over to the new year had made us both focus on what was coming — Stormseye was going out on tour, and Maya was staying in New York and finishing school. I worked on her — oh man, I worked her over good, trying to talk her into taking a semester off and following me around on the road. And it completely backfired. We started fighting, these really ferocious fights where we'd barely speak to each other and then we'd both be yelling and then one of us would leave and then the next day we'd get through maybe an hour together before it'd start up all over again. I absolutely wanted her to go with me and she absolutely wouldn't.

One night in the middle of January, a couple of days before the semester was going to start, we sat around her place and smoked a J and drank a bottle of wine and started up again with the same old argument, except it just got worse and worse, more and more intense and angry until finally she told me I was an arrogant prick who didn't care about anyone but myself and I told her she was a controlling bitch who needed to back off. And she picked up the baggie with the rest of my weed and a couple of quaaludes in it and threw it at me and told me to get my shit out of there and I ignored her and walked out.

I came back a long time later — like, three in the morning — wanting to apologize, wanting to work it out somehow. And I knocked on the door and there was no answer. So I used my key and let myself in and started calling her and there was still no answer. And I went into the bedroom and all her clothes were on the bed, but she wasn't in it, and I said man, that's weird, unless she changed and went out or something, and then I saw the bathroom light was on and I went in.

* * *

There was a break in the clouds above us just then and the moon shone through, big and bright and troubled with roiling gray clouds pushing by all around, tracking with the still-steady wind. Jordan was staring into the fire, blinking hard at the memory that was about to come, and I saw right past the armor for a minute, past the easy façade and caught a glimpse of the man underneath, the real person, the wounded spirit who had to fight every day to keep himself going, keep moving forward, don't look back.

* * *

She'd decided to take a bath. She did that sometimes when she just wanted to chill, take some time alone. She'd drawn a bath and gotten in and then she'd fallen asleep. And it wasn't just normal sleep, because she'd slipped under, and never woken up. She was lying there, knees up, head resting on the bottom, her hair all splayed out, brushing against her bare chest, looking so quiet and peaceful and beautiful that I wanted to scream. And I think I did, but then I was reaching in and pulling her up and over the edge of the tub onto the bathmat, sloshing water everywhere, opening her mouth and trying to get her to breathe but her lips were purple and her hands were all swollen up and her legs — oh, Christ.

Her knees wouldn't bend back down. Her body was already getting stiff and it was so unnatural and just, God, hideous that I pretty much lost my mind for a minute and just crawled into the corner and beat my fists on my thighs and I don't know. I don't know.

And then after a while I did the only thing I could think of. I took out my phone and called Jim. I called our fucking manager, who'd never left town, he was still working on the album packaging and promotional stuff, and I told him where I was and what was going on and I said Jim, what do I do? And he told me to just stay there, don't move.

And I sat there with Maya's body on her bathroom floor for at least half an hour like that, until someone knocked on the door and it was Jim with two cops and I let them in and they checked Maya and looked around the place and checked everything else and didn't find anything that didn't belong, because I'd done exactly as Jim told me and grabbed the bag of weed off the bathroom counter and flushed it, except when I was doing that I saw the two 'ludes were gone and there was an empty glass on the counter and I knew. I knew she'd taken them and with the wine and everything, it was too much, she'd passed out and slipped under, just like that.

The cops brought me into the living room and talked to me for a few minutes, asked me a bunch of questions I don't even remember until I couldn't talk any more, and then Jim asked the older one if he could have a minute with him, and they went in the bedroom. And when they came back, the two cops went off and talked for a minute. And then they came back in and asked me to repeat my address and asked me if I'd come down to the station the next day and I said of course and that was that. Jim put me in a cab and told me to go back to my place at the Dakota and not talk to anyone but him.

I still don't know how he did it – and the more I thought about it, the more I didn't want to know – but somehow, Jim managed to keep my name out of the papers. When I went down to the station the next day they brought me in through the back and right into a room so only the detective who'd gotten the case even saw me in the building. He went over it with me again for a couple of hours and everything checked out and that was that. I'm sure the tox screen came back showing barbiturates and alcohol and all that in her system, but I never saw it, it went right to her family and of course they never released it. I doubt anyone asked. After all, it was just another spoiled, partying college student dying stupid. No headline there.

Her family didn't know I'd been there that night, that it was my drugs she'd taken, but they knew we were involved, and they knew the band's reputation, and her brothers wouldn't speak to me at the funeral, wouldn't even look at me. Afterwards I went up to her mother to say something and her dad stepped in front and told me to leave her alone, I'd done enough.

That was the end of that part of my life.

24

The fire was still crackling away. The wind would stir occasionally, nudging us closer to the searing heat of the coal-bed, but the snowfall grew spottier and spottier and disappeared completely in the very dead of night. I was exhausted yet brilliantly awake, wired on a mixture of cold, dread, adrenaline and revelation. And for a while longer, Jordan kept on talking.

* * *

After Maya died, I just sat in my place in New York staring out the window for a couple of weeks. I used to go down to some of our favorite places and walk around and eat and hang out feeling her presence, smelling the air, watching the angle of the sun, catching myself after a while wondering when she was going to come around the corner to meet me. I'd see someone across the street who looked like her and my heart would pound until I remembered it wasn't her, it couldn't be her.

And then it was February and the band started gearing up again. We had photo shoots and promo appearances scheduled, and rehearsals for the tour. I was wasted for every single one of them. Just ask the guys. Every single one. The last week of rehearsals Seth pulled me aside in the studio — Seth, who's probably abused his brain cells more than any human being I've ever known — and got up in my face and said "Jordan, you've gotta get your shit together, man. Don't go fucking Jim Morrison on us." And I told him to get off my case. That was when they hired Ray to try to keep an eye on me, not that it helped that much. He couldn't be with me every minute and at that point I was a pretty determined drunk.

By the time we got halfway through the tour they were giving me B-12 shots and feeding me bennies to get me through the shows. We were supposed to go to Europe that fall, but after the guys saw how bad off I was in the spring they postponed the whole second leg of the tour. We thought it'd be until the next spring. Instead it was five years.

I told them I couldn't handle the whole scene, the big tour, the expectations, the media. It was all too much. That winter I holed up in my house in Oakland and basically didn't talk to anyone but Sharon for about four months, other than ordering delivery food and letting the housekeeper come in once a month. I was actually starting to clean myself up by then — off the road, away from the promoters and roadies and groupies and all that, I'd smoke half a joint around dinner time every night like the businessman coming home for his evening cocktail, but that was it. The thing is, inside I was worse than ever. Stoned or sober, awake or asleep, I couldn't stop thinking about her, couldn't stop blaming myself.

After spending a couple of months talking to walls in my house, I finally got sick of how I felt and started forcing myself to take walks. I'd go down the hill my house sits on and then back up. After a week I started going farther each time, until I was walking halfway down to the water, then all the way to the bay's edge, then going north or south from there. I'd be gone all day sometimes, just walking. By then I'd let my hair and beard grow out so most people didn't even give me a second look. I mean, it was south Berkeley; I fit right in.

And then one day I made it all the way to downtown Oakland, and ran into a bunch of protesters marching up and down in the little triangular plaza in front of the old City Hall building. They were mad about some infill development that was happening, something upscale that they said was going to start driving out the regular working folks who lived in the area. I was just kind of standing around with the homeless people and street musicians watching the whole thing unfold, the protesters marching around with their handmade signs chanting, when I saw a woman standing near the podium they had set up for speakers who was wearing the same puffy peasant blouse Maya'd been wearing that first night at the club. She didn't look like Maya at all — she was tall and black and striking, with a round face, a close-cropped 'fro and really fierce eyes. And then she got up to the mike and started talking and I swear to God, people stopped a block away at the sound of her voice and gave these looks like "Who IS that?" And I'm sure some of them couldn't even understand her over the lousy p.a. system and most of them probably didn't even care about affordable housing or anything like that, but her delivery was so passionate that people were just kind of mesmerized.

At the end of her speech she stopped for a second and looked around at the handful of people gathered in front of the podium, and then at all the people out on the fringes, the bystanders she'd stopped in their tracks. And as she looked at them, really trying to catch each of them right in the eyes, she said "You're the ones who can make a difference. I can stand up here all day shouting at y'all and it's nothin' but noise. You're the ones who have the power to change things. Will you?" A few people shouted back "Yes!" "Will you?" she pressed. The whole group answered her again, louder, more firmly now. "Yes!" "WILL YOU?" she demanded.

And I said yes.

* * *

After that the world started coming back into focus for me. I started working on a couple of songs that ended up on the Mountain Blue *album. At first I thought about calling Nicky, testing the waters with the band, but Sharon kept telling me to take it slow, one step at a time. She was right. I wasn't ready to deal with the band scene again, not yet. I worked on that first solo album for a year. In the middle of it we did a big Stormseye New Year's Eve show here at the Coliseum. After the show I told the guys I'd been working on a solo album, that I wasn't quitting, that I wanted to keep the band going, but that I needed to slow down and take a break from the grind. They were pretty much okay with it – Nicky'd been working on a side project with Glen and a couple of the guys from Velvet Revolver, and Wayne was traveling a lot with his family. Seth was pissed, but that's normal, so whatever.*

So I did the solo thing, hired Natalie to manage, started doing more and more charity stuff, and built it into some kind of new life, a slower, quieter, simpler life that was about music and connecting with people who cared as passionately as Maya had, and not much else. Every time we'd have a successful event, raise a bunch of money for a good cause, I'd feel a little better, a little less disappointed in myself.

What I said before, about when I knew you were alright? That was true, but there was more to it. I saw something in you. You were hurting, man, you were practically bleeding on the carpet when we met on that plane. You lost somebody, and it was like they took a chunk out of you when they went. And I knew that feeling too well. I lived through it and came out the other side, but it's still fresh, it's been fresh for five years, and I wanted to help you through it if I could, but I also wanted to see how it ends. See if I could figure out how you finish grieving, and get back to living again.

* * *

In the darkest gully of night the wind faded, surrendering to the fire that now held us within a perfect cone of radiating, life-giving heat. I thought about bears and coyotes at one point, thought about the fact that we were sitting out in the open with absolutely no way of defending ourselves if a wild animal came along before we were found. But what choice did we have? There was nowhere else to go.

I couldn't sit by a fire – not even when Jordan was in the midst of unburdening himself – without thinking of Dad. Camping had been the best part of our time together. Dad was still healthy then, we hadn't started fighting, and the universe spread out above us felt rich and full of possibility. Over the past few months I had begun to feel his presence slipping, moving farther and farther away from me, but huddled by the fire under the night sky, he was back at my side, whispering in my ear of barbecues and Beatles records and the meaning of existence.

"Have you figured it out yet?"

Jordan gave me a sideways look, hair hanging forward into his face, the wispiest tendrils like little dancing corkscrews. "How to finish?"

"Yeah."

"No. No. All I've figured out how to do is keep going. You have to keep going. Because if you stop, if you just sit and wallow and let it immobilize you, that doesn't honor what you lost. You don't honor someone you cared about, and who cared about you, by sitting on your ass moping. You have to get back up and get moving again.

"You know, I've thought about it a lot. Probably too much. And I still don't know what I believe about God and all that; it's too big and part of me thinks we aren't supposed to understand it, aren't capable of it. Hard to argue with that when we've got all these nut jobs running around saying God wants them to blow up kids or God hates gays or God has forgiven them for cheating on their third wife with their fourth mistress. When you start using God as an excuse for whatever foul idea your human mind comes up with – well, that's why I'll never be part of any organized religion. The middlemen, they screw it up every time.

"Anyway. Didn't mean to get off on that subject. I really only ever figured out one lesson to take from death, and it's the simplest one of all: life is finite. Maya's, your dad's, mine, yours. We get so much time on earth and no more. It's so easy – SO easy – to fritter it away on things that don't matter. Possessions don't matter. Status doesn't matter. Ego doesn't matter. Getting high doesn't matter. Rude, ignorant, unhappy, superficial, materialistic people – they matter, because they're people, however deluded or toxic they may be, but ultimately they matter less than your time does, so don't spend any more of it on them than you have to. When you quit letting all that extraneous crap distract you and get back to living, that's how you honor your loss.

"That's what I figured out. But even that – man, it is so hard sometimes to turn that knowledge in my head into a feeling in my heart. I knew Maya for six months. Six months! And it's been ten times that long since she died and some days I still miss her so damn much. And sometimes, some part of me thinks those are the best days, because even though I'm sad, I feel close to her, I feel like she's there with me again for a second or two."

I brushed my eyes with my shirtsleeve and said nothing.

"Don't wallow. It's no good for you or anyone else. But do remember. Always remember."

* * *

A while later – maybe minutes, maybe hours, who knew anymore? – the world began to grey up again. Somewhere beyond the shoulder of mountains to the East, a dull glow began wiping the slate sky above us clean once again. As soon as I could see ten feet into the trees I got up and got more wood. I figured it couldn't hurt to get the fire as big as we could possibly make it by sun-up.

On my third trip back with fresh wood I found Jordan had adjusted the blanket over Henry and stood up. He was pale and I could see now there was a thin trail of dried blood running past his ear and down his jawline. But he was wide awake and as vividly alive as the day I'd met him.

We stood like that for a long time, watching the gray twilight bleed into a kind of screened color, the pines gradually sharpening their green contrast against the brilliant white of the snow all around. The final tally looked to be about six inches of fresh powder. There were still clouds around, but they were puffier, far less dense and foreboding than when we'd taken off the night before.

I turned silently and went back for another load of wood. As I reached the deadfall again – I'd stripped it practically bare overnight, but there were still a couple of medium-sized branches I could break down – I caught a flicker of color out of the corner of my eye and turned. Far up the shoulder of the ridge, through a gap in the dense grove surrounding me, a pair of eyes locked with mine. The doe would probably have been shoulder high to me standing nearby, but she was hundreds of feet away, frozen, staring down through the trees at the invader crashing around in the depths of her forest, her world. I waited unmoving for a long time, feeling the snow underfoot, smelling the sharp, rich scent of pine, watching the big round impossibly brown eyes watch me. Finally, with a little flick of her back legs she disappeared, bounding out of sight in the blink of an eye.

A minute later I set my last load of wood down by the fire and rejoined Jordan.

"How about you?" he said.

"Hmm?"

"You figured anything out yet?"

The core of the fire was burning white-hot now. If it got any bigger I was going to have to wake Henry and move him back a couple of feet.

"I don't know. A little bit."

"What?"

I sighed. Part of me still didn't want to say it out loud, but we were deep into it now.

"I was mad at him."

Jordan said nothing.

"When I was a kid, my dad was everything to me. He knew everything, he was so smart and so fun and so, I don't know, reassuring. He was my friend. He made me feel safe. And then I started to grow up and he started getting sick and having all these problems. And I'd get so frustrated with him because he couldn't keep up and I always had to worry about him and I used to blame him for not taking better care of himself. And I'd get so mad.

So mad.

"And how could I be mad at the person who was everything to me?"

I looked at Jordan. He didn't have an answer. There wasn't an answer. No one could answer a question like that.

Of course, being Jordan Lee, after a while he tried anyway.

"You have to let it go."

"What?"

"You want to fix it, resolve it, make it right. I understand wanting that. You know I do. But you're spending all your time wanting something you can never have, and that's nothing but a trap, and the only way out is to let go."

I stared at my hands. "I'm afraid. To let go."

"Of course. You live with a need long enough, you start to feel like it's part of you and if you let it go, you'll be incomplete. But you won't. You'll be free, man."

I looked over at him, at the damp, shaggy hair, the penetrating blue eyes, the granite cheekbones. I studied his face for any sign of doubt and tried desperately to will myself to buy this line. But there was a fundamental contradiction.

"You haven't let go."

"No." He looked down now, picking a stray yellow leaf from the tip of his shoe. "Not completely. Not yet. It's hard. It's incredibly goddamned hard. But I work at it every day, and I know it's what I have to do if I want to get my life back."

* * *

The sun had been up for a couple of hours when Henry began to stir. I knelt down next to him and his eyes twitched open. He looked up and around, startled, and then let his head rest down on the blanket again, his thick, close-cropped hair black and glistening.

"What time is it?"

"Nine or so."

"Can't believe I slept this long."

"Vicodin's good stuff."

"The weather – looks like it's eased off. Have you seen anything? Heard anything?"

"Nothing yet."

"Is he alright?" Pointing at Jordan, who was standing off to the side looking downslope, away from the fire.

"Yeah." I smiled to myself. "He's good."

"Okay. We just need to sit tight. Search and Rescue will track us down."

"Here," I said, offering Henry one of the granola bars I'd salvaged from my bag the night before. "Breakfast."

* * *

Jordan was looking down the gentle slope we'd climbed the night before, staring at the wreckage of the plane. The sun was burning through the cloud cover at a rapid rate now, cutting shadows and sharpening corners and edges all across the long bowl of meadow and up into the peaks surrounding us. The blanket of snow had muffled much of the low-lying geography, but the shape of the plane was unmistakable, a missile-like lump with a few markings visible and a battered wing jutting out away from us. The door we'd exited through still hung open like a disembodied mouth.

We stood there for probably half an hour, just absorbing the scene and everything it represented. Eventually, my mind began to wander out of the strange limbo we'd inhabited all night and focus on the world outside once more.

"Oh man."

"What?"

"Natalie must be completely tweaking."

Jordan sighed. "Yeah. Well, worrying's one of the things she does best. She'll be alright."

It got quiet again for a minute while I considered our circumstances and came to a decision.

"Look, I just want you to know, Natalie and I talked at the after-party our last night in New York, and she asked me not to say anything, but —" I gestured at the landscape surrounding us as if it both changed and explained everything. "I just wanted you to know that I think it's great."

I looked over at Jordan, anticipating a look of relief or maybe some residual trace of a poker face. Instead he was peering at me like I'd just starting speaking in tongues.

"What?"

As he said it, the air around us seemed to get heavier for a second, as if some sort of vibration, dim and far off, was straining to reach us.

"You and Natalie. I think it's great. I wish you guys the best, really."

"Me and Natalie?"

"Yeah." But he was shaking his head.

"Bro, you got your wires seriously crossed somewhere."

The vibration grew stronger and became a sound, a low, distant throb.

"But — she said —"

"Dude."

"Yeah?"

"Natalie's with Ray."

I looked at him for a long, silent moment as everything I'd observed, every conversation I'd had and every assumption I'd made played back in my head. He watched me without a word until I added it all up in my head and came up with: "Shit."

Jordan laughed, and it was big and full and hearty and by far the most beautiful sound I'd heard since we'd crawled out of the plane's wreckage fifteen hours – half a lifetime, it felt like – before. And then, as it faded out, a new sound faded in right on top of it, the distant throb blossoming into an unmistakable thrum, a sound that in that moment was maybe even more beautiful to my ears. An engine.

25

Things happened fast from there.

The plane – a Cessna with striping I couldn't quite make out, but it must have been the colors of the California Highway Patrol – passed over our bonfire once, twice and then began to circle. Twenty minutes later, the plane moved off and a second engine approached. The helicopter came in low over the ridge to our west, swung a quick loop around the fire at 500 feet, and then settled slowly to the ground a hundred yards off towards the center of the meadow, blowing a thick mist of fallen snow in every direction.

A stern figure wearing a navy watchcap and aviator sunglasses emerged from the chopper and clambered up the small incline toward me carrying a bulky shoulder bag over his down parka. He had to shout over the rotor noise now filling the valley. "Are you hurt?"

"I'm fine. The one lying down by the fire, that's the co-pilot. Broken ankle, looks pretty bad. We gave him Advil and Vicodin to get him through the night. My friend there with him has a cut on his head that might need a couple of stitches. That's it."

The EMT – a sturdy, fiftyish guy with what looked to be a permanent five o'clock shadow decorating his square jaw – glanced off to his right at the wreckage of the plane. "Damn." And then he was focused back on me, all business again. "Just the three of you?"

"Yes. Except – the pilot – he died in the crash."

"You're a passenger?"

"Yeah."

As we crunched through the snow towards Henry and Jordan, the EMT glanced over at me again, his eyes crinkly at the corners. "You build that fire, too?"

"Yeah."

He nodded and kept moving. "Nice work, kid."

A half hour later, with Henry strapped onto a stretcher between us, we were soaring over the peaks we'd spent the night trapped within, wearing thick headphones to cut the rotor noise, staring down at the jagged, snow-dusted landscape below us. We flew west, sliding down the face of the Sierras into the foothills and then the flat expanse of the Central Valley. In an absurdly brief snippet of time – half an hour, maybe? – we were over the urban hardscape of Fresno, then swooping low toward a CHP building at its very center.

As we came in, settling over the back corner of an expansive parking lot a few yards from the freeway, I whistled to myself. *Damn.* There were fifteen patrol cars parked in the back lot, but they were now outnumbered by TV news satellite trucks. Every cable news outlet I'd ever heard of, all the Fresno network affiliates and who knows who else. The small forest of transmitter dishes deployed high over the crowd could have been the posts of a missing carnival tent.

As we touched down, Jordan and I both shook Henry's hand and thanked him yet again. The paramedic crew arrived first, loading him out of the chopper and straight into the back of the ambulance. As it pulled away, lights flashing, the sightlines cleared between us and the roped-off crowd, and I saw two shapes break free from the mass and begin running toward us.

Natalie ran straight up to Jordan, heels clacking comically on the asphalt the entire way, and wrapped her arms around him. Jogging up behind her with coattails trailing, Ray grabbed my hand and pulled me into a bear hug.

"Good to see you, too, man," I said when I could breathe again.

"We thought –" I couldn't quite believe it. He was choked up. "It was a long night. It was a long night."

"Yeah. Us too."

Then they traded places and Natalie was hugging me hard and I wasn't even thinking about all the needless, stupid crap I'd put the two of us through over the past few months, I was just accepting the comfort.

"I talked to your aunt a couple of times," she said after a minute. "You need to call her."

"I will."

She stepped back from our embrace, still holding onto my arms. "And who's Terry?"

"She's – a friend."

"Well you need to call her too right after you call your aunt I think your aunt gave her my number and she must have called me twenty-seven times!"

* * *

Ruth was brief, mostly relieved that I was okay, and knowing I'd have a lot to deal with there. Terry was unlikely to be that composed, so I checked that Jordan was still on with Sharon and edged off to one side before making the call.

"Hello?!"

"Hey. It's me."

"Oh God! Oh God, it's you, oh shit you scared the living shit out of me Tim Green!"

"I'm sorry. I'm okay. I'm fine."

"That – Natalie – she said they were taking you somewhere in Fresno."

"Yeah. We're here now. The CHP wants to talk to us for a few minutes, but after that Natalie got a limo to take us to Oakland. No more planes this week."

Her laugh was halfway to a sob. I didn't wait for more.

"Listen. I want to see you. Can you come to the show tonight?"

"Show?"

"The band, they're playing in Oakland tonight. Meet us at the stadium. You can come backstage with me."

"They're – he's – they're still going to play?"

"Yeah. Jordan's fine. They had to cancel Vegas, but the thing Jordan wants more than anything right now is to do the show tonight. To keep going."

"Okay. Okay, I'll be there." And then she paused, and surprised me. "You sound different."

* * *

On the four-hour drive from Fresno to Oakland the cabin was never quiet, a constant murmur of conversations on the phone or among our group, with the television low and squawky underneath it all.

The disappearance of Jordan's plane had been the lead headline on the overnight and early-morning newscasts statewide, and had made it into the top five on all the cable news outlets. His safe return was a sensation, the kind of feel-good story TV news increasingly looks for to balance out the steady stream of death and disaster that is otherwise their stock in trade. Jordan's brief statement before the cameras was pitch perfect, thanking the CHP, our pilots – carefully omitting names or status pending the CHP contacting Garrett's family – and everyone who had put us in their thoughts and prayers.

A half hour into the ride, after we'd watched Jordan give his little speech on three different channels, I dialed one of the flurry of numbers that had shown up on my "Received Calls" list when I turned my phone back on.

"Chambers."

"Hey, it's Tim."

My phone went silent for a long moment. "Son of a —. Is that you, Green?"

"In the flesh."

"Good. That's really good." This, coming from Amy Chambers, counted as an emotional outburst of near-epic proportions. "Where are you?"

"In a limo heading north on 99."

"Did you get my message?"

"Haven't had a chance to listen to them yet."

"Alright. Before all this other stuff happened I called and gave you the details for the endorsement speech. We set it up for a rally tomorrow at noon in Justin Herman Plaza, the foot of Market Street in San Francisco. We're expecting six thousand plus cameras."

"Nice."

"Is he still okay to do this?"

"He wouldn't miss it."

"Alright. Alright then. Drive safe."

"We will."

There was another long pause. Then:

"Green?"

"Yeah?"

"I just want to say —"

"Yeah?"

"I'm really glad you're not dead."

* * *

Four hours and four freeways later, our limo rolled through the gates of the Oakland Coliseum, moving slowly down the center aisle of the massive parking lot as the early-arriving tailgaters screamed and whistled and let off air horns and shook their fists in triumph. The echoes faded as we pulled around the side of the stadium to the cordoned-off loading dock area, where a smaller crowd of band and crew had gathered to greet us. Another cheer went up as we came to a stop, the group surging forward as Jordan and I climbed out. Before they could get three steps towards us, though, the front-running Seth was knocked halfway to his knees by the Terry-shaped rocket that came shooting out from behind him and straight into my arms.

I was still holding her tight when Seth jogged up to Jordan, stopped short and stared him down.

"You missed soundcheck again, man."

Jordan laughed. "Well, fuck me."

And then Jordan and Seth were hugging like brothers and everyone else had closed in all around us, Wayne and Glen and Nicky and Jim and Bill and Arjun and Denny and half the rest of the crew, slapping backs, hugging and high-fiving, and when I looked around again I saw Natalie watching me with Terry, who still hadn't said a word, she was just holding me, just pulling me in. For a second I thought Natalie might be about to wink at me, but then instead she turned around and gave Ray a hug and then – what the hell – a kiss, too.

* * *

The show Stormseye put on that night is hard to describe. It's like you've been following a basketball team all year, your favorite team. And sometimes they've been pretty good, and sometimes on the off nights a step slow, and sometimes – the best times – they've cranked it up a notch and been great. And then one day, with no warning, they walk onto the court and play out of their minds, play like the Harlem Globetrotters against the Washington Generals, full-court alley-oops, underhand swishes off no-look passes, between-the-legs, behind-the-back, 360-degree windmill jams. One, after another, after another. That was the show that night.

Terry and I watched sidestage in a kind of delirious trance as the band rocked the audience back on its heels again and again. Five songs in, with the stage lights up and bright, a face towards the front of the crowd caught my eye. Jordan had given the campaign a bunch of tickets, but I'd expected them to go to A-list contributors. And yet there, standing on a chair in the second row, was Amy Chambers. Amy Chambers, with her steel jaw gone slack, mouth hanging open, eyes like saucers, staring up at Jordan Lee like he was some kind of golden god, like…

I laughed out loud. Terry looked over at me. "What?"

"Nothing. Nothing. It's just – I think this is going to be the best after-party *ever*."

Ninety minutes and about fourteen standing ovations later, Jordan strapped on an acoustic guitar, strolled to the front of the stage and just stood there for a while, beaming as the crowd let loose with its ecstasy, the noise overflowing everywhere until he finally, slowly, brought his finger up to his lips. Which caused a whole new round of raucous laughter and hoots, but at least left him an opening to talk.

"For our last song –" at which no one in the audience even bothered to shout out a protest, since it was perfectly obvious this was merely the end of the main set of what was destined to be a multiple-encore evening – "I asked the guys if we could play something we've never actually played live before. It's a song I wrote five years ago, a song about that moment – that amazing, time-altering, life-changing moment – when you really connect with someone. This is for the family of the pilot who died last night –" Now the crowd was fully silent, still as a church in prayer. "– saving my life and the lives of two other people on his plane. And it's for everyone –" looking over, right at me, making sure our eyes locked – "who's ever lost someone they loved."

With that he stepped back from the mike and began to pick out a gentle melody that grew into strummed chords over a subdued beat, Nicky playing soft rhythm on his electric as Wayne's piano decorated the fringes, moving them steadily toward the moment where the lyric would kick in.

At sidestage, Terry held my hand up in hers. "You're shaking."

"Yeah." I swallowed hard. "It's 'September Serenade.'"

*   *   *

After three encores of two songs each I knew they'd finished off not just the entire set list, but just about everything they'd ever played on that tour. But the crowd wouldn't let them go. The stomping, cheering mass was implacable, unstoppable, and the minute they came off the stage, they huddled up yet again.

There was something about that moment, the five of them hunched together, arms casually draped on each others' shoulders as they talked it out, the crowd shaking the floor with a torrent of stomping applause, that finally squeezed the words out of me that I'd been thinking since I'd first stepped out of the limo and spotted Terry running towards me. I leaned in close so she could hear me.

"I know what I want now."

She turned and studied my face, serious, searching.

"I swear to God, Terry, I won't screw it up. I know what I want. And it's not going to change."

At that moment, the huddle broke and Jordan strode back onto the stage with a spotlight tracking him to the front. The other four followed and dispersed to their posts, tuning and preparing. Jordan took the mike and just stood there smiling for a moment while the noise continued to wash over him. Finally, he put his hands up, and then brought them together in front of him, and gave a little bow before beginning to speak.

"Thanks. Thanks. This – man. You guys really put us on the spot here." He laughed as the crowd applauded itself. "See, we don't actually *have* any more songs." Which naturally triggered shout-outs of several different song titles. "At least, songs that we've practiced lately. But there's one we played a few times in rehearsal this spring that we never did bring out. It's a cover. It's a song that feels like it was made to be played live, and it's by

Switchfoot."

Seth counted them in over the ensuing cheers and Nicky led with a firm, ringing sequence of chords, G-D-Em7-C2, a repeating, anthemic clarion call that the crowd responded to instinctually, every last person on their feet, fists pumping, a frothing horde of joyous fervor. Then the song dropped into a lower gear for the first verse, Glen and Seth laying down a steady backbeat that Nicky embellished with sharp, chunky chords until Jordan came in over the top, wistful at first but gaining power with each line:

All rise
All fall
I'll fail
You all

We built these cities
To stand so tall
We've lost
Our walls

and then it breaks down to just Nicky and Seth again, the drums loose but steady, circling the melody

I don't want to lose it, coming down
With the whole world upside-down
I don't have a soul to trust in now
With the whole world upside-down

and on the last syllable Seth plants a thundering fill that drives all five of them headlong into the chorus

We are one, tonight!
And we're singing it out
We are one, tonight!
And we're dreaming out loud
And the world is flawed
But these scars will heal
We are one, tonight, tonight -
Toniii-iiight!
Toniii-iii-iiight!!

and then another verse, another chorus, a third verse, and then the very best part, the cherry on top, the bridge, where the whole band falls back and it's just Jordan over a soft strum-click backing, cajoling the song down to a near-whisper

Let's slow the evening down
Slow it down
Slow down

and then as the music behind him gradually starts to build again

Please slow down
Down
Down

and then Seth slams out a fill and Nicky twirls a knob and hits the fattest power chords of the night and Jordan cuts loose with

The stars are comin' out!

and the song explodes and every light in the stadium – it feels like every light in the world – is on and fifty thousand people are on their feet singing at the top of their lungs

We are one
We are one
We are one
We are one tonight
We are one tonight
And we're singing it out
We are one tonight
And we're dreaming out loud
And the world is flawed,
But these scars will heal
We are one tonight, tonight!
Toniii-iiight!
Toniii-iii-iiight!!

and the goosebumps on my arms are big as beestings and I'm singing so loud I can feel my voice cracking and I look over and Terry is, too, and then she's looking back at me with tears in her big brown eyes and we're kissing again and I don't know anything anymore because it's too much it's all too much and I'm dancing on top of a wall of sound and touch and feeling and I'm dancing dancing dancing

26

When the final show of the closing Oakland run was done, the band split for home with a series of quiet, almost reverent goodbyes. Nothing was said about when or even if they'd get together again. I honestly don't know if they'll ever play another gig as Stormseye. It could go either way. I know this much – the tour tore them apart and put them back together in ways I think they're only beginning to understand. They all recognize that there's something special about the group, some secret combination to the music that only that precise set of five distinct individuals can unlock together. But they're not hungry young kids anymore and when people start looking in different directions, setting different goals for themselves, it takes a lot of effort to keep remembering the things that bind you together, and to have that be enough.

As for the election, in the end, Jordan didn't spend anywhere near sixty million dollars. He didn't need to. The wave of publicity that carried over from his disappearance and rescue through the rally with Frank – which was attended by a raucous, chanting crowd of twenty thousand, three times Amy's guess – put Jordan in the middle of every newscast for a week without him having to spend a dime. And after that first day back, every single time a microphone was thrust in his face he took the opportunity to remind people to vote, to pass the Clean Futures initiative, and – though those close to him might have detected a certain dropoff in enthusiasm when he got to the last point – to support Frank Cassini. We ended up doing several rallies with Gene and making a very respectable ad buy of $32 million.

At the end of the last Clean Futures rally, after most of the staff had cleared out, I caught a final minute with him in the UCLA office building lobby we'd used as a staging area. In a quiet corner of the simple space, bare but for a bulletin board filled with posted notices for tutors and credit cards and roommates needed, we took a moment. I shook his hand and we hugged. Words, for the moment, felt unnecessary. As we lingered in silence, knowing this was the end for now of a long road we had traveled together, I considered how many questions he'd answered, as well as the few I had that were still left. And then, at the door, I turned back and asked him one more.

"Did all this –" the rallies, the ads, the effort spent for a greater purpose "– help?"

"With –?"

"The moving forward. The letting go. Everything."

Jordan took a long time to answer, and I could almost feel the memories flashing through his mind, the strain of the tour, the fissures within the band, the *Times* profile, our meeting with Frank, our night in the snow, and this final week of speaking up and speaking out. I thought maybe he was getting ready to flash one of those million-dollar smiles at me, the ones that make the women forget what they're saying and the men clench their fists with envy, and say something glib. But he didn't. He just nodded.

"Yeah. Yeah, I think maybe so."

*　*　*

For those keeping score at home, the final tally was a three-point win for the Clean Futures initiative and an eight-point victory for Senator-elect Frank Cassini. On the phone late that evening Gene was effusive as ever about Jordan's role in the initiative campaign. As for Frank, I don't remember receiving a thank-you call from him – but then, I wasn't expecting one.

*　*　*

The next morning, sitting in my father's office in Santa Rosa, letting my eyes move slowly around the room, I could feel his presence lingering between every page in every file, behind every poster on the wall, shadowed on the shiny face of every cassette and CD. By now I had at least glanced at every scrap of paper, loose folder, notebook and pad, but I still hadn't figured out what the pieces made when you tried fit them all together. It was his life's work, and I had to find a way to make it mean something. Was it simply a collection of music reviews and interviews, or something more, something bigger?

The obvious selling point was the stars he'd gotten close to. But was this about the artists my father had sat with in bars and planes and studios and dingy backstage dressing rooms for thirty years, trying to see and hear the world through their eyes and ears? Or was the real story about him, about a writer and the life he lived through music. No, not through music – *in* music. A life in music.

I picked the lighter up off his desk again and flicked it open and shut a few times.

Bernie Green: A Life In Music.

I smiled.

Foreword by Jordan Lee.

I smiled wider. "It's a start."

And then I glanced around the room again and there was the picture, the one from the front table in my apartment, the one that had still been in my bag when we crash-landed in the snow, now perched on top of my dad's old rolltop. There it was, and I was a kid again. I was three years old, and Daddy was throwing me up in the air and catching me and I was squealing and it felt like I was flying and I never wanted it to stop. And then my gaze settled on my dad, the thirty-year-old man in the picture, still young, ten pounds too heavy and awkwardly put together, but strong and real and devoted.

I'd told Jordan the truth up in the snow when I said I was mad at my father. But there was more to it than that. I was scared. I was scared because it really was just the two of us, and he was all I had. I never could get past that stark reality. He was stubborn. He was odd. He didn't take care of himself. He did embarrass me. And he never stopped acting like he knew just a little bit more about – well, everything – than I did. But he was all I had.

And so, when he started his long downhill slide, I just kept going back and forth between mad and scared, scared and mad, until he was gone. And then I was numb, and in the moment, that felt better than mad or scared, so I did my best to stay that way – numb.

And what I realize I have to do now, is forgive him. Forgive him for being a parent. Forgive him for being human. I wanted him to be more than just a "sweetheart," a kind, strange, lonely, fun, obsessive, clever iconoclast; I wanted him to be a hero.

I could spin that storyline to myself; it was what I'd done all my adult life – make people believe what they already wanted to. But whatever heroic acts my father may have performed, he was just a man, like any other, with no more fairy dust running through his veins than anyone else on the planet. He was just a man, who loved me, and gave me the best that he had, for as long as he could.

I believed in him, but that was about my need, not his. He only ever wanted one thing from me, to do what I was only able to do after he was gone: believe in me.

ENCORE

I am standing in a quiet glade decorated with monuments. I know Ruth has been here every month like clockwork, obeying the commands of her Torah. For me, it is the first visit since the day we buried my father. The headstone, which I chose but have never seen in place until this moment, is of grey marble, speckled as a cardinal egg. A muffled breeze stirs the lower branches of the oaks around me, now nearly shorn of leaves as the Northern California fall ambles to another mild end.

I reach into my pocket and unfold a piece of paper. The words on it are foreign to me. I don't know what they mean or even if I really believe what they say I believe. I don't know if I can do this. I'm not completely sure why I'm doing this. I only know that I have to.

I take a deep breath and begin to read, sounding out the syllables from the phonetic representation I have found on the Internet and printed out:

Yit'gadal v'yit'kadash sh'mei raba
b'al'ma di v'ra khir'utei
v'yam'likh mal'khutei b'chayeikhon uv'yomeikhon
uv'chayei d'khol beit yis'ra'eil
ba'agala uviz'man kariv v'im'ru:
Amein.

Y'hei sh'mei raba m'varakh l'alam ul'al'mei al'maya
Yit'barakh v'yish'tabach v'yit'pa'ar v'yit'romam v'yit'nasei
v'yit'hadar v'yit'aleh v'yit'halal sh'mei d'kud'sha
B'rikh hu.
l'eila min kol bir'khata v'shirara

toosh'b'chatah v'nechematah, da'ameeran b'al'mah, v'eemru:
Amein.

Y'hei sh'lama raba min sh'maya
v'chayim aleinu v'al kol yis'ra'eil v'im'ru
Amein.

Oseh shalom bim'romav hu ya'aseh shalom
aleinu v'al kol Yis'ra'eil v'im'ru
Amein.

Last January when I stood on this very spot, I didn't know the words. I don't truly know them now. I only know what they mean to me, here, today.

"Goodbye."

As the word falls from my lips and rides off on the breeze, I feel a loosening, as if something inside me has, for the first time in almost a year, unclenched. I step back and as I do, Terry steps forward, takes my right hand in both of hers, brings it up to her face and kisses it.

"That was beautiful."

"No," I say, intercepting the tear that's tracing a path down her cheek with my other hand. "You."

She looks up at me, this child I have known since before I understood anything at all about the world, and I finish the thought. "You are beautiful."

And she holds me and I hold her and we melt together into that oneness that is both a fiction and the truest thing we will ever know.

ACKNOWLEDGMENTS

Many years ago, I was extraordinarily fortunate to work for three elected officials who inspired me with their integrity, commitment and personal warmth—in other words, none of them bears the slightest resemblance to Francis J. Cassini. Thank you to Mel Levine, Gary K. Hart and the late Leo T. McCarthy for giving a kid a shot, and for never letting me down.

Thanks also to the many former colleagues from the Capitol scene whose friendship and freely offered insights contributed to this story. That means everybody, but especially the friend who became part of our family, the extraordinarily talented Dave Sebeck.

I've been fortunate over my parallel career as a music writer to meet and/or interview several of my musical heroes, and cross paths in one way or another with many more "in the business." I'm grateful to each of them for sharing a little bit of their lives with me, but especially to the late Ronnie Montrose.

Stadium-sized thanks to my music writing brothers and sisters, the staff of the Daily Vault (www.dailyvault.com), publisher of album reviews, interviews and other creative nonsense since 1997. You rock.

Several friends and fellow writers improved this manuscript with their candid comments along the way. Everlasting gratitude for your wisdom and encouragement to Allison Bradley Fleming, Benjamin Ray, Viola Weinberg Spencer and Roger Trott. And then there's the man who was review subject, then friend, then reader, then advocate, then publisher. Mark Doyon, I'm glad to know you, not to mention grateful to have such a determined creative sage at my shoulder.

Never doubt that teachers have the ability to make a difference in the lives of their students. Arthur Feinsod believed in me before I believed in myself; I will always be grateful.

Unlike Tim Green, I have a great big noisy, diverse family. Thanks to each and every one of you who offered love and support along the road, but especially to my mother and my brother Gerry, fellow travelers both.

Finally, four people stood by me through every step of this journey. To Josh, Sarah, Eric and Karen: my love and thanks for being who you are, and meaning what you mean, which is everything.

October, 2011
Seaside, California

ABOUT THE AUTHOR

Music has played a central role in Jason Warburg's life since he sat in his older brothers' bedroom at age three listening to them play *A Hard Day's Night* over and over again. A recovering political junkie, in his thirties he moved into the non-profit world, while enjoying a parallel career as a music writer. The latter includes 15 years with independent music review site The Daily Vault (www.dailyvault.com), where he has served as editor since 2003. He is the author of more than 600 album reviews, interviews and feature stories, in addition to dozens of op-ed pieces and speeches. Jason and his wife Karen have three grown children and live in Seaside, California with three spoiled cats.